Andy and the Summer of Something

Andy and the Summer of Something

JESSICA K. FOSTER

NEW YORK | LOS ANGELES

Jacket design by Rejenne Pavon

Jacket design Copyright by Winding Road Stories

Interior book design by Winding Road Stories

ISBN#: 978-1-960724-24-3 (pbk)

ISBN#: 978-1-960724-25-0 (ebook)

Published by Winding Road Stories

www.windingroadstories.com

To Andrew—my favorite cinnamon roll.

1

Follow the Leader

I've never looked forward to summer more in my life.

I rolled down the window to breathe in the smell of freshly cut grass as the wind whipped through my hair. Something about this drive made me feel like anything was possible. As I stretched my arm out, warm summer air slipped between my fingers.

A throat cleared.

Glancing over at Eric, I rolled my window back up. *Whoops.* I'd forgotten the air conditioning was on. My wild mother would rather roll down her windows—even in the rain. But she wasn't the one driving me today. Would I ever become accustomed to the peppermint air freshener, or the careful way Eric inched forward at intersections, his hands cemented in a perfect ten and two?

He smiled. "You okay?"

I nodded. The longer we dated, the more I talked to him, but chatting didn't come easily to me. I put a lot of effort into making sure I matched his mood when I spoke. And I was okay with that. Half of my life existed inside my head. It may as well be taken up with thoughts that belonged to Eric.

"Thanks for signing up with me," I said. "You totally didn't have to."

"And miss a chance to spend time with you? Never." He held my hand to his mouth and gave it a brief peck.

Warmth spread through me. Everything was tiny touches, small moments that made me feel special. His hand on my lower back as he guided me to sit down at a restaurant. Fingers threaded together in public. Soft kisses in his car when he dropped me off after a date spent browsing the bookstore or walking barefoot along the beach. I'd crushed on him for so long, I couldn't believe this was real.

Eric Phan was my boyfriend.

I touched his dark sweep of hair, tucking a stray piece behind his ear. He preferred his hair shorter and would probably cut it soon. He was so precise, so reliable. Everything about him felt like a warm hug. The smile he leveled at me now was blinding, like I'd given him a present. I didn't often initiate contact. He always beat me to it.

"I'm excited to meet the famous Paige," he said.

I turned to the window so he wouldn't see me roll my eyes. Paige called me at least five times this week. He'd gotten a faceful of her perkiness on our last video chat.

"They always need more guy counselors," she told Eric. "You should sign up. And Lucas won't be there, now," she said before I could shush her. "He got recruited for a college swim team and their conditioning is at the same time. Too bad. He would've given you some competition with Andy."

Eric turned to me. "What does she mean by that?"

Paige paled, her eyes darting between me and him. "Just a joke." She frowned at me. "He's a hot guy, and you've got a hot girl, there."

Eric chuckled. "You're not wrong about that."

"Are you ready to lead a bunch of Victims, Andy?" she joked, using one of her famous classifications from last year. Victims, Converts, and Volunteers. I hoped, for her sake, she got a bunch of Volunteers—kids who liked camp.

But I couldn't think about all of that while my heart hammered so hard it might beat out of my chest. I never told Eric about my romance with Lucas last summer. Lucas was the coolest guy at camp, my first kiss, and my first painful heartbreak. He just... never came up. And now I didn't want to dive into my naïve mistakes from last year. It was so different from what Eric and I had started. Separate.

And anyway, this summer wouldn't be about me. I knew exactly what it felt like to be forced into activities I didn't want to participate in. I imagined about a thousand ways I could make leadership camp more bearable for any Victims. We wouldn't waste time on embarrassing icebreakers everyone hated. I'd give them more breathing room than I'd had and more choices.

By the time Eric and I ended the call with Paige, he'd caught the excitement and was ready to sign up.

I smiled as the paved road outside my window gave way to a dirt driveway. The massive brown camp sign welcomed us to Camp Follow the Leader, which was still a ridiculous name. Coaching teens wasn't a romantic thing to do with my boyfriend, but it would keep Eric and me near each other. We wouldn't have much time in the same zip code once college started in the fall.

I picked at the cuffs of my navy-blue Middlebury sweatshirt as we crunched over the fresh gravel. Mom and Dad lived a half hour away from Middlebury College. Far enough to make me feel independent, but close enough to celebrate the holidays together. Eric would attend Norwich University, a full hour away, but he swore we'd make it work. It wasn't that far.

Part of me wanted to say come with me to Middlebury, but he was from a military family. Norwich was in their blood. He never even applied to another college. I couldn't imagine quiet, reserved Eric in any branch of the military, but what did I know? All the images in my head came from commercials and movies. And he never questioned the path that was chosen for him. Not for one second. He was always so sure of everything. Fit brain, fit body, he'd joked as he pushed his glasses up the bridge of his nose. Would they give him contacts in the service? The thought made me sad.

We pulled around the circle drive in front of camp, and I couldn't control my wide smile. Sure, last summer was tough, but magic happened here, too. I could still hear the Camp Director Dana's voice in my head. *We could use someone like you next year, Andy.*

Eric gave my hand a squeeze after putting the car into park. "Ready?"

Yes. "Let's do it."

He killed the engine, and I opened my door to sunshine and the smell of water and pine. Of course, I was ready. I had everything I wanted. What could possibly go wrong?

2

Coffee Reunion

At least twenty cars peppered the large parking lot. Counselors arrived a day before the campers for training.

"I thought the email said to be here at ten," Eric mumbled. "It's nine-forty. What gives?"

"Maybe some of the people are janitorial and cooking. I doubt it's just us here today," I tried to comfort him.

"Okay." But his tiny frown said he was thrown. He liked to be on time.

I went to grab my duffel from the trunk, but he stopped me. "I've got it."

I squinted at him through the harsh glare of the sun. "But you have your bag, too."

"Andy, it's okay. I've got it." He smiled. "Do you want to grab the pillows?"

I picked up the pillows, a bit annoyed.

"Andy!" Paige's scream echoed across the parking lot. "You made it!" She sprinted to us from the door of the cafeteria.

I rocked back as she smashed into me, pulling me into a long, tight hug. "Why is everyone here so early?" I asked when she pulled away.

"Oh, half of us are here so far, I think," she said. "You're right on time."

This seemed to please Eric, who dropped our bags and held out his hand. "Hi," he said. "Nice to meet you offscreen."

"Oh, my God, Andy, he's so polite. Does he have a brother?" She shook his hand.

I grinned at her tan skin and signature ponytail. It was as if the past twelve months never happened. She looked exactly the same, so sporty and outgoing.

"Nope." I hugged his shoulder. He leaned down to kiss my forehead.

"I'm going to die from sweetness overload," she said. "How about you get your man to grab the luggage while we snag some seats in the cafeteria? He can pile them with the other stuff next to the picnic benches."

Eric gestured for me to go ahead before pulling the pillows from my arms. He was so capable. I met his gaze for a moment, raising my eyebrows.

He nodded. "I'll meet you in there."

Paige squealed and yanked me down the path. "Aren't you dying of excitement, you little Volunteer?"

I snorted as our feet crunched over the fresh gravel. "I didn't turn into a cheerleader overnight."

Paige pulled me to a stop. "But wait. That's why you're here. To cheerlead your campers, right?"

Oh, yeah. "Of course. You know what I mean."

Paige squinted her eyes, skeptical. "Sure."

Time to change the subject. "I wish Emma was here." It wouldn't be the same without her assertiveness from last year.

"Oh, I called her," Paige said. "Guess where she is?"

Knowing Emma, anywhere. I hoped she wasn't cooped up with books and summer classes while working a job or something equally stressful. I shrugged.

"Studying abroad in Spain. Lucky duck."

I laughed. "Spain sounds like Emma."

"I miss her, too. But we're going to have a great summer together, and you brought your boy." She nudged me, and I almost fell off the path. "I knew you had it in you, you player."

"I'm not a player," I mumbled, face burning. "Eric is... was my crush at school even before last summer."

"Oh? Before Lucas?"

I nodded. How could I tell her to calm down about the Lucas thing now that I was with Eric? That should be part of girl code, right?

"I like that," she said as she shielded her eyes with her hand against the morning sun. "Fairytales do come true."

I smiled. Maybe I didn't have to say anything. "What about you?"

"Me? I'm flying solo. As you can imagine, Marshall and I didn't last long." She rolled her eyes.

Crap. I never asked her about Marshall when we talked. Last summer they'd been inseparable, competing with each other at every activity and turning it into flirting. "I'm sorry."

She shrugged. "It's cool. Summer romances, right?"

"Right."

Lucas's arms around me as we lay under the moonlight. His fingers in my hair, his lips on my neck...

"I'm not that worried about dating right now. I want to enter into freshman year of college totally free. Um, not that, you know, it's a thing that you have to do," she backpedaled.

I blinked. "No, I get it."

As we approached the cafeteria, I realized it was subtle, but Paige did seem a tad different. Her hair was a shade darker than I remembered. She had on a sedate T-shirt rather than the skimpy tanks she'd worn last year. And she wasn't looking for a guy now. Maybe people changed, period.

Wasn't the fact I was here voluntarily evidence of that?

We pushed though the cafeteria doors. A bunch of people milled around, and... wait, was that the smell of coffee?

There were coffee machines *out in the open*. Caf and decaf just sitting there next to a basket of creamer cups. Last year, they kept the coffee under lock and key like a prison camp.

"Coffee?" Paige asked through her laughter.

"Obviously." I practically floated to the table. I had a cup in my hand and was waiting my turn when a familiar voice rumbled behind me.

"Thought I'd find you here."

Every hair on my arms stood on end. *Lucas.*

I turned and our eyes collided. His lips curled into a smile. "Surprise."

For a second, neither of us moved. Last year when we were campers, he was all wiry muscle and large, open smiles. He still had all of that, but definition now molded his muscles, and he'd shot up at least two inches. Now he towered over me, his jaw more angular, his hair longer, falling in shaggy waves past his ears.

He stared at me, too, and I wondered if he saw the same girl as last year; whether he'd notice the subtle difference in my curves, the way my cheeks had thinned a little, the fact I now wore trendier jeans.

The line jerked forward, and I remembered why I was there. Who cared what Lucas did and didn't notice about me? I busied myself pouring coffee, adding creamer. Lucas grabbed a cup of decaf. Why bother with coffee if you were going to drink decaf? Last summer he said he didn't drink it at all.

He smiled at me again. "I wanted to—"

"I thought you—"

He gestured for me to go ahead.

"I thought you were on a swim team."

He shrugged, looking away. "They moved the conditioning dates. Something about pool maintenance."

"Did you get a scholarship?" I blew on my coffee so I didn't have to meet his eye. This was so awkward, but I couldn't just walk away after asking him why he showed up. That would be so rude.

"Yeah. Full ride. They'll take anyone these days." He chuckled.

It wasn't funny. It was a huge accomplishment to be able to go to college for free. I couldn't think with him looming over me. I got back in the coffee line.

"You need another cup already?" Lucas grinned. "You didn't drink your first one."

"No, I—" forgot Eric's coffee. Lucas didn't know about him. And Eric didn't know about Lucas because it wouldn't have mattered if Lucas wasn't here. I shook my head as I poured another cup. Now, Eric would find out about him before I had a chance to make it less of a big deal.

I added two sugars to Eric's coffee.

Lucas frowned. "That's not how you take your—"

"Hey." Eric grabbed a lid for the coffee and snapped it on. "Thanks for thinking of me."

"Lucas, this is..."

Eric stuck out his hand. "Eric," he said firmly.

Whoa, what? Why was his voice so low all of a sudden?

"Boyfriend?" Lucas asked me with arched eyebrows.

I swallowed a scalding sip of coffee and nodded, unable to keep myself from staring at both guys. When put side by side, there couldn't be two people more different. Where Eric was a tall, wiry bookish type, Lucas had jock written all over him. In the fluorescent lighting of the cafeteria, even Eric's short black hair contrasted sharply with Lucas's messy blond.

Lucas peered down at me for a long moment before shifting his focus to Eric. "Well, hey, Boyfriend. I'm Luke. Andy and I—"

"Know each other from last year at camp," I cut in, giving Lucas a warning look. Since when did he introduce himself as Luke?

Neither guy said anything for a second as Lucas grinned and Eric placed one stiff hand on the small of my back.

"We should find our seats," I whispered to Eric. "Good to see you again," I threw over my shoulder at "Luke."

We settled in next to Paige on the creaky folding chairs. Her eyes were as big as basketballs. *You didn't tell him?* she mouthed as the lights lowered and Dana took the stage.

I shook my head.

She raised her eyebrows, but she didn't have to. I knew I was in deep crap for not preparing Eric. I didn't think Lucas would be here, and it didn't come up before because I wanted to keep camp life separate from real life. Eric was my dream guy, and being in a relationship with him was everything I'd always wanted. He was hot, considerate, kind, and a whole host of other things. He would never lie to me all summer and break up with me like... I didn't want to think about it. I'd moved beyond the messy drama of last year's summer camp.

"Heya, Counselors!" Dana called as she ran up the stairs to the cafeteria stage.

"Heya!" I chanted back even though my inner snarky girl rebelled. Eric looked at me in surprise, and I shrugged. I was a Convert, what could I say? And so what if Lucas and Eric didn't know about each other? Eric and I were dating now, and Lucas was...

...heading straight for the chair beside Paige.

3

Marching Orders

The cafeteria vibrated with tension. Lucas's blue eyes burned a hole in the side of my head even though I sat crammed between Paige and Eric. Paige tilted her head to hear something Lucas muttered to her. Why was she grinning? What did he say?

Dana tapped the mic on the stage and the screech made us all groan and cover our ears. "Sorry about that," she chirped as the lights lowered. "Welcome to Camp Follow the Leader. Today we'll give you your marching orders. Whether you're cafeteria staff, activity staff, or bunk counselors, I know you're going to make this summer an amazing experience for our campers!"

I nodded, only half paying attention. Was Lucas asking Paige about me? I nudged her with my elbow, but it was like elbowing a stone statue. Her biceps were rock hard. Guess she still kicked butt in the sports department.

A hand touched mine and I nearly jumped out of my skin before I realized it belonged to Eric. He didn't look down at me, his dark gaze fastened on Dana as she spoke. Warmth spread through my chest. I didn't need the fortification, but how incredibly kind of my boyfriend to try to anticipate my needs. He was so great.

"As you lead your campers through their experience here this summer, I want you to remember that it's about their development as a leader, but it's also about yours. How better to hone your skills than to sharpen those of our tenacious teenagers?"

The cafeteria exploded in cheers, and I clapped along. I didn't know how much more I could develop as a leader, but surely Dana was right about some other people here. Would Lucas be able to lead a guy who wasn't sporty? Would Paige? Maybe I could help them.

"If you're a new counselor this year, there's nothing like it, believe me." Dana's face split into a wide smile. "We pride ourselves here at camp in allowing each counselor to decide what individual activities best fit their cottage while participating in group challenges that can benefit all. You'll have a chance to adapt to the needs of your campers through listening and cooperative activities."

I couldn't help my nod. I was a great listener. Dana was right. They needed me. I tuned her out when she began to talk to the cafeteria staff.

"It's hard to imagine you here," Eric whispered after a minute. "Everyone is so peppy." He grinned, waiting for me to share in the joke. Normally, I would. God knew I could be sarcastic when I wanted to. But all I could manage was another nod, the spell of camp broken for a brief moment.

It *would* be hard for him to imagine me participating in some of the activities Dana explained, especially teambuilding. But somehow, him saying it out loud jarred me out of my giddy excitement. I knew I'd be a good counselor this year, even though I might have been a terrible camper last summer.

Eric squeezed my hand, warm and reassuring. I squeezed back. He was trying to lighten the mood after the weird Lucas run-in. Eric always tried to keep it light. I liked that about him.

"Andy!" Lucas whispered over Paige's shoulder.

Speak of the devil.

I turned to face him rather than let Lucas yell over Dana's presentation. He'd be the type to do it if he thought I was ignoring him. I raised my eyebrows, still holding Eric's hand tight. *What?* I mouthed.

"You're going to kick butt this year, Counselor Andrea!" he mocked in a hyper-cheerful voice that my counselor from last year used.

I wanted to laugh, but Eric stiffened the smallest bit beside me. I squeezed his hand again and gave a tight smile to Lucas instead. Paige covered my foot with hers, and I realized my leg was shaking. This was already more stressful than last year.

When the lights went up and Dana separated us into cafeteria staff, custodial, activity specialists, and counselors, I began to realize how small this camp was. Lucas and Paige split off from us to make a beeline for the refreshments table, and

I counted. Twenty-five counselors milled around, grabbing cookies and chatting. I stood with Eric, his hand still fastened to mine. For the first time, I started to worry for him. He was quiet like me. Would he be okay this summer, leading a troop of unruly boys?

Lucas came over, holding a steaming cup of heaven. He passed it to me.

My traitorous hands accepted the coffee before I had a chance to think about it. "Thanks." Lucas had put vanilla creamer in it, too. How did he remember that?

"Didn't you just have a coffee?" Eric asked in a quiet voice.

Lucas snorted. "You're kidding, right?"

I shrugged, trying not to look at either of them. It was difficult since there was nowhere to divert my attention besides the cement bricks of the cafeteria wall. Where the heck did Paige go?

Man, the coffee smelled amazing, though. Like a warm, rich hug in a cup. It took everything in me not to take a drink of happiness. Eric didn't know the extent of my addiction the way Lucas did. He'd never seen me coffee-less like Lucas had, so he wouldn't have tracked how much I drank.

Dana hopped off the stage, her blonde hair bouncing as she made eye contact with me. *A distraction. Thank God.* I smiled. She'd been the one to put the idea of being a counselor in my head.

"Hey, Andy," she said to me before glancing up at my boyfriend. "And you must be Eric Phan. Did I say that right?"

Eric nodded.

"I'm afraid we have a bit of a problem with your application, Eric. I know we sent you a confirmation stating you would be a counselor, but..." Dana bit her lip. "Unfortunately, one of our previous campers signed up at the same time, and they receive preference in assignment because they're familiar with the terrain here at camp. I would have emailed you, but we didn't catch the mistake until this morning, and..."

Eric loosened his grip on my hand as blood pounded in my ears. Another counselor signed on at the same time? One who maybe couldn't come originally? My eyes flashed to Lucas, who had backed off a few suspicious feet.

"There are other positions if you'd like to stick around, but I'm afraid Counselor isn't your assignment. I'm sorry; this is very unprofessional." Dana looked like she might cry.

Relatable. I might, too.

Eric stepped forward, laying a comforting hand on the older woman's shoulder. "That's all right. I did sign up rather late." His eyes crinkled in the approximation of a smile. Always putting others at ease.

"We have several positions open in the kitchen," she said hopefully. "We're very short-handed this year, and I planned to pitch in a few days to help as it is. Or maybe..."

"I'd love to work in the kitchen. I have experience since my mom owns a restaurant."

But he had come here to get away from helping with that. I opened my mouth to protest, but he squinted at me, and I closed it again.

Anything to not make waves. And he *would* be a huge help to them. But then, what about us? My whole vision of lying out on the beach with him, taking our campers on hikes together, laughing as we cheered them all on from the sidelines of their activities went up in flames. Would we see each other at all?

That was selfish. I shouldn't be thinking like that.

"Oh, that's wonderful!" Dana bobbed her head in a grateful nod. "Thank you so much for understanding. I can introduce you to Annie right now if you'll follow me."

I wanted to grab his hand again. I imagined myself pulling him back, refusing to let her separate us, throwing a fit over the whole thing.

...but that wasn't me. And that wasn't him. We weren't those people. He was calm. Considerate. Polite. Empathetic. And I kept everything inside.

"I'll find you later," Eric whispered, kissing my temple.

I watched him walk beside Dana, his face calm as she led the way to the kitchen. My hands clenched my coffee cup as I choked back my disappointment.

What a disaster.

4

Here We Go Again

When Dana came back from the kitchen, she passed around paper packets and activity manuals. I peeled off my sweatshirt and tied it around my waist before skimming over mine, my brain spinning. Eric was gone. It took me a whole minute to realize we had actual schedules to follow. Last year seemed so loose, I couldn't believe there were specific times for food and camp-wide activities versus bunk activities.

Lucas stayed away from me while I seethed and drank his now-lukewarm devil's brew. I didn't feel sorry for him. He had no trouble finding people to talk to. A bunch of counselors surrounded him, one patting him on the shoulder as he spoke in a tone too low for me to hear. Lucas shoved his hands in his pockets and rocked back on his heels as he listened.

Huh. What's that about?

I shook my head. I shouldn't care if he looked uncomfortable with whatever conversation they were having over there. He was responsible for the fact I'd be separated from Eric for most of camp.

Before I knew it, Dana clapped her hands. "It's time to nest!" she cried. "Get settled into your cottage, and I'll see you on the archery field in an hour for activity training!"

I capped my third cup of coffee, because who was counting at this point, and waved to Paige as she exited the bathroom. Then I slung my stuff over my shoulder and began the long trudge to the cabin marked with an X on my map.

13

As I crunched over the gravel path, tension began to leak out of me. Without Lucas towering over me, or even Eric, the thrill of being back at camp began to seep into my bones. I wasn't the same girl who came here the first time.

Sweat soaked my shirt, the beautiful, hazy hot of summer seeping through my clothes and making me warm all over. The air smelled like earth and water, and a tiny breeze tickled the small hairs of my arms. I would be okay, whatever happened. Camp was magical. Life here was hilarious and hard and perfect at the same time. I would get the chance to help other girls embrace their confidence like I had last year. Nothing could top that.

Once I stood in front of the familiar shutters and sign, the humor of the whole situation sank in. "You've got to be kidding me."

Beaver cottage. The exact same place I did time in last year. I dropped my duffel on the ground and covered my sudden laughter with one hand. What were the odds?

"Hey, neighbor," Lucas's voice registered over my giggles. He stood on the porch of the next cottage over.

Seriously? Last year my counselor had paired with another cottage so their campers could do a variety of bigger activities. When Eric signed up and mentioned me in his application, I had assumed they'd make us partners. But now Eric wasn't a counselor. That meant...

I grabbed the schedule from my pocket and unfolded it. In small, sloppy handwriting I had missed before, it spelled out my new fate.

Partner Counselor: Lucas Johnson

I snorted. Of course.

"What's so funny?" He jogged over, grabbing my bag like he might carry it into my new palace of beaverdom.

"Put my stuff down, you... you..." I couldn't finish. It was like the universe was determined for us to repeat last summer. "I can't."

Lucas set down my bag. "Now, Andy..."

"Don't you *Now Andy* me!" I half-hissed, half-laughed. "You're the reason I can't have Eric right now. And you... and that shirt..." I wasn't making any sense, but his baseball tee was practically painted on. Buy a size up, for Pete's sake.

"My shirt?" He looked down. "Are you okay?"

"Fine. Perfect. Great. Happy Hippo nesting."

"Cheetah." He pointed to his cottage. "They changed the sign."

"They changed the guys' Hippo sign but not the girls' *Beaver* sign?"

"What can I say? Not everyone has your dirty mind." He wiggled his eyebrows.

I sighed. "Of course. Of course, they did. Happy Cheetah-ness. Whatever. I'll see you later."

Grabbing my crap in the most awkward way possible, I thumped it up the stairs. Then I nudged the squeaky cottage door open with my shoulder and dropped my stuff in the center of the floor with a thud. I didn't look back to see where Lucas went.

Focus on what you came here to do—help girls be awesome and find their inner badass like you did last year. I circled the room, trying to figure out where to sleep. With a laugh, I found myself choosing the same lower bunk that Suzie had last summer. It was near the door so I could catch shenanigans. *Huh.* Maybe she hadn't been such a terrible counselor, after all.

It was crazy to think that only one year separated me from being a camper. Crazy to think I'd ever been the one causing problems. Eric would never be the boy who asked me to do something that would get me kicked out of camp. He was too good to me. And now he was stuck in the kitchen, and I was back with Mr. Let's-Meet-After-Curfew-And-Kiss-On-The-Beach. Well, I wouldn't fall for that again, even if he did remember my coffee order. I had a boyfriend now.

I spread out my sleeping bag and plopped my pillow on top. Then I taped a picture of Eric and me to the bedpost. It was stupid and silly, a selfie we took of him giving me bunny ears with a carnival in the background. The day we took it had been such a great date. Our first date. He'd been so reserved and shy while asking me, and when we got there, neither of us knew what to say. It took a whole hour for us to warm up to each other. I touched the edge of the photo. We laughed a lot about that now.

A knock on the cottage door startled me out of my thoughts, and I bounded over to answer it. We didn't have to be at our first training session for another half hour, so it had to be Eric. I grinned—I needed his calm energy to quiet my unsteady heart.

And that boy did not disappoint. As soon as I opened the door, Eric held out his arms and I collapsed into his hug. He rested his chin on the top of my head as I snuggled into his crisp black T-shirt. He smelled like mint.

"It's going to be okay," he murmured.

"I should be comforting *you*." I pulled back to see his face.

"It's fine, honestly. They're so disorganized in the kitchen. No wonder they're short-staffed. I'm needed. You know how I love to feel needed." He graced me with a small smile.

"I need you," I said in a tiny voice, returning to his warm arms.

He squeezed me tight. "I know. But this won't change our plans, Andy."

"It won't?" I mumbled into his shirt. I was never leaving this hug. He would have to cut vegetables in the cafeteria around my body.

"Of course not. There are breaks. We'll find each other. We'll make it work."

I wanted to believe him. "Okay."

His arms dropped, but mine stayed locked around his waist.

"You're not going to let me go, are you?" he joked.

I grinned up at him. "Are you complaining?"

He pushed his glasses up. "Never. But I have to get back, and you have to..."

Do all the things he wanted to do this year. My face fell.

"I know," I whispered.

He kissed the top of my head. "Come on. Let's go be awesome."

I stood in the doorway after Eric left. I wanted to watch every careful step he took back to the cafeteria. When the door swung shut behind him, I sighed. He was right. Time to go be awesome.

Before I could close my own door, Paige sailed by me, holding a piece of lined paper. "I told him I wouldn't do it, but then I felt sorry for him. You know how he is." She shoved it in my face.

I followed her into the cottage. "Who did you tell..." Wait. I backed away from the note like it was made of acid. *No. Absolutely not.* The last time I got a written note at camp, it was from Lucas. I couldn't do this again. Eric *just* left.

"Go ahead and read it. Then we can decide what to do," she said.

"Nope. You read it." I already knew what I would and wouldn't do. If it was something with Lucas, the answer was a hard no.

Paige unfolded the note. "*Canoes. 8pm,*" she read. "Wow, that's romantic. Doesn't waste any words, does he?"

Lucas could've texted me and didn't. I knew he still had my number. This was purposeful. He wanted to show me he remembered. It was word-for-word the same thing he wrote to me last summer.

I sank onto the edge of my bunk. "I can't go."

"You don't have to go," Paige agreed. "But you're going to, anyway. You and Lucas... there's something unfinished there, and you should know—"

"It's finished," I said in a hard voice. "We finished it last year."

She leaned against the bunk post. "He doesn't seem to think so."

No kidding. "How's it going to look when I sneak away to meet a guy who isn't my boyfriend? I can't go." I wasn't going.

"Whatever you say," she said. "Guess what time it is?"

I looked at her blankly. It was nowhere near eight, that was for sure.

"Time for leadership training, Counselor Andrea!"

I laughed. "Shut up."

She pulled me up to stand and linked arms with me. "You're different this year, you know. Happier. More confident."

"Thanks." I pushed down my frustration as we trekked to the archery field. I *was* more confident. That was the whole point of this summer: helping campers be sure of themselves, too.

I had a job to do.

5

Leadership Training

The cottage leaders trickled into the archery field like water dripping from a faucet. The grass beneath our feet crunched, unlike last year when the wet and moss crept into every article of clothing I'd brought. This summer, we hadn't seen rain for weeks, and the dust that kicked up across the open space took me by surprise. I rubbed my eyes, but that seemed to make it worse.

"Try blinking a lot," a low voice suggested behind me and Paige.

"Thanks," I muttered, turning to see Lucas.

A ball cap and sunglasses hid his eyes. "No problem."

I shouldn't be annoyed by it, since a hat and glasses were my normal M.O., but this was Lucas. Sure, the sun might bake us into the ground, but when had he ever worn either of those things last summer? Never, that's when.

Dana clapped her hands. "Okay, crew." She was calmer off-stage, her smile genuine as she made eye contact with each of us. *Interesting.* My memories of her consisted of constant screaming through microphones and bullhorns.

"In order to get you used to leading activities, it's a smart idea for us to perform some of the things we'll ask the campers to do. It isn't a contest to see who does something better or faster," she warned with a smile. "Just try to have fun and absorb what it feels like to complete the tasks. As you can see, there are different stations set up around the perimeter of the field." She gestured to numbers staked into the ground in equally spaced intervals with lumpy trash bags attached to them. "We'll number you off and get this party started." Dana proceeded to walk around the group and bop us on the head counting numbers one through six. "Andy, you're a six," she said as she patted my head. "Lucas, you're a one."

18

The knot in my stomach unraveled a little. Good. I needed a break. Not seeing his eyes unsettled me more than I wanted to admit. Was he indifferent now that I'd shut him down? Or maybe he was waiting for a sign that I'd meet him later…

When Paige got bopped as a six, we smiled at each other.

"Okay, head to your numbers. I'll call time in a bit, and you'll rotate to the next station."

Paige and I walked to the number six sign. We didn't have far to go, since it stood closest to where we were already grouped together.

"So," she said while we dumped out the contents of the bag. Fly swatters and papers fluttered to the ground.

"So," I replied.

"Lucas tonight. Let's make a game plan. You know that he—"

"Nope. Next subject."

She blew a piece of hair out of her face. "Fine, then. Eric."

I used my hand to shield my eyes from the sun as I squinted up at her. "I wish he was here with us right now."

"He's so hot!" She fanned herself.

I toed the ground, smiling. "Yeah."

She arched an eyebrow. "Hmm."

"Hmm, what?"

She shrugged. "I don't know. You're different around him."

I rolled my eyes. "Different how?"

"It's not bad, it's… you're reserved. Even when we talk about him. He's not a creep, is he? I don't have to protect you?"

"Wow. Tell me how you really feel," I deadpanned.

"I'm serious!"

I put my hands on my hips. "A: I can protect myself. And B: if he was a creep, I would totally let you pound him."

She nudged me. "Good." We both laughed.

"I… I *like* him, okay?" I said in a soft voice.

"Okay," she said. "Then I do, too."

I smacked her on the arm with one of the flyswatters, then picked up the directions to the activity. Two guy counselors joined us, both I'd never met before. Or maybe I had. I didn't pay attention to many people last summer.

"Hey, James. Derrick," Paige said.

I rolled my eyes. Of course, she knew them.

"So, what do we do?" Paige asked.

"Slap things we think are stupid." I set down the paper.

"There has to be more to it than that." Paige leaned over the directions. Ten seconds later, she had us organized into a line. She called out a statement and we had to run and slap it if we disagreed, then rate our disagreement on a scale of 1 (a gnat flies up your nose) to 10 (bologna breath on a first date).

"Men should always wash their hands after using the restroom."

I stayed on the starting line, but both guys ran and slapped the paper with their fly swatters.

"Gross," Paige said.

"I don't think you're supposed to comment on their choice."

Paige made a face at me. "Okay, give us a number, James."

"Two."

She sighed. "It could be worse. Why two?"

He shrugged. "Sometimes the sinks are grosser than my body."

I snorted.

"Derrick?"

He folded his arms. "Eight."

"You... do know how this works, right?" Paige asked incredulously. "You're saying you strongly disagree with washing your hands?"

"Yeah. When I pee, I don't touch my urine. And, like, natural immunity, you know?" He flexed his arm.

Paige looked like she might be sick, so I didn't bother asking about when he had to go number two. I smothered laughter. Eric wouldn't have swatted the paper. He had perfect hygiene. He always smelled like bathroom soap. But Lucas... I didn't know what Lucas would have answered, or why I glanced across the field to where the Ones participated in a hula hoop contest. My eyes definitely didn't get stuck on how he jutted out his hips.

Derrick followed my gaze. "Still into Lucas, huh?"

"What? No."

He started to laugh, but he sobered up fast when he saw my face. "It's just kinda sad."

What was sad? Me liking Lucas? I never said I did, and he better not start that rumor.

"At least he gets to go to college close to home, though," James said thoughtfully. "And with his brother. That might make it easier."

"Lucas is going to the same college as Tyler?" I shouldn't be surprised he planned to stay in West Virginia. Of course, they would have scouted him for a swim team. But why did he need anyone to make anything easy for him? He was *Lucas.* If I googled the word confidence, his smiling face would probably be the example picture.

Both guys looked at me like I'd sprouted two heads. Neither of them said anything.

Well, fine then. "Read the next question," I said irritably.

On it went. I swatted papers and filled out worksheets and sat in circles that looked more like squares since there were only four of us. By the time Dana called time on our last activity, sweat coated my arms and back. I needed a shower and a good, long dive into a book.

But when I looked over at Paige, I was proud of the work we'd done. And James and Derrick would be great counselors. I could imagine how funny they'd be with kids. Dana was right. We were more confident with the activities now.

As I entered the cafeteria, I half expected Eric to be there waiting for me, but as I passed through the burger line, I didn't see him. I didn't know the proper girlfriend etiquette in this situation. I bit my lip as I filled a cup with coffee. Maybe now wasn't the best time to try to see him. Maybe I should wait.

A loud laugh startled me out of my thoughts. Was that... yes, Eric's voice echoed from the kitchen. A throaty chuckle followed, obviously female. He was with a woman? He never laughed that loud. Or maybe he never did with me.

I frowned as I added creamer to my coffee and set it on my tray. I stirred it for a long minute before Paige joined me.

"What crawled up your butt?" she asked.

I shook my head. Nothing, except my boyfriend having fun with someone who wasn't me. Was this what jealousy felt like? He should try to have fun. That's what we were supposed to be doing this summer, and he'd already drawn the short straw moments after arriving. Why not find joy wherever he could?

"Seriously, what's the problem?"

"Nothing. I'm fine." I took a long, scalding sip and my brain regulated itself. We were eighteen. I should act like an adult right now.

"Huh. I thought he'd sit with us."

I followed Paige's stare to where Lucas sank into a seat next to James. He'd pushed his sunglasses up to hold back his hair. But he didn't smile. Not his normal smile. His eyes drooped, and he pressed his lips together in a way that reminded me more of myself than him. Did he still want to meet at the canoes tonight? Maybe I *should* go, to see what was wrong with him. I didn't want to deprive him of friendship if he needed someone. Maybe something got screwed up with his swimming scholarship.

"Earth to Andy. You're hardcore staring at Lucas right now. People are going to notice." She lowered her voice. "What if Eric walks in?"

Now she was team Eric? I averted my eyes and focused on spearing some ranch-soaked salad with my fork. Paige was wrong. No one noticed me. It was easy to be invisible. It's what people expected.

Wait, hang on. That was last year at school, not here at camp. People did notice me here. Dana did. Paige did. And... Lucas.

This year, I'd also have a cottage full of teenage girls looking to me for their activities, counting on me to make their leadership camp experience count. The lettuce scraped against my now dry throat as I swallowed. I could handle that, right?

"Let's go to the beach after this. It will be the last time we can do anything camper-free. Please, Andy? I know you hate swimming, but..." Paige blinked her puppy dog eyes at me.

I smiled. "Sure." I'd bring a book. Reading on the beach was practically my chosen sport.

I breathed in deep the smell of fresh-cut grass and lake water before returning to my book. Prince Stephen was about to be crowned king, but it wasn't the real Stephen. It was an imposter, and once his royal seal was on the papers to evict Marietta's family from the kingdom...

"Hey." Paige kicked my foot.

"What?" I snapped before I remembered we were supposed to swim together.

"Oh, I forgot how you get with your sex books, you little perv."

I placed my bookmark and sat up. "Historical romance novels, not sex books."

"They're sex books, and you know it."

"Mmhmm." I sighed as she laid her towel next to mine. "You're not going to let me read, are you?"

"I'm glad to see you've upgraded your wardrobe to something less sister-wifey," Paige teased.

I smiled as I rested my head on my hands and let the sun bake into my back. It was so hot this summer. Vermont cycled through rain and snow so often that it was foreign to me to reapply sunscreen the way I had lately. At this rate, I'd run out before camp ended. Especially with my bathing suit covering less of my body. The bikini I wore wasn't the sexiest the store had by a mile, but it suited me. Boy shorts and a sports bra-like top made me look cute while keeping me contained. The bare stomach was new, however.

Was it wrong to dress different now that I had a boyfriend? The thought made me uncomfortable. I was happy ten seconds ago. Then she had to throw down her towel and start being all... Paige.

I blamed Brynn for my new wardrobe. Now that I'd "joined the land of the living" by being in her extensive social circle, I had to go shopping. A lot. I was bound to pick up some new pieces along the way. And maybe even repair our friendship. Kind of.

"I like it," Paige said. "Different, but still black. Still kind of you."

That's what Brynn had said, too. Everyone seemed to know me better than I knew myself these days—even a girl I went to summer camp with once.

I just smiled.

Paige shook out her hair. "Man, it's beautiful today, isn't it?"

It was. Heat shimmered off the lake, and the sky was a pure, deep blue. Not even a wisp of a cloud dared to ruin our time at the lake.

"Can I persuade you to swim with me out to the floating dock?" Paige asked. "We can get you a life vest."

I shook my head. I didn't plan on swimming. Just being warm.

"Fine, but your boy is already out there."

I laid back down on my towel. "Lucas isn't my boy."

Paige paused. "I was talking about Eric. But Luke's out there, too. Looks like they're having a cozy little chat."

Wait, what? I rolled over and sat up, shielding my eyes from the sun as I peered out to the floating dock. Paige was right. Eric sat on the dock with his feet slung over the side, and Lucas sat beside him.

My heart jumped into my throat. I should've known Eric would have some free time, too. Why didn't he text me? He knew now about Lucas and me. He had to. They were talking! I had to do something. I had to swim out there. I got to my feet.

"Hell yeah," Paige said as I sprinted to the water and dove in headfirst. I hadn't done much this year besides date Eric, but I did manage to squeak in some swimming lessons so what happened last summer would never, ever happen to me again. Once I hit deeper water, I did my best impression of a breaststroke all the way out to the dock. I climbed up, feeling proud of myself and sick with worry at the same time. I sat down next to Eric, who stared at the water with a pensive expression.

"Look, I can explain—" I started, but Lucas cut me off as Paige swung her legs over the edge next to him.

"Explain that you've grown fins this year? That was so great, Andy!" Lucas beamed like me learning how to swim was the equivalent of earning the Nobel Peace Prize. It seemed he'd gotten over his mood from earlier. He reached over Eric for a high five.

I returned it silently, our wet hands touching for the briefest of moments before I pulled away. A chill swept through me.

"You couldn't swim?" Eric asked.

"I could," I said.

"Not well." Lucas laughed like we had some secret joke.

Paige slapped his chest. "Cut it out. She was fine."

Eric got to his feet.

Yikes. How do I fix this?

"Hey, I risked my life to swim out here for you, and you're leaving?" I teased in what I hoped was a casual voice.

Eric smiled tentatively. "Risked your life, huh?"

"To be with you." I nudged his leg. "I must like you or something."

A corner of his mouth lifted.

Lucas stood. "Uh, cool. I'll see you guys back at camp," he said and dove off the dock, barely making a splash. The water churned as he swam with even strokes until he reached shallower waters near the shore. I could see why he'd gotten a scholarship. It made me feel better about last summer when he could swim circles around me.

Paige whistled a funny little tune and swung her legs. I widened my eyes at her.

She took the hint. "Yeah, uh, me too," Paige said. She flopped into the water with a giant splash and swam away.

"Think they're trying to tell us something?" Eric laughed, sitting beside me again.

"Maybe they're trying to give us time together." I held his hand and laid my head on his shoulder. "I don't mind."

He leaned his head on mine. "Me neither."

I wiggled my head in further until it was sandwiched between his shoulder and cheek. The pressure made me feel safe, like I belonged somewhere. Like I belonged with someone.

"What were you guys talking about out here?" I asked casually.

"Huh? Oh, I asked that guy how he knew you from last summer."

"Oh," I said. My throat clogged with the follow-up question I didn't want to ask.

"We talked about why he signed up late. Kinda sad. He said you were on the same team. Like your cottages were together."

I swallowed. It *was* sad that Lucas had to sign up late and ruin our time together. "Yeah."

"I wish I'd been at camp with you last summer," he said in a quiet voice.

I sighed. "No, you don't. I was so awkward." God might strike me dead at the vastness of that understatement. I'd had an actual panic attack halfway up the rock wall. I'd almost drowned myself at the swimming test. I clammed up every time anyone talked to me. It was a wonder I'd survived, and that I was here now.

"You're not awkward, Andy."

"I'm sorry about the whole counselor to kitchen thing," I whispered.

"I told you, it's all good. Honestly, I don't care where I'm placed as long as I get some time with you." He laced his fingers between mine.

My face heated. Intertwining my hand with his felt so intimate.

Time passed, and still we sat, touching but not speaking. A small breeze created miniature ripples in the lake around the dock. The smell of barbequed meat floated over to us, making my mouth water. I could have lived in that moment, the camp surrounding me like a hug, so warm that the water drying on my skin didn't chill me at all. But it couldn't last forever. Like some unspoken timer, everyone on the beach stood and shook out their towels.

"I don't want to go," I said. I didn't want to sever Eric's unspoken connection with me, trading it for all the drama I thought I'd left behind last summer. This time it was supposed to be about fun, about Eric and Paige and not pushing anyone to climb a darn rock wall.

"Me neither," he said as he slipped into the water. "Come on."

He paced me all the way back, probably worried I'd drown myself after Lucas's comment. When we got to the beach, he nodded at my book. "Is it a fantasy?"

"Uh, no. I read historical stuff." Historical *Romance*. I never read anything else. "This is one of my favorites."

He scoffed. "You read books more than once?"

"It's comforting," I mumbled. It didn't occur to me until this moment that re-reading the way I did might be odd. People rewatched their favorite TV shows, right? Oh, great. Maybe they didn't. Now, I wasn't sure of anything.

He helped me gather my towel and book, and we walked together to the edge of the beach. I tried to clear the gross feeling in the pit of my stomach with some self-logic. *Eric was teasing me. He wouldn't judge me. That's just his sense of humor.*

Outside my cottage, he pressed a kiss to my temple and said, "I like your bathing suit, by the way."

My body flooded with warmth. He noticed. Brynn was right—this moment was worth it. "Yeah?"

His eyes blazed as he scanned me from head to toe. "Definitely. Yeah."

I ducked my head, smiling all the way back to my bunk. It wasn't until I'd changed back into regular clothes that the ring of my phone startled me out of my PG-13 thoughts about Eric.

"Hello?" I answered, cradling the cell in the crook of my shoulder while I toweled off my hair.

"Geez, I've called about twenty times. You didn't tell me if you got to camp or not, or if Mr. Hottie with a Body got you alone in the woods yet."

I sighed. *Oh, Brynn.* "I got to camp. Sorry I didn't text." Because I hated talking on the phone, even if counselors were allowed to have them when campers couldn't. I could only imagine the thrilled looks on the faces of my own Beavers when I asked them to turn off and surrender their devices this year.

"Well, fine. But did Eric get you alone yet? He's so hot, and totally into you!"

"Brynn, come on. You know that..." That what? That I sucked at this type of girl talk? I didn't want to give up the dirty details of my every move with my boyfriend.

"No, I don't know anything, other than the fact that you went to this magical camp last year and came back a literal baller bitch. It made me think about signing myself up this year."

"Uh huh." Because Brynn would give up time on the beach to mentor kids in a place with communal bathrooms. "I have to get back. I'm sorry that I'm going to miss the party tonight." Was there a party tonight? Oh, who was I kidding? With Brynn, there was always a party.

"No biggie." I could almost hear her shrug through the phone. "But don't skimp on the details when you get home. I'm dying to know what goes down!"

I rolled my eyes. "Sure. Slumber party at my place when I get back?"

"Andy! We're eighteen! You don't have to keep calling it a slumber party. But sure. We can do manis and pedis and you can dish. Sounds like fun."

"Cool."

I got off the call with minimal promises made. Brynn had welcomed me back with both arms this year, but she was different from how I remembered her in middle school. Pushier. Less into real stuff. More into gossip and what happened between Eric and me. It was Brynn, so it was okay, I guess, but it was never my style. I knew relationships between girls could be more than that. Emma and Paige proved that to me last year. I threw my phone back on my bed and pulled a brush through my hair. I had an awkward evening to get ready for.

6

8pm. Canoes.

Dinner tasted amazing. The kitchen staff let Eric sit with me while I ate a delicious stir fry that I knew was all him. He smelled like spices and smiled while telling me about the funny ladies in the kitchen. The throaty chuckle I'd heard earlier belonged to the infamous Annie, who wasn't a day under seventy and chain-smoked cigarettes—but never in the kitchen.

Paige remained quiet while we exchanged cute little stories, but it was probably because she was adapting to me having a boyfriend.

"I wouldn't have swatted that paper," he said after I told him about James and Derrick.

I beamed at him. I knew he wouldn't.

"I wouldn't want you to think I was anything less than hygienic," he said in mock-horror.

Paige snorted. I smirked. I knew she'd like him once she gave him a chance.

"Well, these guys aren't trying to date me, so it looks like you're safe," I said to Eric.

Paige snorted again. This time I met her eyes. She jerked her head to the side, and I knew what that meant. I should tell Eric about last summer with Lucas. But I didn't want to.

And after he walked me back to my cottage, I paced between the empty bunks, muttering to myself for half an hour. I shouldn't meet with Lucas, but there was something wrong. I could sense it. And what kind of person would I be if I ignored that?

Despite every cell of my body rebelling, I walked to the beach and stood waiting for last summer's mistake to waltz over to me and say God knows what.

The longer I stood under the stupidly romantic sky full of the light of a thousand stars, the larger the knot in my stomach grew. I shouldn't be here. It wasn't too late to go back to my cottage and pretend I hadn't seen the note. Then his blond head appeared behind the canoes. He walked toward me with short, uncertain steps, like he wasn't sure if he should be here, either.

Well, okay then.

Lucas rounded the end of the canoes, and we stood a few feet apart, watching each other. He shoved his hands in his pockets while I stared at him. When he didn't speak, a weird feeling bubbled up inside me. He was the one who sent me the note. I had a boyfriend. He knew better—we were supposed to be focused on being counselors, not caught up in this stuff.

But what came out of my mouth was, "Are you okay?"

He burst out laughing. Not the reaction I'd expected. And not the kind of laughter that meant it was funny, either. It was harsh, almost desperate.

"You have a boyfriend."

What? That was the reason he wanted to talk to me? There was no crisis? His voice sounded different, too. Older. I guess I was, too.

"Yeah."

He threw his hands out at the same moment I did.

I found myself unscrewing my smile, unfiltering my response. "And?"

Though I'd never been one for big speeches, I could pack a lot into one word when I wanted to. And Lucas had always been perceptive. *And* meant: What are you going to do about it when you dumped me at the last second of camp last year? *And* meant: Why do you care? And it also meant: Don't ask me to come out here in the middle of the night when you're fine. You scared the shit out of me.

Lucas sighed. "I knew you were mad when you left last year. I told you, you're different."

My body rebelled against confrontation even as anger rose inside me like a deadly wave. "What are you saying?"

Was he trying to tell me he dated nobody all year on the off chance that the pool at his future college would be undergoing maintenance during training, and we'd end up here together? Because we both knew that wasn't true.

His eyes dropped to his shoes. *Yeah, that's what I thought.*

"You thought we'd pick up where we left off last year?" He gave me zero credit, didn't he? Just waiting for me to fall right back into his arms.

He shoved his hands in his pockets. "It was a shock seeing you together. The way he treats you."

Oh no, he didn't. I balled my hands into fists. "Eric is amazing to me."

"I bet. He handles you like you're made of glass."

"You're mad because my boyfriend is *nice* to me?" That was monstrous. "No, but..."

I folded my arms. "If that's all this is, we're done here." I turned to leave.

"Please, Andy. Hang on. I'm not saying this right. I want us to be..." His voice broke, but I couldn't turn around. It wasn't fair that he still had this effect on me. That his pain somehow felt like my pain. His desperation, my desperation.

"Friends like last summer?" My voice faded into the light wind that pushed ripples into the lake. "I'm not the same girl I was last year, Lucas." I'd never be that naïve again.

"You are to me."

I didn't know what to say to that. I couldn't explain how he made me feel. Mad. Hurt. Broken. Incomplete. I was taken, darn it. Eric and I were both headed off to in-state colleges in a month. We had it all planned out. I shook my head.

Lucas stepped forward, closing the space between us. I threw my hands up in front of me. "Stop. You're not my boyfriend. Eric is. He gets me."

Lucas stopped inches from my fingers, but he was still too close. "And I don't?" he whispered. "I get you more than anyone ever has, and you know it. There's still something between us. You can't ignore that." A primal spark blazed behind the cool blue of his eyes. "Andy."

I didn't want him to say my name like that, like it was all he needed to remind me of an entire summer of longing that I'd tried so hard to forget. He didn't get to do this to me. Not this year. "There is no *we.* There's you, and there's me and Eric. Eric likes me. He wants what's best for me." My voice caught. "He's not getting me in trouble for doing stuff we shouldn't or... or..." I couldn't come up with another example of why Lucas was terrible.

He reached out and took my hand. "I texted you. So many times."

"It wasn't the same. I couldn't... just don't," I choked out. "It's over."

"It's not. It was never over." But he let my hand go. My brain whirled with the inconsistencies of this conversation. "Andy, I—"

"Lucas, I shouldn't. I can't. I won't." It came out so garbled, I didn't even know what I meant. "You weren't supposed to be here!"

"I'm exactly where I'm supposed to be," he said, his voice calm.

"No," I said firmly. "If you're serious, we can be friends." It was all I could offer, and I wasn't sure I could even do that.

He barked out a laugh. "We can't be friends. You know that."

Enough. I turned to leave.

"You *know* that," he said again with more emotion, but I pretended not to hear him.

My hand tingled all the way back to the cottage. The building was lonely and cold without the voices and snoring I'd gotten used to last year. I snuggled under my same purple sleeping bag and pulled out my phone.

Four missed texts from Eric.

I tamped down the guilt of leaving my phone in my bunk. It seemed wrong to have it with me after not being able to have it at all last year. I couldn't believe I hadn't seen them after answering Brynn's call.

> **The kitchen is so hot! (But you're hotter)**

> **Annie is hilarious. She's almost a million years old, but she swears like a sailor. Nothing beats spending time with you, though.**

> **Did training go okay today?**

> **Settling in alright? I miss you already.**

I chewed on my lip. Was it bad that I missed all his messages?

> I forgot my phone today, sorry! I'm all settled. I'm still so sorry about kitchen duty. I know you needed a break from all that.

Three dots appeared, indicating he was typing me back. Shame sat heavy on my chest that he'd been waiting for me. My sleeping bag rustled as I turned on my side. Should I go visit him? I already went out once tonight for Lucas, and we weren't even dating. Where did Eric even sleep if it wasn't in a cottage with campers?

> It's okay. I'm enjoying the kitchen.

Was he? He'd say that even if he wasn't. He was such a good sport. Sometimes I wondered why he ever decided to date me. I slithered out of my sleeping bag cocoon. He needed me. I should go to him. It was the least I could do after meeting with Lucas tonight. Maybe we could snuggle before parting ways to go to bed.

My phone buzzed again as I pulled on a hoodie.

> We both have an early morning tomorrow. I'll let you sleep. Miss you.

I sat down on the edge of my bed, one arm in my sweatshirt and one out.

> Miss you, too. See you tomorrow maybe?

He didn't answer. I took my sweatshirt back off. Eric wouldn't break any rules to meet with me. He cared too much about our positions here, about making a good impression.

It took forever, my brain still moving at lightspeed hours into the night, but eventually I fell asleep, my hand curled around my phone.

7

First Dibs

At breakfast, Dana pep-talked us all within an inch of our lives. I didn't see Eric between all her *You can do it* speeches, and Lucas didn't sit with Paige and me, for which I was grateful. I headed back to my cottage with a steaming cup of coffee and the optimism that today could be a zero-drama first day of camp.

Counselor Suzie put stickers on each of our bunks with our names last year, but I wouldn't be as weird about it. I could memorize the girls easy enough. There were eleven of them, after all, and I had their names on a list.

But I couldn't tell if they fell into one of Paige's categories. I tapped my clipboard with my pen. Were they a Victim like me last year, pushed into camp by overzealous parents? Were they a Volunteer, willing to do any activity and level up in leadership the way the camp brochure promised? Or were they a Convert, a veteran of camp like Paige and Lucas, and like I'd become after a transformational experience here? If I knew, it would be easier to get a handle on what they might need from me this summer.

I studied my list as I walked through the bunks and ensured everything was ready. I could do this. Dana told me at the end of last summer that I'd be a great influence, that I'd lead through example. The girls would love me.

The faint squeak of old brakes in the parking lot and the sound of voices welcoming people to camp made me pause my nervous pacing. *Showtime.*

"Hi," I said to the first girl to walk through the door. She towered over me, her blonde hair falling in waves halfway down her back. It reminded me of Paige.

"You're my counselor?" the girl asked, more inquisitive than mean.

"Yep."

"Cool." She looked past me into the cottage. "I'm the first one here?"

"Yeah, but that's okay," I rushed to reassure her. "I'm sure the other girls will be here in a minute or two."

But she'd already walked past me. "Sweet. I get first dibs."

I hadn't thought of that. When she chucked her stuff onto the bottom bunk closest to the back door, she smiled as it bounced. "I'm Sarah. You want my phone?"

"Um, sure. Yes." Of course, I needed their phones. I should have remembered that.

She powered it down and handed it over, unphased. This was not how I saw this going. She didn't appear awkward to be here by herself with her counselor. Wouldn't she miss her phone for the next ten days? *Volunteer.* I penciled a VOL next to her name on the list.

I set her phone on my bed. I should get a freezer bag or a bucket to put them all in. What an archaic rule, taking all their cell phones. It would make me look like a jerk if I used mine to check in with Eric.

Less than a minute later, a trio of girls slammed through the door. They didn't pause when they saw me. They sprinted for the beds to stake a claim.

I watched them, trying to figure out who was who. From their screeching, the shorter girl with pronounced hips and strong calves was named Abby and the tall, dark-skinned girl with hair twists was Destiny. The third girl with short black hair and a mammoth suitcase talked a mile a minute about the ride over and her boyfriend back home and her new sleeping bag, so I didn't catch her name.

I should probably check them off the list and take their phones. I walked over to the corner where they'd set up camp. "Hi, I'm Andy."

They ignored me, still listening to the loud one's explanation of how her brother thought he needed her sleeping bag for his youth group camping trip, but over her dead body would she miss the chance to show it off.

I cleared my throat. "Hi. I'm Andy."

The girls turned as one, and I had the same weird, sinking feeling I always got at school when I hung out with Eric's friends. I brushed it aside. They were younger than me. I didn't need to be liked by them. Right? I smiled.

"Are you the counselor?" Destiny asked.

"Yep. Destiny, right?" I crossed her name off my clipboard.

"Aren't you supposed to, like, be wearing a vest? How else would we know you weren't another camper?" the loud girl pointed out.

"Great catch," I said, trying not to blush. I'd forgotten to put it on. "What's your name?"

"Maria."

"Hi, Maria." I smiled. "And you're Abby?" I asked the shorter girl.

"How'd you know?"

"Oh, I thought I heard…"

"Ugh, she's one of those." Maria rolled her eyes. "Are you going to be listening in to all our conversations and ratting us out all camp long, then?" she interrogated.

I opened my mouth to respond, unsure of how to answer that question. I had to report if I thought they were in danger or causing distress.

"Be nice," Destiny said. She turned to me. "Maria isn't mean, I swear. She's just cranky from the trip."

"Oh, do you all know each other?"

Destiny nodded. "From last summer. We bunked together then, too."

I hadn't thought of that. Of course, some of them had been to camp before. How else did you become a Convert? And I knew Paige and Lucas and even Emma had all been to camp together before last year. I guess I didn't count on my campers already having friendships coming in. How would that affect the girls who weren't here last year or who had friends in different cottages?

This might be more complicated than I thought.

I made a mark next to all their names on my list, and they forked over their phones without being asked. I laid them in a neat line with the others on my bed and stood at the door, propping it open with my back. Maybe if I kept my distance, I wouldn't be labeled a horrible eavesdropper during Maria's loud conversation about skittle flavors.

I breathed in the scent of dirt and pine and stared at the blue, blue sky over the lake. Still no clouds in sight. Lucas jogged over from the parking lot, wearing his vest, of course.

"Alright, Andy?" His voice cracked. Was he getting sick?

I shielded my eyes from the sun to see him. I guessed he'd decided we were still on speaking terms even though I'd reamed him out last night. "Yeah."

He nodded, then sprinted the rest of the way to the door of his cottage, fist-bumping the guys hanging out on the porch.

"Who is that?" a tanned girl asked as she bounded up the stairs. "He is *fine*."

"A counselor," I said quickly.

"Taken. Got it." She powered by me to get into the cottage.

"No, I—" Crap, I didn't get her name. I tapped my pen against my list in agitation. I still had time.

"Stressing you out, already?" another camper asked through perfect black lipstick as she breezed by me into the cottage. "That's not good."

Maybe *she* was a Victim.

Ten minutes later, I had every camper marked off my list and all their cell phones sat in a mismatched row on my bed. Time to lead.

"Okay, the schedule says we have enough time for a cottage activity."

"I can't even hear her," Maria muttered.

"Can you talk louder?" Destiny asked, elbowing her friend.

"Sure, sorry." I cleared my throat. "We have some time, so I thought we could play a game like quiet ball or maybe settle into our bunks. Chat or read, maybe?"

"Quiet ball?" Destiny arched an eyebrow. She made eye contact with a few other girls in the circle. "I don't even know everyone's names. Can we, like, start with that?"

Every atom of my body rebelled against the idea of an icebreaker, but she had a point. It made sense for them to get to know each other.

"Okay, let's do that." I smiled bigger than felt natural. "Name and favorite activity?"

A few girls nodded, and Destiny volunteered to go first.

"I'm Destiny. I'm into soccer. I play forward."

Obviously.

The next girl, a perky petite blonde, went. "I'm Taylor, and I play soccer, too!" She high-fived Destiny. "But um, let's see. I'm into dirt biking. Little, but fierce!" She rolled up the left pantleg of her jeans to show a grotesque scab ringed by an angry-looking bruise. "Got it at my last Freestyle."

"Wow. That's... something." Maybe these girls should be leading themselves. *I'm a counselor for a reason, though*, I reminded myself. *They can learn from me.* But learn... what?

"I'm Summer," another blonde said. She squared her shoulders. "I'm on the debate team back home."

I opened my mouth to give an encouraging comment, but Maria beat me to it.

"A smart chick! We'll need you in competition this summer." She beamed.

I nodded, trying to keep my smile even. "Totally." So much for her being a mean girl. Maybe her pointed comments only applied to counselors who—*gasp*—forgot to wear the stupid vest.

One by one, the girls listed their impressive, outgoing activities. I kept waiting, halfway hoping there'd be someone who I could help, someone I could relate to. Someone like the girl I'd imagined leading when I saw myself as a counselor.

That never happened. Caralyn was a cheerleader, Megan played volleyball, Leah starred in her school's musical last spring, Mallory was in show choir, and even the girl in black led the drumline section in marching band. They were all confident, self-possessed young women. No one needed me for encouragement. Regardless of race, culture, and sexuality, every girl was welcomed into the circle. I was... useless?

My stomach twisted. I was useless.

Thankfully, some of the girls needed to nest more after we chatted, so I dumped out my mesh swim bag and used that to house their phones next to my bed. When I checked my own phone, I was shocked to see that it was almost time for our first activity with our partner cottage. Instead of feeling panic, the thought of Lucas helping me out with the girls was like a weight lifted off my shoulders.

But first I had to get their attention.

"Hey, Destiny. Sarah. Maria. Caralyn. We're going to meet on the porch." I went around and told each girl the same thing. They gave me weird looks, and I wondered if they were asking themselves why I didn't call it out. But it wasn't my style. They'd get used to that, right?

They all moved to the porch as a loud, raucous group. Maria talked a mile a minute about... cats? Yep, it was a whole diatribe about the care of a sick cat back home.

"Girls," I said. But no one heard me. "Girls, your attention?" This time Megan turned to me. I smiled at her, but I needed everyone's attention, so I clapped my hands together three times. That got a couple more of them to look my way. They clapped back three times. Oh, like at school. Sure.

I clapped twice. This time more of the girls clapped back. Most everyone finished talking. I had their attention. Awesome.

"Some of you who were here last year might already know this, but we will be paired with another cottage this summer to complete some of the activities. Uh…"

"Is it the hot guy you said was taken?" Megan asked.

"I didn't say…"

"Counselor Andy has a crush on someone?" Summer grinned.

"No, that's not…"

"Where are they? Are they coming over here?" Sarah said.

"We're going to meet them in the courtyard. Let's go." Maybe if I ignored their comments, they'd knock it off. I didn't know how to deal with them saying things like that without making it worse. "Please be nice," I said as an afterthought.

"To you or them?" Abby laughed.

My face flushed. I could handle this. They were joking.

I started toward the field, and they fanned out around me, talking about all the food they hoped the cafeteria would make this summer, about how it would be helpful if the camp served them hot guys on a platter, too. I sighed to keep from laughing out of frustration.

"And how are the Beavers doing so far?" Lucas asked with a scratchy voice as we strolled into the courtyard in the center of camp.

I wanted to kick him. Even with half the volume, he still commanded the attention of all the guys in his cottage. They sat cross-legged in a circle surrounding him, chatting with each other, whereas my girls… Blair pulled on Mallory's braid. She screeched at her to cut it out. Destiny and Abby stood next to a clump of trees more than fifty yards off deep in a secret-sharing session. And where did Leah go? She was walking with us a second ago. The sheer volume of giggling and gossiping from the rest of the Beavers would be enough to drown out anything I'd say back to Lucas.

I gave him a sarcastic thumbs up.

"Guys, make some room for the girls," Lucas commanded in a low voice. "Ladies?" He gestured for them to sit.

They all shut up to do as he asked. My mouth dropped open in shock as even Maria stopped talking to squeeze in beside the guys. Lucas held his hand out to help me step between them and into the center of the circle.

I ignored him. I couldn't touch another guy when my boyfriend was at camp. It wouldn't be right. I took a huge step and lost my balance, windmilling my arms to keep from falling on my face.

Lucas sighed. More giggles.

"Rejected!" one of the guys jeered.

Lucas pretended not to hear him, clapping his hands together. "For our first activity as a full group, we have a few options. We can go with something mental, something physical, or both. What do we all think?"

"Mental!" a few of the guys yelled while a resounding "Physical!" rose up from the rest of the group, including most of my Beaver girls.

Leah materialized from the woods and sat next to Abby. I narrowed my eyes. No way she got lost. We walked here *together*.

Lucas looked at me. "Haha or Human Knot? They're both a hybrid."

I stared at my shoes, remembering the touch of our hands, the way he'd coached me through the Human Knot exercise last year even though we'd both been campers that summer.

"The Haha one," I said, though I couldn't for the life of me remember what that was.

He nodded gravely, like maybe he remembered the same thing I did. "Do you want to kick it off, or should I tell them the directions?"

"Um, you," I said, trying not to feel guilty I was making him speak with half a voice.

Destiny snorted from the second row. I ignored her like Lucas did when his camper made a crappy remark. So what if I let him do it? I couldn't remember how it went anyway. I didn't study the handbook like there was a midterm on it.

"Okay, guys. It's lucky that it's nice and dry out here today, because we're going to be getting down on the ground. The Haha game is all about not letting yourself laugh."

"That's not that hard," Destiny said.

"You wouldn't think so, but you'll be laying your head on the stomach of the next person in line. We all lie in a zigzag that way. The first person has to yell "Ha" once, then the next twice, then the next three times, and so on. Our stomachs tense when we yell, so your head will bounce, and it's funny."

The campers looked at Lucas like they couldn't imagine what he was talking about.

"But if you laugh, we have to start over," he said.

"How do we win?" a lanky guy asked. Destiny smiled at him like she wouldn't mind if he was the prize.

"Great question, Josh. We win if we don't laugh by the time we get through all the Ha's."

"I think we should lie down girl-boy-girl-boy," Maria said. "I won't laugh if it's guys around me. No offense, Beavers."

"None taken," Destiny said, eyeing Josh. "I'm for it."

Some of the guys looked a bit uncomfortable at this, and I had the sudden image of tigers stalking baby gazelles. These girls were something.

"Sure. Andy and I will start the line, and then you all can fill in."

Wait, what? I had to lie on his stomach, or he had to lie on mine? That wasn't part of the deal, here. But when all our campers looked at me expectantly, what else could I do?

Lucas stretched out on the crunchy grass. I hesitated a second before placing my head on his stomach. It wasn't that bad. Kind of warm. Kind of moving when he breathed. One of the guys put their head on my stomach, but the layered shirts I wore made a stranger touching me more bearable.

"Everyone ready?" I called, putting effort into projecting my voice. A bunch of thumbs shot into the air and the Beaver girls cheered.

"Ha!" Lucas yelled. His stomach contracted and bounced my head up.

It startled me, and I almost laughed before I caught myself. "Ha Ha!" I yelled.

The guy lying on me let out a "Ha Ha Ha!"

Caralyn, whose head perched on his stomach, dissolved into giggles. "It's like a boy trampoline! I'm sorry! I don't know why it's funny!"

We had to start over.

The sun blazed down on us, and I regretted my decision not to bring my sunglasses as the game went on. Lucas and I adjusted ourselves a few times until my head rested more in the concave part of his stomach and not on the jutting bones of his ribs or hips. I found it hard to concentrate, knowing how close we were. Even though this whole thing was innocent, we were still touching each other. It felt super unnecessary and wrong, even as his gravelly voice mumbled encouragement to the kids down the line every time they screwed up by dissolving into laughter. By the time we mastered it, my cheeks burned hot from all the sun.

Lucas's strong hand practically scalded mine as he helped me up. We all brushed the dust off our shorts, though it didn't make much difference. Half of it stuck to our sweat.

"Okay, Beavers. That was fun!" I said with more enthusiasm than needed. "Let's head back to the cottage to get cleaned up before lunch."

Lucas cleared his throat. "Right," he said. For a moment, his voice came back. "Us, too. Let's go, Cheetahs."

I raised an eyebrow. Was he sick or not?

"I'm okay," he said to me in a more normal tone. "Just need water."

I nodded and trailed behind the Beaver girls until we shut the cottage door. Then they exploded.

"Oh my God! Did you see the way she touched his hand?" Megan squealed.

Maria nodded. "And that whole thing at the end? She was super concerned."

"His voice lowers around her. It's like a movie!" Summer yelled.

I was lost. "Who are we talking about?" Did they have crushes on these boys already?

Destiny rolled her eyes. "You. Duh. Why didn't you tell us you and Counselor Luke were a thing?"

8

Landy

These girls thought Lucas and I were... that we had...

I had to shut this down now. "We were campers together last year. We're friends now, and that's it."

"Oh, I heard all about that," Sarah said. "How he stood up for you at the rock wall challenge. Our groups passed by each other that day."

Great. "I don't like heights," I mumbled.

"But you do like Luke," she teased.

"Lucas," I corrected before what she said sank in. Sarah smirked.

"Oh, I know! You guys can be Landy!" Abby gushed. "Lucas and Andy, get it? Or we could do Andas, but that sounds like—"

"Girls. Stop," I said with more force than intended. It was great that they all gathered around me now like they'd accepted me as one of their own, but the cost was too high. "Lucas and I are friends," I repeated. "I already have a boyfriend, and he's here at this camp."

"Ooh, scandalous. It's always the quiet ones that turn out to be such players." Maria wiggled her eyebrows.

A low pressure built inside me. They didn't get it. They could spread this Landy thing all over camp and Eric would hear, and then... I rubbed the center of my chest.

"Knock it off," Destiny drawled, heading to her bed. "You're bullying our counselor."

"So, who's the boyfriend? Counselor James? It's James, isn't it?" Abby asked, oblivious.

"His name is Eric," I replied, walking to my own bunk. How many minutes were left before lunch? Six? It may as well be six thousand at this rate.

"Wait, is that the new cafeteria guy?"

I nodded, though I had no idea how they'd seen him already.

She gave a low whistle. "What a body."

I shook my head, uncomfortable that she'd noticed his body. They were only a year younger than me, but it was still weird.

"He can hand me a hamburger any day," Megan teased.

"How are you pulling the two hottest guys at camp right now?" Maria demanded.

I took out my phone and texted Paige.

Are you free?

She didn't immediately text back. I don't know why I thought she would. We had responsibilities. I imagined her sitting in a circle with her campers, doing something leadershippy. I needed to be mature about this.

"Okay, we won't rat you out to Cafeteria Eric. I still like Landy, though," Abby pouted.

I gave her a thumbs up, too overwhelmed to do anything else.

Destiny frowned. "Let's go. I want to get a good spot."

I grimaced. I hated that a camper had to be nice to me. It should be the other way around. The girls filed out, even Sarah, who wasn't a part of that posse.

Gratefulness washed over me, and I knew that made me a horrible person. What a mess. I sat down hard on my bed, but I didn't have long to feel sorry for myself before my phone buzzed. *Paige.*

Where are you? Come to the cafeteria and I'll help.

I sighed, pocketing my phone. I couldn't panic or get wrapped up in boy drama this summer. I didn't have that luxury. I had a job to do.

With determined strides, I made my way to the cafeteria and got in the food line. It smelled... amazing. Wow, what *was* that? My mouth watered in anticipation as the line moved at a snail's pace. And then Eric stood in front of me with a dorky hairnet on, spooning a spicy chicken dish onto my tray.

"Hey," he said softly.

My heart melted. "Hey."

For a long moment we stared at each other, my heartbeat settling as he smiled my favorite calm smile. Someone cleared their throat farther down the line. I jolted—I was holding everyone up.

"Sorry," I said to the people behind me, sliding my tray along the counter. I grabbed milk and an orange and prepared myself for the inevitable teasing of my campers. No way they missed my interaction with my boyfriend. When I set my tray down at our table, Maria opened her mouth to speak, a sly look on her face. I tried not to wince.

But before she could get anything out, Paige announced, "Age before beauty, Beavers! I need to talk to my bestie." She wheedled in between them, and I didn't even try to mask my relief.

"I'm here," she said, forking a piece of chicken into her mouth. "What's the SOS for?"

I shook my head, my face flaming. Like I could tell her with the girls surrounding us right now.

She tapped the table with her fingers. "Want to sit at the counselor table?"

I followed her eyes to the table in the corner where Suzie and Tyler spent most of their lunches last year. Garrett had James in a headlock while James pounded the top of the table, yelling 'Mercy.'

"No, thanks."

Maria squirmed in her seat. I ignored her.

"So, what's up?" Paige asked. I sighed.

Maria couldn't take it anymore. "She's here with Cafeteria Eric but she should be with Counselor Luke, and she knows it. It's like a soap opera!"

"They should have given us popcorn," Taylor said.

"You mean Eric should give us popcorn." Sarah's eyes wandered to the food line. "It would probably taste like heaven. He's so hot and polite."

"I still like Landy," Abby pouted.

Paige choked on her milk. "Landy?"

"Isn't it perfect?" Abby said, misinterpreting Paige's reaction. "They're meant to be. There's so much chemistry there."

"Uh..." Paige looked at me.

Help, I mouthed, my shoulders hunched over like the worst doormat possible.

"You might want to keep the Landy thing quiet unless you want to be responsible for the first breakup at camp," Paige said.

The girls fell silent for a second.

"Huh," Summer said. "I didn't think about it that way."

"You didn't notice your counselor went quiet?" Paige asked. My face blazed as the girls contemplated.

"She did tell us to stop," Destiny admitted.

Paige and I locked eyes. She smiled. "Good for you," she said. I knew she remembered last summer when I struggled to stick up for myself at all.

Leah slid her tray next to mine, late again. "What are we talking about?"

Paige made eye contact with each of the girls surrounding me. "You need to respect her telling you to stop. She shouldn't have to repeat herself."

Summer and Abby looked down at their food. Paige was the master of calling people out, letting them know what was and wasn't okay.

I glanced over to where her campers sat. What was the name of her cottage again? Clownfish? That wasn't even a woodland creature. Neither were Cheetahs. Who oversaw the cottage naming at this camp? Two of her Clownfish read books at the table while eating, and one had nodded off. I stared at them. How much easier it would be if Paige and I could switch cottages.

Maria whispered something to Abby who whispered to Destiny. They all giggled. Paige arched an eyebrow.

"We'll be good," Maria promised. "Right, girls?"

"Right," most of them said.

I narrowed my eyes. Why did I get the feeling they had their fingers crossed under the table?

Paige left, giving me a thumbs up before patting the shoulder of her sleeping camper to wake her up. I stared at the over-the-top smiles of the Beavers surrounding me.

"This is gonna be the best summer ever," Caralyn said cheerfully.

Oh, boy.

I bit my lip as I texted Eric on the way back to the cottage. We'd been dating for the better part of a school year, but I still couldn't shake the butterflies, like whatever I'd type would be so cringe that he'd roll his eyes and wonder how he'd ever thought such a dork would make a fun girlfriend. *You texted him yesterday. This is no different. Just do it.*

> **What are you doing later? Do you get any free time?**

Right after sending, I swiped open my Kindle app to soothe my nerves. A stolen moment of period romance would go a long way to remove me from my current issues, even if only for the two-minute walk back to the Beaver cottage. But no sooner did I click into the app than a text appeared.

> **I can duck out around 7 for a bit. You okay?**

I smiled. Eric was worried about me. Seven was right after dinner when the campers had free time. Perfect.

> **I'm fine. Meet me by the snack shack?**

It would be more romantic to meet by the lake, but I wanted it to be convenient for him, and memories of Lucas already filled the lakeshore.

9

Beaver Bonding

I had ten seconds of silence in the cottage before the girls trickled in behind me. The schedule dictated that we do an individual cottage activity next, which was both challenging and a relief. I inhaled, channeling my inner Paige. As I exhaled, I imagined her chuckling as she chatted with her campers in a circle. I could do this, too.

I flipped through the handbook before settling on an activity that made me laugh out loud. They'd struggle with it, but it would play into their competitive streak. *Perfect.*

"Okay, girls," I said after they began to gravitate toward the center of the room. "I've got an activity for you, but it might be difficult."

"*Please.* I'm in." Maria nudged Abby, who smiled.

I grabbed a small, pre-made bag labeled Activity C from under my bed. "Okay, so we split into teams, and you will get toothpicks and mini marshmallows to try to build the tallest free-standing structure you can within five minutes."

"What?" Sarah called from the back of the group. "What are we doing?"

"We're building toothpick towers," Destiny called back. "Maybe we should sit to get directions first," she said to me. I nodded, heat flooding my face. I should've thought of that.

They sat in a haphazard circle, and I repeated myself, trying hard to be a tad louder than normal.

Taylor snorted. "I've done this before."

I raised my eyebrows. "But none of you are allowed to speak."

"What?" Maria squealed.

"Don't worry about it." Abby patted her knee with a mischievous grin.

I narrowed my eyes. "And..." This next part wasn't in the rules, but they needed it. "I'm eating one of your marshmallows every time I hear you talk."

Abby gave me a death glare, but I caught Summer nodding. Fair was fair.

I numbered them off, splitting up the grumbling trio of Abby, Destiny, and Maria in the process. I handed each team a sandwich baggy of toothpicks and marshmallows and waited for them to settle in different corners of the room.

"Go," I said.

Leah flipped her hair back. "Did she say to—"

"*Shut up*," Destiny said. "We're starting."

"Well, it's not like I could hear that," Leah grumbled.

I let that go and didn't take their marshmallows. Was I that quiet? It felt like I had yelled it.

Silence descended in the room as the tension ratcheted up. It was the weirdest, most hilarious thing to walk around, watching the girls try to argue with their arms while frantically spearing marshmallows with toothpicks.

Destiny, Taylor, Leah, and Mallory worked quickly, Destiny constructing the tower while the other three girls stuck together one marshmallow and one toothpick to make a pile of kindling for her to work with.

"Yes!" Maria hissed when her team began their top tier. I floated over to them and plucked a marshmallow from their dwindling pile to pop in my mouth. Summer and Sarah stared daggers at her. She mouthed *Sorry* at them.

I suppressed a laugh but reigned in my expression. Remorse looked out of place on Maria's face.

"One more minute," I called, pleased I didn't have to shout to be heard in a silent room. When I called time, I had to scramble for the measuring tape to see who had won.

"With fourteen-and-a-half inches, our winners are..." I paused, and the girls smacked their knees in an approximation of a drumroll. "Destiny, Taylor, Mallory, and Leah."

"Thank God! I need to talk!" Maria burst out as they all clapped.

I took a seat and the girls followed suit, creating a circle in the center of the room.

"How do you think you won?" I asked, popping an unused marshmallow in my mouth while the rest of them feasted on their own towers. If my mouth was full, I could hide my nervousness about asking the after-activity questions.

Leah shrugged, looking uninterested. My stomach twisted. They totally thought this was stupid.

"We had a plan," Taylor said.

"How did you figure out the plan?" I expected them to turn to Destiny, but to my surprise, they all looked at Mallory.

"Assembly lines work best, and I knew Destiny would stay focused if we gave her the most responsibility," she said.

"How did you know that?" Destiny asked.

I sat back, smiling.

"You were calm during the Haha game, and I thought you'd want to win against Abby and Maria," Mallory said.

Destiny opened and closed her mouth, thinking.

"Very observant," I complimented.

"So maybe..." Summer paused. "Maybe leadership is about noticing, kind of?"

"Not just talking." Destiny smirked at Maria, who stuck out her tongue.

I laughed as I got to my feet. "Maybe. We have time for one more activity before dinner. How do you feel about something a little more physical?"

"Hell yeah!" Taylor said as we headed outside.

"Then prepare yourselves for Duck, Duck, Goose," I said in a dry voice.

They all cheered. Not one of them didn't. It was a joke, but they wanted to play it? Of course. I followed them out the door. Passing the time with the girls until dinner didn't feel as forced as I thought it would. I found myself wanting to get to know them better.

Taylor tripped over her feet every two seconds, but she was an awesome sport about it. I headed back into the cottage when she scraped her knee, and when I emerged wearing the safari vest with a pocket containing Band-Aids, the girls all cheered. Blair had sarcastic comments for everything, but she was the first to stick up for someone who got interrupted or talked over. Megan was the most boy-crazy girl I'd ever met in my life. She always tried to bring up Eric and the whole Landy thing in between talking about the muscles of this guy and the smile of that one. But Destiny...

Destiny might be the best leader out of all of them.

She diverted Megan's attention, comforted Taylor, listened to Blair, and provided a much-needed balance between all the girls. It was a sight to behold, and I found myself sitting back to appreciate each of them for the wonderful leaders they already were. In no time at all, they'd talked through dinner and took off for free time.

I sat down on my bunk in the empty cottage, smiling. I liked them. All of them. I laid back on my pillow, my eyes drifting closed in pleasant exhaustion before they snapped back open.

"Eric," I whispered. Without changing, I sprinted out of the cottage. As I rounded the corner of the Snack Shack, I slowed so I wouldn't appear out of breath. How would he feel if he thought I had to rush because I forgot to meet him? I texted first. And there he was, right on time, looking as perfect as he always did.

He smiled his shy smile, and I ran to him, throwing myself into his arms. I belonged here. Safe, enclosed in his gentle, comforting embrace. And it wasn't because he thought I was made of glass. He cared about me, respected me.

"Whoa, there." He rocked back as I continued to squeeze him. "You sure you're okay?"

"I just miss you," I said, blushing into his sweatshirt. Camp was getting to me. I was usually so much more put-together.

He chuckled, and I relaxed. "I miss you, too."

"Want to get a snack and walk along the trails? There's one that has these Cottonwood trees I wanted you to see."

He grimaced. "There's a lot of prep to do for breakfast tomorrow. I have to chop a ton of veggies for morning fajitas."

"Oh." I tried not to look disappointed. "So how much time do you have?"

He shrugged, not meeting my eyes. None, but he wanted to see me.

"I don't want you to get in trouble," I fretted. But I wanted us to connect, to hang out. We hadn't done that, and I knew it was the main reason he wanted to come here with me.

"I won't be, but..."

"But you have to get back," I whispered.

He straightened his sweatshirt. "Yeah."

I grimaced. "This wasn't what you had in mind at all, was it?"

He squinted against the harsh sun. "Honestly? No, but it's okay."

"It's not. I'm sorry." I didn't know what to say. I had spent my day having fun bonding with my Beaver girls while Eric suffered for real.

"I've got five minutes. Let's just..."

Just what, though? Be stressed next to each other? I leaned into him again.

We stayed that way for a long minute. Then finally, he released me. "If I can get an Andy hug every day, it might solve everything."

I smiled, but we both knew it wasn't true. "I'm sorry it turned out this way. If you want to... If you want to leave, I get it."

He stared at me, his eyes dark and serious. Did I say the wrong thing? He wanted to be a counselor. Doing what he did at home all the time wasn't a break, and it wouldn't be easy to get time together. It was logical to give him the out. I'd miss him, but I didn't want him to be miserable.

"I'm sorry," I said again, at a loss.

His face softened. "Stop apologizing," he said, pushing a lock of hair behind my ear. "You haven't done anything wrong."

I nodded, though I wasn't so sure.

10

Color War

I only half-heard what Abby droned on about the next morning as I picked at my breakfast. My morning run had been breakneck since I wanted to get back in time to be Counselor Andy. I'd thought that a quick sprint might help me come up with a solution to Eric's problem, but it didn't. It just made me sweaty.

"Your boy has leveled up the cafeteria experience," Destiny said through a mouthful of food.

I forced a smile. She was right. The fajitas smelled delicious. "I'll pass that along."

"You should." Abby stabbed a watermelon cube. "Even the fruit salad is better. He's like, a kitchen guru."

I nodded. He was an everything guru. I was the one falling short. And a part of me resented that I felt this way. Why did I ever think it would be a brilliant idea to bring my boyfriend to camp? If he wasn't here, I could concentrate on being a better counselor. If he wasn't here, there'd be no buffer between me and Lucas. But I didn't need a buffer. I was strong enough to resist Lucas on my own.

I took a bite of my sausage, veggie, and hollandaise fajita and about died from happiness. That just made it worse.

"Heya campers!" Dana boomed from the stage.

"Heya," I said along with the girls and everyone around me.

"This year at camp, we have a surprise for you!"

I tuned in fully. Nothing in my instructions said anything about a surprise. After the girls came in last night, I read the rest of the handbook. Okay, I skimmed it. Half of it. Was this "surprise" yet another thing I would have to learn how to do?

"Drumroll, please!" Dana cupped her ear with her hand and waited.

We all stomped our feet, and the table shook with the force of a dozen hands banging against it.

Dana cut us off. "We're having a color war!" she crowed. Everyone clapped and cheered, including me, but what the heck was a color war?

"Yes! Finally, a reason to get competitive!" Summer yelled over the noise.

Oh, great. All these girls needed was a reason to become more aggressive. *Please let there be rules.*

"Every team will get a color that goes with the animal of their cottage," Dana explained.

"So, brown. Because we're the shi—"

"Maria," I warned.

"What?" she asked with innocent doe-eyes.

I tried not to smile. At least she saw the bright side of it.

"... until you can no longer pair with them and have to duke it out to determine the one true winner."

Great, I'd missed half of what Dana said. Some counselor I was.

"More reason to hang out with Josh," Megan teased Destiny.

Destiny elbowed her. "Shut up."

Okay, so we'd work with our partner cottages until we couldn't anymore.

"Every day, in addition to your normal group challenges, we'll be adding one more that will determine the points for the color war. The cottage that wins our first ever camp-wide competition will get their names etched on the new trophy."

"I want the Beavers to be the first name on the trophy," Caralyn said. None of the girls laughed at her. They all nodded along.

"And of course, infinite bragging rights."

Both of those prizes seemed trivial to me, but I could tell the girls were dying to compete their guts out. Maybe being a good counselor would be more about reigning them in. How could I accomplish that? It was so opposite from what I thought I might do this summer.

After Dana finished telling us the specifics, Lucas slid into the seat next to mine. Today he'd pulled his hair back in an actual man-bun and wore one of his signature baseball tees. Green and grey, this time. Somehow, he pulled it all off. "You don't like the food?" he asked, looking at my half-eaten tray.

I sighed. How very Lucas. "Looks like your voice is back."

"Water. Drink of champions." He winked. "Thanks for caring, counselor."

I snorted. "You know they allow you to go up for seconds," I told him as he picked up my fork and ate the rest of my meal.

"I know. But watching you get all worked up over it is more fun." He swigged a drink of my carton of milk. "We're going to pulverize your team."

Destiny opened her mouth to lay into him. I raised my hand for her to wait.

"Sorry, what?" I said to him.

"The color war. How would it look if the first ever team to win was a beaver? Come on, Andy. Your color is brown."

"What's wrong with brown?" Destiny asked with an arched eyebrow.

Lucas almost swallowed his tongue. I let him sputter for a few seconds before sighing. I should save him. He wasn't racist. He was just trying to get a rise out of me.

"Sounds like maybe you're over here to trash talk because you're *yellow*-bellied," I said. "But don't worry, I won't tell the guys."

"Oooh," the Beaver girls jeered.

His eyes twinkled as he forked some of my fruit salad into his mouth.

"No comeback? Too busy eating my food? That's okay, you'll need your strength."

He sat back, trying hard not to smile. "There she is," he murmured.

I rolled my eyes. He did *not* get to say that to me. "There who is? The girl whose team is the most competitive at camp? We have the most diverse skills, the most drive, and the most reason to win. You're screwed, my *friend*."

He chuckled, but I knew he hadn't missed my emphasis on that word. "You do realize we have to work together on some of the competitions, right?"

I looked down my nose at him the way he had at me with his stupid *there she is* comment. "And you're welcome for pulling you along."

Mallory choked on her water.

A guy counselor whose name I didn't know walked by but paused when he got to our table. He looked at Lucas. "You okay, bro?"

Lucas stared at him for a second. "Yeah, I'm fine," he said in a serious voice. Then his expression cleared, and he smirked. "I'm about to finish Andy's food."

The guy snorted and kept walking.

Oookay. I guessed we were all going to pretend that wasn't strange.

"Why wouldn't you be okay?" I hissed to him as the girls talked over each other, dissecting Abby's makeup routine this morning.

Lucas didn't answer as he finished my fruit salad and stood. Half of me wondered if my last comment went too far and that's why the other counselor stopped to check on him, but my Spidey senses were tingling. He came over to eat my food and trash talk, so he got what he deserved. Something else was up.

My table exploded in cheers when he sauntered away from our table, Blair laughing the loudest. "You were so savage to him, Andy! Holy crap!"

I grinned at them, but a secret part of me worried Lucas might take it personally. He just... wasn't allowed to talk about my Beaver girls. No one was. I tracked him as he walked to the trash with my tray. After a moment, he winked over his shoulder at me. I grinned back, relief flooding my body.

After he sat back down at the Cheetah table, I spied Eric on the other side of the room. Replacement coffee cups filled his arms, and a hairnet covered most of his forehead.

I stood. "Eric!" I waved. He must not have seen me, because he walked back into the kitchen after setting down the cups. I sank back into my seat, the girls around me talking a mile a minute.

"Here she is, all quiet and calm, but then Lucas says one thing and bam! Instant extrovert!" Megan said.

I sighed. *Really?*

"Yeah, it's like he brings out the best in her," Summer gushed.

"Or the worst," Maria said, stabbing an egg with her fork.

"Or," I said a bit louder than my norm, "I was defending my Beavers."

"Aww," they all said.

"You love us." Caralyn hugged my side.

"Of course, I do. Now let's crush those Cheetahs until the farthest they can run is back to their little cottage."

"Dark," Blair said.

"I like competitive Counselor Andy," Taylor added.

Leah chose that moment to jog over to the table. "What did I miss?"

I laughed. Maybe they'd rubbed off on me. Or maybe I was getting the hang of this counselor thing after all.

11

Capture the Flag

Dana wasted no time pitting cottage against cottage. Before we could even start to strategize, she'd passed out flags in different colors and told us we were going to do a version of Capture the Flag. Only the campers could compete to find each other's flag. They'd steal it if they could and bring it back to the center of camp. Each camper also had a smaller flag tucked into their waistband. If another team grabbed it, they were out. A counselor could only play if one of the campers got hurt and needed to tag us in.

"Are they anticipating a bunch of injuries?" I muttered under my breath as we circled up in the central courtyard.

Of course, Lucas heard me. "Plan for the best, prepare for the worst."

"Sounds like a Dana motto," I said, lamenting the fact that my team's flags were, in fact, a tannish brown nightmare. They looked like baby poop.

He nudged me, and I stumbled.

"Stop trying to cozy up to me, *Luke*," I said as I shoved him back. "We're still going to kick your ass."

"Language, Counselor *Andrea*," he mocked.

Megan and Taylor whispered back and forth. No doubt strategizing. Across the field, Paige stood with her hands on her hips, her eyebrows raised.

What? I mouthed.

She smiled, then turned to where her campers lounged in the grass. "Come on, girls!" she encouraged. One of them gave her a dry look.

Lucas's Cheetahs sat in the grass too, looking like they didn't have a care in the world. These teams didn't have a chance against mine.

"...and your ten minutes begins... Now!" Dana yelled through the mic attached to her vest. My girls took off running, all in the same direction. I knew they'd have a plan!

I saluted Lucas and sprinted after them as he sat in the grass with his guys. His laughter trailed behind me as my feet ate up the distance of the nearest hill. I pretended that the sound didn't tug something deep inside me. Something that made me want to laugh, too.

When I caught up to the girls, Summer had her shorts half-off on the beach.

"Whoa," I said, bracing my hands on my knees. "What are you doing?"

"I have a bra and underwear on. We know the best place to put the flag. Under the dock!" she squealed. The Beavers shushed her.

"Sorry!" she said in a whisper yell. "Under the dock!" she repeated. "Isn't it brilliant?"

"Is that allowed?" Sarah asked me.

Heck if I knew. I hadn't paid much attention to the directions. I should do that more now that I was a counselor, but Lucas was always being so... Lucas.

"Sounds good to me," I said instead. "But maybe keep a corner of it showing so people don't complain as much when we win?"

"That's the spirit!" Summer said, thumping me on the back. She grabbed our baby poop flag and waded into the water.

"So, I think we should take out the weaker teams first while avoiding the Cheetahs," Destiny said.

"What makes you think they're the stronger team?" I asked.

She rolled her eyes. "We already sized them all up. If we save them for last, they'll be tired from chasing everyone around. They'll make mistakes."

"But won't we be tired, too?"

"No. We're smarter than that."

I pressed my lips together, trying not to laugh. Watching them figure things out might be my favorite part of camp.

"Okay, Blair, Summer, and Sarah will run recon on the Clownfish team and report back. We'll use the woodpile by the archery field as home base to psych them out and make them all think that's where our flag is," Destiny continued when Summer got back from the dock.

I winced at the fact they considered the Clownfish team to be the weakest. That was Paige's team.

"We should still have someone here to defend in case one of the teams figures it out. They can hide behind a tree or a bush," Summer said, her voice muffled by the shirt she pulled over her head.

"I'll do it," Taylor said.

"Perfect. Okay, and Andy?" Destiny made eye contact with me.

"Yeah?" I was part of this now?

"You should stay in the courtyard in case we need you. It's right in the middle between here and the woodpile."

So, I'd need to run back to where we'd started. No wonder Lucas wasn't in any rush. He'd already figured out the best place to stay. "Got it."

"The rest of us will look for opportunities to eliminate other teams, but no one get aggressive until closer to the end. We can't risk our flags being pulled."

The girls nodded. Sarah tied her hair back in a can-do ponytail.

"Huddle up?" I suggested. We got in a circle and put our hands in. "Whisper," I reminded them. "Let's not give away our location."

"One, two, three, Beavers!" we chanted under our breath.

"Let's kick some Cheetah butt for Andy!" Caralyn said.

I laughed, then pointed back to the center of camp. "Come see me if you need me. Remember to be a good sport."

Megan and Taylor traded a smirk, but I didn't have time to find out what that was about because Dana's voice echoed through the camp. "Your ten-minute strategy time has elapsed. Let the game begin!"

I trotted back uphill to the center of camp. When I broke through the trees, most of the counselors still milled around in the grass. Lucas had his arms folded, staring at me as I sprinted the last hundred yards up the hill.

"Alright, Andy?" He laughed.

"Shut up." I flopped onto the scratchy grass. For a long minute, all I did was breathe and sweat.

"You seem winded, counselor," he said as he sat beside me. "You wouldn't be coming all the way from the lake, would you?"

I sat up. Like I would give away our location. "Just out of shape," I lied. He didn't need to know I'd rejoined the track team my senior year.

"Mmhmm."

"It's so bright out here," I said, shielding my face with my hand. Why did I never remember to put on sunscreen?

"Take my hat," he said, pulling it off his head and offering it to me.

I rolled my eyes. "I'm fine."

"I have sunglasses. It's no big deal."

"Fine." I took the hat he held out to me and put it on. "Thanks." It made a huge difference. It had to be, like, ninety degrees out here.

We sat in silence a few minutes under the glaring sun, neither of us moving toward or away from each other in the heat. I tried not to think about how worn in and perfect his hat felt or how I shouldn't be using it. Wasn't that more of a boyfriend-girlfriend thing? I should give it back, but then the sun would blind me.

"So, I was thinking—" he began, but cut off as Taylor came into view, limping up the hill.

I scrambled to my feet and so did Lucas, both of us running down to her.

"I still have my flag," she panted as Lucas slung her arm over his shoulder and supported her. I did the same, and together, we took her to the nearest picnic table for medical attention.

"Andy," she said as soon as we sat her down. "Take my flag."

"What? How did this even happen? I thought you were…" I stopped, realizing I shouldn't give away our spot in front of Lucas. He was the enemy, after all.

"Take my flag," she said again and handed it to me. "You know my job." She sucked in a breath as Lucas touched her ankle.

Oh. I was "in." And no one was guarding the dock. I took her brown flag. "Are you sure you—"

"Go!" she yelled.

I shoved it in my shorts and took off like a shot, leaving both her and Lucas squinting after me. As I got closer to the dock, I darted between trees, looking for a place where I could see the water and intercept anyone who came by. I set myself up behind a large oak tree, panting. No one was here yet. At least I didn't think so. If I checked our hiding spot, I'd risk a camper seeing me do it. Better to guard an empty dock than to give it away like that.

After a couple of minutes, I adjusted Lucas's hat on my head and began to breathe normally. No one would think to come this way. I was the failsafe like Taylor had been. How did she hurt herself this early in the game? Did she get bored, walk around, and trip over a root in the woods? So random.

Time passed, and I was grateful for the shade from the trees. With no wind, I would have baked out in the open, hat or no hat. Squeals, groans, and cheering echoed from near the woodpile, so the Beavers' fake home base must've been found, or maybe they attacked someone.

I leaned against the tree and soaked in the quiet hum of nature, trying not to think about anything but my job. Protect the flag, be a good teammate. Be a good counselor. They liked me better when I was competitive, but that side of me only surfaced when I was around Lucas.

Why was that?

After a while, I wished I had brought my phone. I could've texted Eric or read a chapter of an eBook. This was boring. I was so unnecessary. Then, a rustle in the leaves down by the lakeshore. I sprang to my feet, my heart hammering. *No.* They couldn't know.

I thought of Lucas squinting after me. Maybe I gave away our position by going straight for the lake on the way here. Darn it! He was too perceptive.

A flash of floppy blond hair darted between two trees, getting closer to my own position. It couldn't be. What a cheater!

"He's going for the dock," I whispered to myself. "Beavers!" I yelled, but no one heard me, because no one was in range.

Lucas slipped into the tree line, one of his own campers trailing behind him. A yellow flag fluttered from his waistband. He was playing? How was that fair? A brown flag trailed from my own shorts, but that was beside the point. Like I was anywhere near Taylor's level of competitive. I was just a warm body to stand near the flag no one was supposed to find.

The Cheetah camper surged forward. I had to defend this thing.

"Hey!" Megan sprinted from the archery field and tackled him to the ground.

"Dude!" he yelled. "Grab the flag, not the guy!"

Lucas darted forward.

"Go! Go!" the Cheetah kid cried. "It's under the dock or she wouldn't defend it!"

Lucas sprinted forward. Crap, now I had to do something. He couldn't see me from my position in the opposite tree line, so I had that going for me. If he got close enough, I could grab his flag before he made it to the dock.

His long legs ate up the distance between us until he veered toward the lake instead of the dock. In one fluid movement, he jettisoned himself over the rocks that lined the shore and straight into the water with a perfect dive.

I sprinted forward. *No, no, no!* He couldn't get there before me! Destiny would kill me—the whole cottage would—but how could I have predicted that he'd power-swim to the flag fully-clothed like a human jet ski?

My feet flew down the waterlogged boards of the extra-wide wooden dock, but he outpaced me. No wonder he got a scholarship. If it was just us, I'd let him win because I don't care about stupid competitions, but I couldn't let the girls down. This was my chance to prove to them I had their backs. Then maybe I'd deserve all the precarious faith they had in me.

I didn't even think. I jumped off the darn dock and into the water with a big splash. I knew the flag's location, and he still had to search. He could have it over my dead body. Water lapped at my neck as I stood under the slimy dock between him and his goal.

Lucas saw me and headed over, his big arms slicing toward me in sure strokes. All he had to do was dunk me and I was done.

Wait. That was it.

He ducked under the dock and stopped a few feet away from where I stood. Darn the rules that said we couldn't move it once it was placed! He whipped his wet hair back over his forehead next to one of the support beams. A dangerous smile broke over his face. "Andy."

I raised an eyebrow. "Lucas."

"Isn't this a little ridiculous?" he asked in his Be-Reasonable voice. "I know where the flag is."

I folded my arms, which was a bit silly since my elbows wanted to float. "Then you should let a camper come for it."

He took a large step toward me, water lapping at his shirt. "You should let a camper defend it."

I pressed one hand against his chest before he got too close. "Guess we're at an impasse."

He glanced down at my hand, then at the goosebumps coating my arm. "Nice word. Did you learn that for your college essays?"

"I like to read," I reminded him.

"And I like to swim." He pushed against my hand, but my arm held strong.

I stared at him. *What now, Mr. Tough Guy?* He had to go through me to get the darn flag and now he knew it.

He sighed. "Come on, Andy. Don't be difficult. I don't want to freak you out by dunking you."

"Aw, how thoughtful," I said sarcastically. "Then don't."

He sighed again. "Fine."

"Beavers!" I yelled out as loud as I could. "Help me!"

Lucas winced at my volume. "They're probably all out at this point. I sent a group after your so-secret hideout."

I narrowed my eyes. "It was a good spot."

"You're predictable."

"You think so?" I hadn't even come up with the plan. And my Beavers weren't predictable. It *was* a good plan.

His hands surrounded the one I used to hold him at bay. "You're kinda hot when you're competitive."

"You're trying to change the subject, but I'm not moving." His hands were big and rough and warm. It was annoying when at this point, my entire body shook with the cold of the water under the shaded dock.

He inched closer to me until his chest and mine had the thinnest barrier of water between us. "You're wearing a white shirt."

I didn't look down, but my face flooded with heat I hoped he couldn't see in the shade of the dock. I *was* wearing a white shirt. How rude of him to mention it like I was in a wet T-shirt contest.

I cleared my throat. "Does that distract you?" My voice came out lower than it should have.

"You've always distracted me," he breathed, his lips descending.

I braced my other hand on his chest, partly to get some space to breathe, and partly... I ran my hands down to his shorts. His eyes widened and his fingers came up to graze my cheek.

I smirked and ripped his flag out of his waistband. "Victory!" I crowed and raised his soaked yellow flag above my head, knocking my fist against the underside of the dock.

Lucas grinned and shook his head as a huge cheer laced with groans echoed from the wood planks above us.

"Oh, my God." They had been there the whole time? How much of that did they hear?

Lucas was already pulling himself up onto the dock where our campers waited.

I crossed my arms over my boobs and walked out of the shade of the dock and onto the lakeshore. Despite being outside, the Beaver girls cheered so loud, I thought I might go deaf.

"You did it! You stuck up for us!"

"That was so smooth! I can't believe you dismissed him like that!"

"Epic. The whole thing was epic!"

"Hos before Bros!"

"Shh," I said. "Be good sports, remember?" I didn't want them gloating over Lucas, especially when my chest tightened at what it must have looked like just now. I wasn't trying to use him. He was the one pursuing me when I had a boyfriend.

"None of this means we won," I reminded them. "We have to get their flag."

"Oh, we already won, but watching you and Counselor Luke was too good. We weren't stepping in the middle of that." Sarah produced the Cheetah team's yellow flag from her fanny pack and waved it in my face.

"You weren't... I didn't have to... Oh, for the love of..."

"Andy! Andy! Andy!" Summer chanted, and the girls picked it up.

They grabbed Lucas's flag from my hand, and we marched back to the cottage together, passing the sweaty Clownfish team as we went. Paige gave me a tired wave as the girls continued to talk over each other about the competition, their voices escalating the longer they recapped. Taylor's ankle seemed to have magically healed. I raised my eyebrows at her, and she looked away. Why did this whole thing feel like a setup?

I never looked behind me to gauge Lucas's reaction. I was too scared of what I might see.

12

Kissing Eric

By the time the girls left the cottage for free time, all the energy from earlier had leaked from my body. I flopped onto my bottom bunk, my head swirling with all the reassurances I'd given them. *Lucas and I are friends. It's not like that. He was teasing me. I already have a boyfriend. Please stop talking about this.* Maybe I could take a nap before they came back. Was that unprofessional?

My phone buzzed. *Eric.* But when I glanced at the screen, the message wasn't from Eric at all.

SOS. My cottage.

SOS? Paige never SOS'd me.

Be there in a sec.

I tucked my phone in my shorts and hurried to Paige's cottage, imagining all sorts of horrible scenarios that would cause Paige of all people to SOS. Did all her hair fall out? Did she fall out of the window and find herself in a survival scenario since the girls had left for free time?

When I stepped through the doorway, Paige sat on her bunk in her safari vest. Not a fire or a screaming camper to be found.

"What's up? I thought all the bunk beds collapsed, and we had to bring in the jaws of life."

"Ha, ha," she said, her voice somehow off.

I crossed the room and sat down on the bed with her. "Who do I need to beat up?"

She peered at me. Her face looked worn, like she'd pulled an all-nighter. I gave her my I'm-dead-serious eyes.

"A bunch of teenage girls?" she said in a semi-joking voice.

Ah. "What's going on?"

She hugged herself. "I don't... I didn't think it would be like this when I signed up. Maybe I'm not as much of a leader as I thought."

What? Paige was the leadery-est leader there ever was. "Why do you say that?"

"I don't get them. They don't want to compete. They begged people to take their flags at Capture the Flag. And nothing I do motivates them. I..." She blinked back tears. "I don't understand why they'd come to a leadership camp if all they wanted to do was sit around. And I don't want to yell at my campers, but they're kind of lame."

I rocked back. "Huh."

She chuckled. "That's all you've got for me? Huh?"

"Can I also interest you in a "that sucks" and maybe a hug?"

She paused. "Honestly? Yeah."

I leaned forward and hugged her. "That sucks. I'm sorry." I wished I had more to say to help her. I wanted to give her a pep talk like she gave me last year. But I wasn't a pep talk person. I didn't know how to give them. And nothing I said would change her situation. She'd ended up with the Andys, and I ended up with the Paiges; life wasn't fair, but we both had to lead people who weren't like us.

When I pulled away, I said, "Camp just started. We've only done one challenge. You have time, and you're resilient. You'll figure it out."

"Thanks," she said, smoothing back her ponytail. "Sorry to SOS you."

"Shut up. That's what friends do."

She grinned.

I made it back to my own cottage after eight more half-formed *you can do its.* Exhausted, I flopped back onto my bed and eyed Lucas's hat, which lay flattened on the other side of my pillow. It was a basic, dark blue color, faded from use, the bill broken in for comfort and maximum shade. I should return it. I never should've borrowed it in the first place. I wouldn't have if it hadn't been so hot out today.

There was a knock on the door. Probably the guy in question. Paige and the Beaver girls wouldn't knock.

I grabbed his hat and trotted over, but Lucas's blond hair and big smile didn't greet me. Eric leaned on the doorjamb, his breath smelling of peppermint and his face radiating calm. I took a surprised step back, my heart hammering. "What are you doing here?"

"My first real break. I thought maybe we could have a picnic?" He gestured to the bag over his shoulder.

Like a date? I grinned. Finally, we would have alone time together!

"I would've texted you, but you never have your phone," he teased.

I winced. "I know. I'm sorry."

"It's okay." He gestured outside. "So, do you want…"

"Sure, yeah. Give me one second." I ran back to my bunk and traded Lucas's hat for my sunglasses. I could return it later.

I followed behind Eric to a quaint, shaded patch next to the tree I'd sat beneath so many times last summer. Its branches welcomed me back, the leaves fluttering in the slightest of breezes. He set down his bag and took his time spreading out a couple of beach towels. After we sat, he pulled food out of his picnic backpack: sandwiches, cut strawberries, bottles of water, chips.

"This is so great," I said, sinking to my knees to grab a plate. "I'm starving."

I was actually too tired to be hungry, but I couldn't resist the strawberries. Fresh food at a summer camp that prided itself last year on sloppy joes and cafeteria pizza was refreshing.

"I'm glad you like it," he said.

We ate in silence for a few minutes, sitting across from each other. Conversations between campers and squeals from the various competitive activities floated over to us, but no one came to pierce our perfect bubble. It was… nice.

He was nice.

When we finished with the food, he packed the containers back up. For a moment, I thought he'd leave, and we'd never talk at all. I frowned.

"How's it going with your girls?" he asked.

I brightened. "Good." *Ish.*

He checked his watch. "That's great." Did he have to get back?

"It's... different than I thought it would be, being a counselor."

He squinted at me across the towels. "I know you'll figure it out. You always do."

I smiled. Did I? I wasn't so sure I'd figured out much of anything at camp this year. Part of me wanted a different response from him. I wanted him to ask me why it was difficult, maybe talk through some scenarios I could be doing better. Be supportive in that way.

But maybe this was enough. I moved closer to him, the fabric of my jeans scraping against his. He held my hand, our fingers cupped against each other. I leaned my head against the hollow of his shoulder.

"I'm glad we get this time together," I said in a soft voice.

"Me too," he whispered. He dipped low to kiss my cheek.

I know it was meant to be brief and sweet, that he was hyper-aware we were in public, but I didn't get to see him the way we'd hoped this summer. My mind was a tangle of conflicted emotions. I didn't want brief and sweet right now. I shifted my mouth, so his kiss landed on my lips.

He adapted to my unspoken demand, one hand reaching up to cup my cheek. It was wonderful and warm and polite. He gave me what I wanted, no more, no less. Kissing Eric reminded me of sinking into a warm bath. It felt comfortable and right, like a hug but for my mouth. It's not like he groped me on the beach or dismissed me by ending it too soon, but...

I don't know.

I ended the kiss. Maybe my nerves were shot from the Landy thing. Maybe I felt guilty for being caught under the dock with Lucas, even though I didn't do anything wrong.

"What was that for?" he asked, his breathing more ragged than I'd ever heard it.

"I miss you," I whispered.

"I um..." He cleared his throat. "I miss you, too."

I twisted my fingers together in my lap. "Look, I—"

"There's something I—" He gestured for me to go ahead.

I blew out a breath. Here went nothing. "The girls in my cottage are being ridiculous about something, and I didn't want you to hear it through rumors."

He frowned. "Okay."

I braced myself. "So, I'm partnered with a guy cottage, right?"

"You are?" Oh, yeah. He had no idea how things worked at this camp.

"Yeah. Every girl cottage has a guy cottage to work with for larger challenges. Anyway, they're trying to matchmake the counselor of that cottage with me, and it's stupid. I'm trying to squash it."

He narrowed his eyes a fraction. Anyone might've missed it if they weren't a super worried girlfriend staring at their boyfriend's every feature for a reaction. "Okay."

"And there was this capture the flag challenge. At the end of the game, I ended up under a dock fighting for a flag with this guy, and they're getting all ridiculous about it. Again, there's nothing to worry about."

He rocked back, bracing his hands on the ground. "Is this the same guy I met on the first day? Luke something?"

My face burned. "Lucas. Yeah."

He raised his eyebrows. "Lucas?"

"Yeah."

He was silent for a moment, watching me. "Okay."

"Okay?"

"Yeah, okay. You said there's nothing going on there?" He raised one dark eyebrow.

"Of course not," I assured him. "I have an awesome boyfriend. I don't need another one." I grinned—maybe too wide.

He smiled, but it wasn't a happy smile. It was forced, like the smile you give your aunt when they buy you clothing you're never going to wear. "Okay."

It didn't feel like the end of the conversation. His okay wasn't real. I could tell. We sat in silence for a full minute, both of us staring at each other. I couldn't take it anymore. "Say something."

"Like?"

"I don't know," I mumbled, dropping my eyes to the green stripes of the towel beneath me.

"I trust you, Andy," he said in a low voice.

"You do?"

"Should I not?"

My eyes flew to his. "Of course, you should trust me."

"Then we're okay." He reached for my hand.

When he touched me, I should've felt all the nerves wash away. He trusted me. Everything was fine. I'd blindsided him, but it was better to be honest, right? Relationships went down the drain when people weren't honest in my books, and I didn't want to lose Eric. But something felt wrong, and I didn't know how to fix it. I laid my head on his shoulder again, and he sighed, offering me a peppermint from his ever-present tin.

I took one, the shock of the flavor making me doubt myself all over again. Was he trying to say that I had bad breath? Was his silence because I had ruined everything by bringing Lucas up? Maybe I shouldn't have said anything about it.

My brain wouldn't turn off, and as we picked up and folded the towels, I had the horrible thought that maybe this would be the last time he'd surprise me with a romantic picnic.

A lot of free time remained when he walked me back to the door of my cottage. "I'm glad we did this," he said.

"Me too," I breathed, looking at his lips. I'd know it was okay between us if he kissed me for real right now.

He dipped his head and my stomach clenched with nerves. His lips brushed mine once before he pulled back. "I'll try to find some more time soon. Text me?"

I nodded, biting my lip.

When I closed the door behind him, I vowed to keep my phone close to me from now on. Eric and I texted all the time back home. It wasn't fair to cut that off because of my busy schedule. I pulled open my text messages on my phone and sent him a heart. A few minutes later, as the girls trickled back into the cottage, my phone buzzed.

"Is that your boyfriend?" Megan sing-songed.

I ignored her and grinned as I swiped into my messages. Eric had sent me a heart back.

13

—————

Hide and Seek

Morning broke, bright and hot. After a breakfast of crepes and fresh fruit more suited to a resort or a fancy bed and breakfast than a summer camp, Dana ushered us out into the heat that already shimmered off the grass.

"Today, your color war challenge is to paint as much of your skin as possible with the colors you are given before we have an epic Hide and Seek Battle!" she crowed through her microphone. She proceeded to tell us the parameters of the exercise which included the counselors being the "seekers." Full participation was a must this year. The counselors were involved in everything. Then, with blonde curls bouncing, Dana turned off her mic and let us get to it.

Sarah frowned at the brown and yellow paint we'd been supplied with. "Like, I know brown is for Beavers, but this feels a lot like putting on black face." Her eyes skated over to Destiny.

"Then don't put it on your face. And maybe use the yellow if you're hiding in a place where that makes more sense," Destiny said with a shrug.

"Yeah, it's about strategy," Josh said. He nudged Destiny and she pushed him back. He laughed. They were so cute.

Lucas's eyes met mine, and we shared a moment of mirth over their puppy love, like we weren't the same exact way last year.

"Okay, but I am not putting it in my hair," Leah said, walking up late as usual. "I can't even get washable color spray out of it, it's so thick. Did I ever tell you about the time I played an old lady on stage, and they made me spray my hair white? It took hours to get out," she complained.

"You have a lot of skin showing. I don't think it has to be in your hair," Sarah said.

I took one finger and touched the brown paint, drawing a stripe across each of my cheeks like a football player. "We've got this, Beavers."

A kid named Troy or Trey on the Cheetah team snorted. "Yeah, but can you be quiet long enough to not be found? You girls are so—"

Maria grabbed a handful of yellow paint and walked toward him. "We're so what?"

"Loud!" he shouted, jumping behind Lucas for cover.

Maria glared at him but didn't dare throw the paint when he hid behind a counselor. *Coward,* she mouthed at him when he peeked around Lucas's back. He smirked.

Destiny drew two yellow smiley faces on her kneecaps. Lucas took a small paintbrush and began creating brown and yellow stripes on his bare biceps. Did he have to draw attention to his tank top and exposed muscles like that? But it didn't matter, because the other Beavers and Cheetahs blocked my view as they strained to get at the buckets of paint.

I moved aside, the paint on my cheeks dried by the summer sun. I sat a few yards away, waiting for the Beavers and Cheetahs to paint themselves. My phone buzzed from a pocket in my safari vest, and I pulled it out.

Alarm: Text Eric

I opened our messages and tapped out a short text about how you're never too old for hide and seek, then shoved my phone back in my vest. Was it pathetic that I had to set an alarm to text him? I pushed the guilt from my mind. No, that made me a good girlfriend. He wanted me to text, and I made that happen even though I had a full schedule.

Lucas chose that moment to lower himself to the ground beside me. I ignored him as he braced his now bumble-bee striped arms on his knees, watching the hormones and silliness play out in front of us as the Cheetahs and Beavers threw paint at each other.

"You know counselors are playing in this one, right?" he asked.

"Seems to be a bit of a theme." Dana insisted on our active participation this year. I didn't remember our own counselors jumping into this many activities last summer. I leaned back on my arms in the grass before realizing how the position pushed my boobs forward. I sat back up. "I forgot your hat."

He squinted at me. "I don't mind. You need more paint, though."

"If I do, you do." Because his two tiny stripes weren't enough to show what team he was on.

He gave a wolfish smile. "I'm game."

I narrowed my eyes. He didn't think *I* would be the one to paint him, did he? "You're just trying to get me to touch you."

"What?" He blinked at me, the picture of innocence. "I can't paint the back of me, and there are paintbrushes. Be a pal."

"I can paint anything I want?" I'd show him what a pal would do.

"I mean, don't Sharpie my face the way you would at a party, but yeah."

Oh, Lucas. Only he would assume I'd ever been to that type of party. "Fine."

He jumped to his feet and offered me his hand. I allowed him to yank me up, and we jogged back over to where a few campers remained, putting finishing touches on their paint.

"Turn around," he said.

I shrugged off my vest. "I thought I was painting you."

"Now who's trying to touch who?"

"Whom," I corrected, turning around.

"No one says whom." He dipped his hand into the brown paint, ignoring the pile of paint-soaked brushes scattered on the ground. I tried not to think about how his fingers would have to skate across my skin to paint me.

He drew over my arms and the backs of my shoulders. Broad, confident strokes of his fingers. The paint was ice-cold, but his hands were so, so warm. A shiver rippled through me despite the threat of sunstroke out here. When his touch stilled, the heat of his breath brushed against the same skin, blowing on the paint to dry it.

Okay, that was way, way enough. A girl could only take so much of Lucas this close to their body. No doubt I'd hear all about this later from the girls. The space around us had cleared more than it should have, and a few campers looked away from us with exaggerated innocent expressions.

Uh huh. They were so very stealth.

I swatted Lucas away, his cheeky grin betraying the fact that he knew exactly what he was doing.

"Your turn," I said.

"Sure, sure," he said, touching a paint-covered finger to the tip of my nose.

"Really?"

"Now you're a brown-noser. One that says whom."

"Gross." I grinned. "No one says that."

He grinned back, the blue of his eyes clear and honest in the full daylight of the afternoon. *Dork.* I grabbed some of the dark brown paint in my hand and my lips curved into a wicked smile.

"That's a lot of paint," he said and raised his eyebrows.

"Is it?" I asked. Then I pressed my hand to his cheek, the wet oozing between my fingers. "It's going to look like I slapped you," I teased.

"Nah," he said, unphased aside from the husky tone of his voice. "That's not what it looks like."

I pulled my hand from his face at the speed of light, my handprint small on his angular cheek. "We're probably good."

"Probably!" one of the Cheetah guys burst out.

All the campers around us laughed. My face burned as I rolled my eyes and shrugged, trying to play it off.

"Aw," Summer crooned behind me. "I love that." She pointed to my shoulders.

I craned my neck, trying to see what Lucas had written, but either his writing was too sloppy, or he'd done it in such a way that I couldn't piece together the words.

I'd ask him what it said over my dead body. At this point, getting the attention off us was priority number one. I never should have touched him. Guilt swarmed like a horde of angry bees within me. What would Eric think?

"On your mark, get set, hide!" Dana's voice yelled through the speakers.

The campers scattered, Destiny and Josh running fastest of all, while Lucas and I walked to the center of the field to circle up with the other counselors. We didn't say anything else to each other, and I sought out Paige so he wouldn't sit next to me.

"Hey, girl," she said, making room for me, her voice louder and more cheery than usual. "How's it going with your Beavers? They are *motivated*."

I shrugged and pulled my knees to my chest as people chatted around me. I couldn't lose myself in a group of twenty-four people. Lucas's low voice rumbled across the circle as he talked to James. What would it take to get a little space around here?

"Well, my campers still have zero get up and go," Paige said glumly. "I'd trade you any day."

I grimaced. "Yeah." The word felt traitorous coming out of my mouth for some reason.

Paige may be more of a Beaver than a Clownfish, and I felt like an actual clown lately, but I didn't wish away my campers. They were different than me, but we were beginning to root for each other.

"Do you need any help?" I asked. I'd been a Victim once. Maybe I could talk to a girl or two for her.

She sighed. "No. I've got it."

I nodded. She did have it. She could do it.

"What a summer, huh?" she said, picking a long piece of grass and twirling it between her fingers.

"Yeah."

I pulled my vest over my dried shoulder paint as Dana yelled, "And, time. Counselors, go seek! Remember to send found campers back here, but don't bust your own cottage. Whoever has the most campers still hiding at the end of ten minutes wins!"

I looked over at the large wooden color war board and smirked when I saw the Beavers still at the top. But right below them, the darn Cheetahs were edging up the list. They didn't try half as hard as my girls. How was that fair?

Game on. We weren't losing the lead on my account. After all, who knew more about hiding than me? I saluted Lucas and sprinted back toward the cottages. I would find all these kids if it was the last thing I did.

Groans and good-natured laughter filtered through the woods as I jogged down the trail. I tagged a red Robin girl who hid behind a tree and a green Gecko kid who thought climbing one branch above her would save him. It was strategic, since the green of his paint blended into the leaves, but she looked up when I busted her.

I continued jogging, pretending I didn't see Abby slipping under the swing of one of the cottage porches.

My heart pounded as my eyes flitted from place to place. I had a few minutes left to find as many campers as possible. Two boys hid behind grass clippings, itching their skin. Yeah, that wasn't too smart. I tagged them, then pulled calamine lotion out of my vest and tossed it to them before they trudged back to the center of camp.

With my hands on my hips, I stood for a moment, sweating in the hot sun while I thought. If I had to hide, where would I go? Last summer, all I wanted to do was get away from everyone else and read my book. One time I sat next a tree to do it, but the other time it took my counselor, Suzie, a while to find me...

I broke into a sprint. The bushes behind the cottages weren't as obvious as the ones in front of them. If a counselor wasn't observant, they wouldn't even know the bushes were there, their scraggly leaves holding on for dear life in this weather.

I started with my own cottage. I spotted sneakers peeking out from the bushes, and the swipe of yellow paint across a shin. My own camper—don't bust her.

I moved to the Cheetah cottage. It didn't look like any campers hid in theirs, except... wait. I backed up. I didn't see any shoes sticking out, but the shadow of the bush didn't match. I parted the branches, and a girl with orange face paint yelped.

"Gotcha," I said. "Time to meet in the center." I offered her my hand. But her eyes blinked, wide and wild, moving side to side, and her entire body shook. She didn't take my hand, but instead hugged herself closer. *Wait, was she...*

She pressed her hand to her chest as if in pain.

Oh, no. Her breathing morphed into short gasps as she warred against tears and began to rock back and forth. *Panic attack.*

What do I do? I didn't even know her name, so I couldn't ground her with that. I scanned the nearby hill for another counselor, anyone who might be able to help me. But I didn't want to admit who I was looking for. Lucas, who helped me out of a panic attack last summer. Lucas, who always knew what to do with other people.

He was nowhere to be found.

Should I like... lift her up? Try to get her to stand? She didn't look that heavy.

No. Breathe. That's not how you help. I took a steadying breath. What would I want if I were losing it? Not a thousand eyes on me as someone sought help for me. I would want to disappear, to find a way to regulate. Embarrassment would make this worse. But I couldn't leave her alone, either. Who knew if she could do it on her own, or how long that would take?

I crawled into the bush with her, the tiny branches scraping the exposed skin of my arms. It was awkward, but I wiggled into the small space against the dirty cottage wall with the poor waif of a girl who looked like she might break in half. She needed someone.

I lined up my shoulder and arm with hers then leaned against her firmly. Sometimes touch helped distract me during a panic attack. Sometimes it made it worse. If she didn't like my arm against her, then hugging would be out.

She recoiled from my touch. "I'm fine. I just need a second, I'm sorry. I'm so sorry."

Okay, so no hug. "My favorite fruit is blueberries. What's yours?"

She stared at me like I'd grown an extra head. "What?"

"Your favorite fruit," I prompted. "Tropical or locally grown?"

"Bananas," she gasped.

"Bananas?"

"Yeah."

"When I have a panic attack, I say my favorite fruit until I can imagine how it tastes." I broke a dead stick off the bush and poked it into the dirt.

Out of the corner of my eye, I saw her look at me in shock. "When you..."

"Blueberries. Once you pierce the skin, you never know if they'll be that perfect amount of sweet and sour, or whether they'll have too much of one or the other. I like that they don't always follow the rules of color. Sometimes the ones that look the best still make you squint."

She didn't say anything as she continued to gasp for breath. Maybe it wouldn't work. Then finally, through the tears, she said, "Bananas have potassium."

I hid a smile. Maybe it *would* work. "Totally."

"And fake banana flavoring tastes good for some reason," she wheezed.

"And blueberry," I added.

She nodded, tears streaming down her face. "Who doesn't like a banana Laffy Taffy?"

"No one." Me. I hated all Laffy Taffy. It tasted like pulled rubber. "Blueberry pie is the most underrated food of all time." Warm from the oven with vanilla bean ice cream on top. My stomach rumbled in agreement.

She loosened her hands on her knees a fraction of an inch. "Most people peel bananas the wrong way."

"Yeah?" *Distract, distract, distract.*

She smoothed her hands down her thighs and back up, slower now. "You're supposed to open them from the bottom, not the part where the stem is longer."

"Huh." I didn't know that.

Her rocking slowed. "Banana bread is my favorite food."

"Carbs are a whole vibe." I grinned at her.

She sucked in a rattling breath. "Right?" Swiping under her eyes, she leaned back against the exposed logs of the cottage. "I hate how my body does stupid shit."

There was never a more relatable statement. She could be me. She *was* me. "Me, too."

"I knew someone would find me. So why does it feel like you're going to kill me when I know you're coming and that I'm not in danger at all?"

I could go into what my therapist said about fight, flight, and freeze, but that wouldn't be helpful when she was still coming down from crying. "It sucks," I said instead.

She stared at me for a long moment. "Yeah."

"And that's time. Counselors and remaining campers, return to center field where we will announce the winners!" Dana's voice echoed across the camp.

I crawled out of the bush and offered the girl my hand. This time she took it. I pulled her to her feet. She was a tiny thing, maybe five feet tall.

She wiped her splotched face again. "Do I look like I've been crying?"

Yes. "Not too much. It will wear off by the time we get to the field."

"Thanks, Counselor Andy."

She knew my name. I smiled, and we walked together back to the center of camp. When we broke through the trees, the girl made a beeline for a couple of other campers wearing orange paint.

"How many did you find, Counselor? I bet I beat you." Lucas fell into step beside me as I homed in on my group of Beavers.

"I'm sure you're right," I said in a chipper voice.

"No trash talk?" Lucas covered his chest in mock surprise. "What happened?"

I glanced over toward the girl who now laughed with her friends. "I took care of it."

"Of course, you did." The way he glanced down at me as we rejoined our groups was...

I batted him away. He needed to stop being so confusing.

"Did we win?" I asked the girls.

Destiny and Summer groaned. "No."

"Did the Cheetahs?" Lucas asked.

"Please. If we didn't win, neither did the Cheetahs," I teased. We'd teamed up for this challenge, anyway.

He looked at where Destiny and Josh had laced their fingers together and now played a thumb war in the grass. "Fair enough."

I snorted.

"Andy!" Paige's voice sounded from across the field. Her orange Clownfish surrounded her, looking more excited than I'd ever seen them.

"Yeah?" I called back.

"In your face!" She pointed to the scoreboard where Dana erased their score and added points to it.

I made a fake crying gesture to her and grinned. Paige finally found an event her girls would compete in. I wondered how often they wanted to hide from *her*. Chuckling, I looked back to my campers. They didn't seem any worse for wear.

14

If You Say Yes

The girls' chatter echoed from every corner of the cottage. We'd finished surprise trust falls (which were somehow different than planned ones), and my arms ached from catching everyone. Now, my heart stuttered, too. Were there any scarier words that a guy could send to the girl he was dating? Okay, fine. He could've texted *We need to talk*. That would have ended my streak of mental resilience, or whatever my therapist had called it, but this was just as awful.

Surprises could range from "here's your favorite coffee from Starbucks"—which would be awesome right about now—to "I've come up with an activity that you'll suck at and embarrass the crap out of yourself"—which would push my anxiety through the roof. And boys were terrible with the clothing factor. What was I supposed to wear? Sneakers and jeans or whatever I'd packed that might be halfway cute? I didn't want to look like an idiot. Not to him. I didn't even know when this supposed surprise was scheduled to happen.

I sat on the edge of my bed gripping my phone like it was the source of all my problems. Dating a guy was so complicated. Here I was, worried to death about a thing he was planning for me—a thing that was most likely very nice.

The lie was justified because it was in the name of being a good girlfriend—a girlfriend Eric deserved. Not a mess like I actually was. He never needed to see that part of me.

I slipped my phone into my safari vest and smoothed my fly-aways behind my ears. I had to plan the next activity, and I intended to hustle the girls at a horseshoe competition. They'd never knew what hit them.

I bounced out the door, trying not to care that my phone hadn't buzzed again, that I should have asked for clues to ease my anxiety. I could handle anything. I was eighteen, after all. I could vote and buy a lottery ticket and drive a car. I was an adult, and the girls were my priority. Eric probably had everything planned out and I was being ridiculous.

I got caught up in Beaver bonding after that. They let me talk them into horseshoes when I told them the winner could have ten extra free time minutes before lights out. I didn't know if I could technically grant that—the counselor manual still gathered dust under my bunk—but Dana was MIA unless a camp-wide activity needed planning. Ten minutes shouldn't be that big of a deal.

Of course, Destiny and Maria won the horseshoe contest once I showed them all who was boss. I wouldn't have worried about anyone else after curfew but those two, or maybe Megan or Leah. But I had to be true to my word, and it put them both in a great mood for the rest of the day.

After a pie-eating contest in the cafeteria, Destiny grinned as we headed back to our bunks. "This day has been great," she said, licking her fingers.

"You're only saying that because you got to sit next to Jo-osh," Maria sing-songed.

Destiny looked down her nose at Maria. "And won."

"You didn't win."

"I ate more than Josh. That was winning."

This reminded me of Marshall and Paige from last year, who'd been competitive in a handsy way. Destiny and Josh were hardcore flirting. Should I say anything as her counselor about maybe not doing that?

Meh. Let her have her summer. There weren't any rules about it... probably. I really should read that manual.

"... excited about it," Sarah said.

"About what?" I asked, tuning back into their conversation as we re-entered the Beaver cottage.

"The movie night, duh!"

"Oh, yeah." Cue the cheesy camp movie with singing in it. The girls were excited to chill with the guys and their friends from other cottages. After all the back-to-back excitement of the color war, a relaxing activity would be a great way to end the day.

"I wonder if they'll make us sit in assigned seats," Summer said.

"No way. They didn't two years ago. It was like a drive-in but in the archery field. It was hard to hear the movie, but no one cared. We all sat on blankets and towels and stuff," Destiny replied.

"Sounds fun," I said, calculating how wet their towels might be from their swim earlier today.

"And we have like, I don't know. A few minutes, right? Do we have enough time to take showers?" Summer looked at me.

"Uh..." I hadn't paid close attention to the schedule; I pulled open a pocket of my vest. The movie started at 9:30. It made sense to wait for it to be darker. I pulled my phone out from another pocket, surprised to see a few text messages waiting for me. It was 8:15.

"We still have an hour."

Summer squealed. "That's like, zero time to be cute!"

Why did she need to be cute?

"Come on!" She yanked Maria's hand, and they fled to the small bathroom with most of the other girls. *Okay, then.*

I swiped into my texts. Lucas had sent one around the time I owned the girls in horseshoes.

> **I can see you gloating from here.**

I smirked and texted him back.

> How many girls can fit in a bathroom at the same time? The whole field is going to smell like hairspray.

> **Yikes.**

I sent him an eyerolling emoji and he replied back with a laughing emoji. Then I swiped into my other messages. Crap, they were from Eric.

> **Your surprise will be waiting for you at 9:30.**

> **Found us a spot.**

Warmth bloomed in my chest. So, he planned to surprise me with time off for the movie. Now primping in the bathroom seemed like a great idea. I couldn't go in a ponytail with sweat dripping down my back. Besides, I still had paint caked on my shoulders from the hide and seek challenge. I strolled over to my duffel bag, happy I'd come more prepared than last year. There were a few cute tops in there, but if I chose one of the frillier ones, my Beaver girls would notice.

Did it matter? I fingered a silky cami. If I wore it under the vest, no one would notice, and then I could take the vest off once my date with Eric began, and it would have the desired effect. I hoped.

I grabbed my shower stuff and headed to the bathroom with my hair in a messy bun. I didn't have time to wash it right now.

"Ooh lala! Dressing up for Luke, are we?" Megan teased.

I rolled my eyes. I should've known it wouldn't be this easy. "Actually, Eric got the night off." Let them think about *that*.

I started the shower, but before I jumped in, I twisted around to see what Lucas had written. Now that I was about to wash it off, curiosity overwhelmed me.

"Den mother?"

"It's so cute, right?" Maria said through the curtain. "Like Beaver den, but also like Cheetah den mother!"

"Uh, sure." I didn't know how to feel about that as I scrubbed it all off in five minutes. I dressed behind the curtain and emerged into a cloud of hairspray and gossip. Destiny froze in the middle of applying her lip gloss when she saw me. Summer's eyebrows rose so high they almost disappeared into her hairline.

"Girl," Maria said. "You look *good*, but that hair... I gotchu. Come here." She gestured to me with her straightener.

"I don't know," I said, trying to squash my nerves. "Maybe I should braid it back at this point."

"Please. It will take ten seconds. Maybe longer if you spill how you met your hottie boyfriend." She snapped the straightener together a few times.

I hid a smile. "Oh, we've known each other for years."

"You've been dating for years?"

"Well, no." But I knew him, kind of. I fantasized about him. It was almost the same thing.

"Then spill." She pulled some of my hair through the straightener and flipped it to curl the ends. How did people learn this stuff? Every time I watched a YouTube tutorial, I got all turned around.

"I uh... was a little shy. We didn't even talk until this past year. Then he asked me out."

"You stopped being shy?" Destiny asked.

"No. I just... I came here. And then I felt more... I don't know. Confident."

"Boys can smell confidence a mile away. Good for you! So how did he ask?" Maria sectioned off a new part of my hair.

"To date me?"

"Yeah. Was it a whole thing?"

I shifted in the seat before remembering she had a hot tool in my hair. Of course, I'd seen the big signs, the elaborate prom-posals and romantic gestures that went down in our school, but Eric wouldn't do something like that. He knew it would embarrass me. "It was at my locker, kind of? He asked me to go to a carnival with him."

Summer frowned, then brightened. "Not in a group? Just him?"

"Just him." I smiled.

"But he has a group of friends?"

"Yeah."

"And you've met them?" Leah chimed in. Where did she come from? She wasn't here a moment ago. This bathroom shrank smaller every second.

"Yeah."

"Ooh. That's a big deal," Summer cooed.

I smiled. "It felt like one."

Eric looked over at me from the driver's seat and smiled. "Don't worry. It'll be great. They'll love you. You already know them all, anyway."

If sitting in the same class counted as knowing them, sure. I stared through the windshield at the white house in front of us that thumped with the beat of a popular song. "So this is…"

He put the car in park. "So this is me introducing my friends to my girlfriend."

"Your… girlfriend?"

He turned to me, his hands still gripping the steering wheel. "If you say yes."

I swallowed. "Yes," I whispered, my voice reed thin. "Yes," I said in a stronger voice.

He leaned over the console to kiss me gently. "I'm glad. Ready?"

"Sure," I whispered. He asked me out! And we'd only hung out twice!

The moment we entered the house, Eric became my anchor. He held my hand, smiling at people who said hi to him, to people who looked at how attached I was to him with raised brows. He accepted it all without comment. Winding through the halls, he led us to a small room lined with shelves out of the way of the chaotic drinking of the living room. Whose house was this? I thought I spied a first edition of a Hemingway on the corner shelf.

He chuckled. "We can come back another time and you can read to your heart's content. I doubt Brody ever comes in here when there isn't a party."

I grinned. "How did you know?"

A blush crept up his neck. "You look at those books the way I look at you."

I blinked. What did that mean, the way he looked at me?

Before I could start to process that, I realized we stood in front of a group of friends lounging on couches in a room away from the general party. Eric was right. I knew these people. I'd worked on group projects in school with half of them, but… I inched closer to Eric at their openly curious stares before Brynn noticed our entrance.

"Andy! You're here! See, I told you those jeans were it! You look amazing!" Brynn said, hugging me. As soon as she found out we'd made our relationship official, she squealed and escorted me to the bathroom to analyze every interaction Eric and I had ever shared. She was my friend again, and Eric was my boyfriend. I'd wanted this for so long.

"Make up?" Summer asked, holding her palette out.

"Huh?" I said, the memory fading as I tuned into what she was asking. "A little bit?" I said when she motioned using an eyeshadow brush on me. I didn't want them to paint my whole face.

"Some trust, please," she said and guided my chin to face her.

"I don't want to look like I'm trying too hard," I whispered.

"I get that," Leah said. "Go easy," she warned Summer.

"Seriously, you all need to chill," Summer said.

"And we need to go in ten. I want you to have enough time to feel confident about your makeup, too," I said.

"Please. I could wear a paper bag and those boys would try to stick their hands under it."

"Summer!" Abby cried.

"What? Like half of them can handle me. I can talk circles around all of them. Lightning-fast tongue."

I got the feeling we weren't discussing her debate skills when she said that.

"You *want* them to handle you," Maria said.

"Ew, stop it. Our counselor is right here," Summer said. She handed me a tissue after capping the lipstick she'd been using on me. "Blot."

I blotted. Them trying to censor themselves was how Brynn acted toward me now that I'd entered her friend group again. Everyone saw me as innocent, as too shy to know or do anything with a guy. I had a stack of period romances that proved otherwise. The girls were under my wing, so I accepted that they were holding back and trying to be appropriate, but Brynn? I never knew what to say around her anymore, either.

"There. What do you think?" Summer said and put down her eyeshadow brush.

I turned to look at myself in the mirror. *Wow.* I still looked like me, but my eyes shone brighter, my hair sleeker than normal. The shirt fit me in a way that accented my waist while still remaining casual. I looked like I cared about my appearance but that I could've done this in a few minutes without fretting over it.

"It's perfect. Thank you," I said, tilting my face side to side. She could make a career out of this.

"Anytime. Tell us all about your date after," Megan begged.

I rolled my eyes.

"I bet Lucas punches Eric right in the face one of these nights. He's caveman-ish like that. Possessive." Caralyn sighed in an exaggerated way.

"Lucas isn't possessive of me."

"Girl, you have got to have a past with that boy." She unplugged the curling iron she'd finished using. "Is he the 'confidence' that made Eric notice you?"

My stomach tightened. Had this conversation crossed the line between counselor and camper? "Let's talk about something else."

"Mmhm."

I bit my lip, feeling like I owed them something since they helped me out when they didn't have to. "Lucas has always been kind to me, even last summer. He's a great guy. But he's not from around here, and I am. I'm going to Middlebury in the fall. It's not going to happen."

"Yeah, except you could light the whole camp on fire when you look at him. You like him."

"He's a great counselor," I said primly.

"Uh huh," Destiny said.

I waved the girls away and let them leave before me to go to the movie. If I'd learned nothing else from the parties Eric had taken me to this year, it was that you didn't want to be too early. That's where the awkward silences lived.

Five minutes, then I'd go. And in the meantime... I fished under my pillow for my favorite novel, flipping to where I'd tagged a well-worn page with a neon pink arrow. I needed some confidence, and it always did the trick.

"You're going to make it," Alexander said in a reassuring tone, his biceps straining to hold the rope steady.

"I'm not!" Amelia shrieked back. Under her, the rushing rapids of the river gurgled and swirled, their depths unknown in the dark of the night. One false move on the rope, and she'd be swept away. She clutched it with her slick fingers and thighs, her hair dipping close, too close to the water below.

"Look at me. Amelia, look at me!"

Amelia held her breath, peering across the space that divided them to his face, shrouded in darkness.

"I'm not going to let you fall."

"You can't promise that! I can't swim, Alex!"

"I know," he said through gritted teeth. How much longer would he be able to hold her? "But you know something else?"

"What?" The rope began to sag closer to the water as the branch it was attached to started to give way. She pulled herself along one more soggy foot, trying hard not to cry.

His voice was hard and determined as it carried across the river. "If you fall, I'm coming in after you."

I closed the book, the sound of Alexander's strong voice in my head as I straightened my spine. He would never let Amelia float away. Eric wouldn't let me drown, either. He'd still like me even if I made a social misstep.

I hoped.

15

Movie Mayhem

I trekked across the archery field to where sheets rippled in the breeze, ready to project the movie tonight. The low chatter of the crowd blended into a comforting white noise and the vast sky overhead gave a calm, spacious feel to the activity.

But where was Eric? I continued toward the screen, hoping he'd grab me when he saw me.

I didn't count on seeing Lucas first.

"Hey, Counselor Andy." He waved from a group of his Cheetah campers, smack-dab in the middle of the field. "Want to sit with us?"

I smiled, waving back. "I'm okay, thanks."

One of the guys elbowed him in the side. "She told you!"

"Shut up!" another one said as a timid tap landed on my left shoulder.

"Hey, Andrea."

I turned my smile up a few notches and took in Eric, clad in an uncalled-for button-down shirt and were his jeans pressed? They were. A line ran down them and everything. I didn't know the camp had an iron. How was he not sweating to death in long sleeves? Even with the sun setting, it still had to be at least eighty degrees.

"Hey," I said.

He laced his fingers with mine. "Ready?"

"Totally."

We left the crowd for a spot underneath a tree on the side of the field.

"We won't be able to see it as well from here," Eric apologized, "but I thought you might like the privacy." He was right about both things.

"It's great." I turned my attention to the food he pulled out of a picnic basket. "Where'd you get all this?" I fingered the checkered waterproof blanket beneath us.

His neck colored. "I uh... brought it with me just in case. Kinda forgot about it last time."

"Oh." Could he get any more perfect?

He pulled out paper cartons filled with every Chinese food I could think of.

"But you hate Chinese!" I laughed.

"It's okay. It's your favorite."

Warmth flooded my cheeks as I stared up at him. *He remembered.* Eric blinked back at me, earnest and thoughtful, as he brought my hand to his lips. I ducked my head and picked up a pair of chopsticks and the Lo Mein, offering them to him.

"Nah. I came prepared." He pulled what looked like a peanut butter and jelly sandwich from the basket. I laughed as he unwrapped it.

Singing echoed from the cheesy camp movie that had started on the big screen.

Eric frowned at the screen in the deepening shadows of just-past-sunset. The cast had broken into a choreographed dance. "Sorry, this isn't as romantic as I hoped it would be. I know you're not that into movies."

I winced. Did he think I was bored? "It's great. I love it."

He grinned, patting my knee. But he was wrong. I loved movies, especially romances. How many times had Mom and I cuddled up on the couch to criticize movie versions of our favorite books? Maybe Eric thought I didn't like them because he'd asked me to go to the theater with him and his guy friends a couple of times, but I said no. It seemed awkward, so I always found an out.

"Hey, Eric." Derrick jogged up to our picnic, and he and Eric shared a fist bump. "How's your hand treating ya, Veggie Master?" He made a chopping motion.

Eric laughed. "Hey, make fun all you want, but I heard my cooking this year is the highlight of the cafeteria experience."

Derrick leaned on a nearby tree. "Okay, can't argue with that."

"How's Teddy?" Eric asked. "He doing any better after that trust fall?"

Derrick rolled his eyes. "You'd think ten kids could hold one of their own up for five seconds. He'll be fine. He was just scared."

Eric laughed. "So much for trust."

I sat, flabbergasted as my eyes bounced between the two guys. They were so comfortable with each other. It looked like Eric had made a friend here. When did he have the time to socialize? We barely had time to see each other. Where was the quiet boy who stood up for me in school projects, the one who pushed his glasses up three times before he got enough breath to ask me out?

I hugged my knees to my chest and glanced over to where Destiny and Maria tickled each other in the grass. Maria put up a good fight, but Destiny was relentless, and soon Maria screamed with laughter. I smiled. Relentless was the right word for all my Beavers this summer. They'd grown on me.

After a few minutes, Derrick left.

"What's making you happy right now?"

I turned to Eric's soft voice. "You are," I said. And it was true. This was the kind of date I wanted with him, not one picked apart afterwards by Brynn. It was real and present. He'd done a lot to be with me this summer, and I didn't take that for granted. Not for one second.

Lucas's laughter floated over to me from the field. He pointed to the screen with one arm, leaning back on the grass with his other. The Cheetah campers next to him pounded Red Bull and popcorn with wide grins on their faces.

Then the girls noticed our picnic. Summer pointed at us. Maria's eyes followed. Then Destiny. Sarah. The whole group began chatting to each other, their eyes never leaving us.

My stomach sank.

Destiny ran over to Lucas. *Oh, God.* She pointed at me and said something. He frowned as he replied, and they both turned to stare at me. I pretended to look away as she nodded and got back up, returning to the other girls.

Something mean and horrible unfurled in me. I didn't need him fighting my battles with the girls. She shouldn't have ever gone over to him, either. What did she even say to him?

My face began to heat. Then I heard it.

"Landy. Landy. Landy! Landy!" The girls yelled, laughing between each word.

I was going to kill them.

"What are they saying?" Eric asked. "Does it have something to do with the movie?"

"I have no idea," I lied, even as their chant became louder.

"I think they're yelling Andy," he said.

I held my breath.

"Maybe you should go over there."

I nodded. This was getting out of hand. I got to my feet and started toward them, but Lucas was already on it. He sprinted over to the girls, his expression thunderous, and said maybe three words. They stopped chanting. Not one of them looked back at me.

"Huh. Guess that Luke guy helped them out."

"Guess so," I said, trying to keep my voice light. He didn't need to do that. They were my campers. "They're just being silly." I sat back down.

"How is leading the girls going? I'm sorry we didn't talk much about that last time. You're in what, the Beaver cottage?" Eric asked.

I smiled. "Yeah. It's going okay." Unless you counted the fact that they were trying to wreck my relationship, and Lucas was making me look bad by going over there to solve my problems for me.

"They're not being crazy or anything? I know how girls can get."

I narrowed my eyes. What was that supposed to mean? "I've got it handled."

He traced a circle on my hand. "I'm worried about you."

"You are?"

"This whole place seems... out of character for you. You're this sweet, shy girl. You know?"

I frowned before I could catch myself.

Even under the darkened sky, Eric caught it. "Not that it's a bad thing," he backtracked. "It was... I was surprised you signed up for this, that's all."

"I can do it." The words came out with more force than I meant to put behind them.

He threaded his fingers through mine. "I know. You can do anything."

I smiled at him. He believed in me. It wasn't his fault he was pressing the buttons of my insecurities. Maybe I wasn't the perfect person to lead these girls. They deserved someone who knew what they were doing. I didn't, but I was trying. Was that enough? The stress of it made my head throb.

We watched the movie for a few minutes, which was a lot easier since the girls had quieted down and tuned in.

"How's the kitchen?" I asked after a bit. If the conversation focused him, I'd be more comfortable.

"It's a lot of prep work. I chop things. Like a ninja," he joked, slicing the air. "Just like at home."

He ran a hand through his hair, looking away from me. "Kind of."

"I'm—"

"Don't say it." He pressed a finger to my lips. "I'm a big boy. If I don't want to do it, I won't."

"Okay," I said around his finger.

He laughed, dropping his hand. "Andrea Stevens, I like you."

"But you don't have to sacrifice your summer for it."

"You have no idea what I'd sacrifice for you," he said in a low voice.

That might be the most romantic thing anyone ever said to me. I frowned in the darkness, knowing he couldn't see it. Then why did it feel ominous? Maybe it was just poor wording.

"Come here?" He opened his arms.

I settled against him, and we cuddled, his minty breath mingling with the woodsy scent that seeped into all my clothes. It was still at least eighty degrees out, and soon I'd be soaked in sweat. It was worth it. Being near Eric was always worth it. I tried to shake off my weird feeling.

"I'm still glad we came," he whispered into my hair.

"Me too," I said.

And who knew how much either of us were telling the truth?

<hr>

As soon as the credits rolled, I helped Eric pack up the leftover food using our cell phone flashlights and said goodbye. He kissed me softly, sweetly, the way that he always did. I tried to enjoy it, but I couldn't get the bitter taste of betrayal out of my mouth. Beaver cottage betrayal.

As soon as he turned down the other side of the path, anger sped my steps until I wound up jogging back to the cottage. I beat the girls there.

They entered, laughing and talking to each other. Until they saw my face.

"It was funny! Come on, you have zero chemistry with that guy! You should be with Lucas!" Megan started. "Yeah, he's so perfect for you!" Caralyn giggled.

Destiny frowned. "Guys, stop. She looks like she wants to say something."

Did I? It didn't feel right to bring up my romantic relationship. The line between camper and counselor felt so thin right now. It was hard to think as my anger bubbled up, looking for an escape hatch.

"Do you care how I feel?" I asked in a quiet voice.

Taylor grimaced. "Andy, we—"

"I'm mortified right now. Maybe I still need a minute." A minute to remember my job. A minute to push down the sarcastic comments that rose to the surface. Mean comments, ones I had no business saying to teenagers I was in charge of.

"Mortified?" Sarah asked. "Like embarrassed?"

One by one, the girls' faces fell. They hadn't thought it through again. They were just having fun.

I blinked quickly, my anger fading into shame. "I'm disappointed. You need to think," I said in a calm voice, "about what you're doing before you do it. Okay?"

"It wasn't funny," Blair said, staring down the other girls.

"We're... we're sorry," Abby said.

"Please stop. Please." My voice cracked, and I hated myself for it. I had done so well up until this point.

"Okay. We won't chant it anymore," Megan agreed.

I sighed. "Thank you."

"I think this is the first time you've been real with us. Like you're talking to us like real people instead of scripted counselor speak," Taylor whispered.

I threw my hands up. "Okay?"

"We like it better," Destiny said.

"You like being yelled at better than me being nice?"

She shrugged. "You didn't yell. And now we know a line not to cross."

"And we're sorry," Megan added, her face red.

"Okay." I couldn't unpack all of that right now. Still wound up, I headed for the door.

Taylor stepped forward. "Are you—"

"Shh, she said to stop," Megan whispered.

I rolled my eyes. "Yes, I'm going to go talk to Counselor Lucas, now."

"We won't wait up," Maria teased.

"Shut up!" Megan stepped on her foot.

"Ow!"

"Lights out is still in ten minutes," I reminded them. Except for my two horseshoe winners, but I couldn't deal with that right now. I stalked over to the Cheetah cottage.

Lucas stood, backlit by the porch light as he braced his forearms on the railing.

"Stand up," I said irritably. I couldn't yell at him when he looked like an Instagram model. "You're always leaning. Stop leaning on things."

"What?" he asked, straightening. "Look, Andy—"

I held my hand up. "No. Stop. You need to stop." My heart threatened to beat out of my chest. So much confrontation might trigger a panic attack if I wasn't careful, but it had to be done.

"Stop what?"

"You don't need to save me. I don't want you to." He was treating me like he did last summer. Like everyone did before senior year. Poor Andy, too weak to fight her own battles. I wasn't that girl anymore. I was stronger.

His jaw dropped. "Are you serious right now? I *helped* you with your little problem. You should be thanking me that I didn't let them out you to your boyfriend."

"Out me for what? What have I done wrong?" I jabbed my chest with one hand.

"I don't know." He crossed his arms. "Have you told him about us?"

"There is no *us*, Lucas." Could he be more frustrating?

In the low glow of the porch light, his jaw flexed as he held his tongue. What would happen if he said what he really wanted to right now? I didn't want to know. I was too disgusted with him and the girls.

"Well, you're welcome," he said.

I followed him to his door. "I'm not thanking you. Let me fight my own battles."

"Then fight them," he said without turning around. The door slammed in my face.

I ran back to my own cottage and slammed the door, too. It was childish and stupid, and the girls looked at me with varying degrees of surprise, amusement, and pity, but they didn't say anything. It was worse than if they had let loose and said what they wanted to. Almost.

I waited ten minutes for my two horseshoe winners, then turned out the lights and buried my face in my pillow.

What an asshole.

16

Turtle Day

The next morning quickly morphed into one of those days where the words I needed to say got stuck in my throat. It used to scare me a lot until I talked through it with my therapist back home. She laughed like it was the most normal thing in the world and called them Turtle Days. Turtle Days were for reading and bubble baths and movies and no people whatsoever. Sometimes I could force myself out of one by sheer force of will, and sometimes that made everything worse. What horrible luck that one happened while I was here.

I didn't want to think about what might've triggered it. Coffee sometimes made me feel better.

The girls didn't notice my silence as we got dressed and brushed our teeth and hair and tromped over to the cafeteria. They chatted away, fully recovered from my lecture last night. I couldn't keep up with their conversation if I tried. It bounced from boys to makeup, back to boys, how the competition was going, and then boys again.

I made a beeline for the coffee machine in the staff lounge and sat on one of the folding chairs, staring into the steam rising from my cup for a long minute before taking a sip. I could do this. I would have to. I had no choice. *Get up. Get up and go be awesome.* They deserved that from me.

I pulled the wrinkled list of activities for the day from the left breast pocket of my safari vest and looked at the schedule. Cottage activity followed by free time followed by group activity followed by lunch. Then a color war activity and more free time, dinner, and back to cottage work. I sighed. One thing at a time.

My coffee was gone. I refilled, then forced myself to walk back out the door from the quiet bubble of the lounge and into the cacophony of the cafeteria. I smiled at the girls, a large, fake counselor smile that I doubted fooled anyone.

"She's still mad at us," Maria whispered to Destiny as I sat down.

"Give her a break," Destiny said.

I tilted my head at her, a small smile pulling at my lips. She was trying to be kind.

The girls chatted around me as I sipped, sipped, sipped my coffee, and then we were off. Time blurred together, and when I spoke, my voice came out scratchy, my smile plastered to my face. I was proud of myself, though. A year ago, I would have curled into a ball and shut out the world on a day like today. In fact, last year at camp I did that exact thing. It might look like I was floating along, but the effort it took was a giant step for me.

I returned to the coffee station every free time, every break, hoping it would grease the back of my throat enough to turn me into a real person for even a second.

It didn't.

But I was surviving. I couldn't do more when every cell of my body wanted to crawl back into bed and forget that I ever had to speak to another soul. I avoided Lucas's intense stare during our group activity and stood on the sideline with, surprise, a cup of coffee.

Finally, the girls and I made it to the last activity. I hoped for a challenge where I could step back and just exist. Cheer a little. Maybe not even that. The girls and I walked to the archery field.

"Get the lead out, Counselor! What's your deal today?" Paige said, bouncing up next to me, her girls shuffling along behind.

I turned to her.

She sobered. "You guys go on ahead. I'll catch up."

"I'm fine," I whispered when her campers melded with my own and walked out of earshot. I couldn't SOS her twice in one week. I needed to deal with this on my own.

"You're not. What's happening?"

I threw my hands out. I didn't want to talk about it. I didn't want to talk at all.

"Are you... overwhelmed? Overstimulated?"

"Something like that," I muttered. I couldn't label my discomfort. Forcing myself out of my shell on a turtle day might cause a migraine, but I would grab myself some painkillers later.

Paige watched me throw my coffee cup in the trash can by the entrance of the field.

"Fake it 'til you make it, right?" I gave her a counselor smile.

"You look kinda scary," she said.

I sighed. "I know." My eyes always gave me away. I had zero poker face.

"Want a hug?"

I was a ticking time bomb. Touch was the last thing I wanted. "Definitely not."

"Noted. I've got your girls if you need a minute." She raised her eyebrows in question.

I strode forward, out of the path's tepid shade and into the full sun of the field. "I'm good." If I walked away right now, I wouldn't be able to return. I was like a wind-up toy, one that would freeze if the energy stopped.

Dana was in the process of finishing instructions on a water balloon relay when Paige and I rejoined the campers. "So, make sure that you work with your partnered cottages to yield the greatest results!"

Great. Just what we all needed. A team thing.

Lucas looked over at me, frowning. *You okay?* He mouthed.

Did I look that stressed? I nodded. I hoped he understood that nodding didn't give him permission to overstep.

He nodded back and then re-centered his attention on where Destiny and Josh passed a balloon back and forth. She squinted at him, and he chuckled. How could you flirt during a water balloon toss? I rolled my eyes.

Lucas walked over to stand beside Paige and me. I hated that the hairs on my arms stood at attention when he was near, even though it had to be a million degrees out. How could my body react that way when sweat dripped out of every pore? This summer was all sun. Too bright and too much.

It's okay. The day is almost over.

Eventually, the Beavers and Cheetahs won. I felt guilty as I clapped with wooden movements. None of them even came close to beating us. Lucas whooped, uncaring that we had a stacked team. I smiled my counselor smile at him and turned to go.

He frowned again, his hand coming up like he wanted to pull me back. Thankfully, he didn't. I needed to get through the rest of the day and coffee my way through dinner until the last block of free time before bed arrived and I could relinquish my counselor duties.

An hour later, I winced as the screen door slammed behind the last girl to leave for bracelet-making or candle-dipping or Flirting 101 or wherever they were going. The sharp sound made the whole room vibrate, made me vibrate. Everything was loud and claustrophobic, and...

I stared at my phone for a second before leaving it on my bunk and heading out the door in the opposite direction of the archery field. Moonlight lit my path over the dead grass and onto the beach. The water rippled against the shore. Fireflies bobbed in and out of sight.

It was quiet. Finally.

I took off my vest and used it as a pillow as I lay on the sand and stared at the stars. I needed... nothing.

Not two minutes later, the scuffing of feet sounded across the sand. So much for being alone.

"Hey," Eric said in a soft voice as he sat beside me.

I sat up, straightening my back and forcing a smile. I didn't know we were supposed to meet, but I hadn't exactly been checking my phone today.

Then he threw an arm around my shoulders. I gritted my teeth and pretended my skin didn't sting at the contact. I made myself lean into him, blinking back the moisture in my eyes. What was another ten minutes? I could do this. I could. I didn't even want to touch the earth below us. I wanted to live in an Andy bubble with zero clothing scratching me, zero air pressing in on me, zero gravity holding me.

Eric anchored me to the sand.

After a minute, I shrugged out of his embrace.

"You okay?"

I drew a circle in the sand, wishing I could read the tone of his voice better. Was he mad? Disappointed? Concerned? I didn't want any of that. "Trying to be."

"What can I do?" Again the neutral voice.

I didn't know what to tell him. My throat closed trying to explain. Trying to figure out how to do it and not be the worst girlfriend ever, not embarrass myself. The Andy he knew was shy, bookish, smart. Introverted, sure, but sarcastic and awesome. He'd never seen me like this. I didn't want him to know this side of me existed.

He bent toward me, his eyes intense, his mouth descending. That was what the neutral voice meant? He wanted us to... but I couldn't right now!

I turned so his lips landed on my cheek, hating myself for it.

"You're not okay at all, are you?"

I shrugged. I told him I wasn't.

"You gotta talk to me here, Andy. I'm not a mind reader." He said it nicely, but frustration radiated from the rigid set of his shoulders.

Anger grew, dark and twisted within me. I didn't ask for his help. I didn't want to explain myself. He wasn't my therapist or my parent. But I knew that wasn't fair.

"I don't... want to talk or do anything. Is that okay?" It took an astronomical effort to say, but I softened the blow by giving him a small smile.

He frowned. "We have so little time together, but okay, Andy. If that's what you want." He got to his feet.

Wait, I should've said. I wanted to. *Wait, I can kiss you. Tell me about your day. I'm sorry you're stuck in the kitchen.* Insert cutesy laugh. Insert fake confidence. Insert the girlfriend I should be. Instead, I watched him disappear into the darkness of the woods.

I lay back down, my head pounding with the headache that had threatened to overwhelm me all day. I didn't try to stop the tears spilling down my cheeks. Why was I like this? Why couldn't I keep going like Paige and the girls in my cottage? My battery was always half-charged compared to theirs. They were probably having a ball together during their free time.

I breathed in and pressed my fingers into the sand. Again, the scuffing of feet, this time louder than the ones that just left me.

Oh my God. Leave me alone!

"Andy."

I squeezed my eyes together, which made more tears fall. I couldn't deal with anyone else being mad at me right now. Lucas sat next to me, but he didn't say more.

I returned to listening to the crickets, to the canoes rubbing together in the lazy waves of the lake. My gaze drifted to the spaces between the stars, and the one wimpy cloud that tried and failed to cover the uber-bright moon. I placed one hand on my chest like I'd been taught in therapy and let the thud of my own heart lull me into a different space. Let myself feel the sand around me cradling my body instead of hurting it. Let myself breathe.

Lucas stayed.

When I looked over, I expected him to be asleep or at the very least, bored. He was staring at the moon. The moment my eyes landed on him, he turned his head to me in unspoken connection.

"I'm sorry," he said. "I was trying to help with the Landy thing."

"I know. I'm sorry, too."

Lucas fisted his hands in the sand.

"Are *you* okay?" I whispered, a stupid echo of what Eric had asked me.

"Not really," he whispered back.

"Do you want to…" Talk? Was it about us? There was no us, but still, he was allowed to feel whatever feelings he had.

"God, no," he said roughly. "It's not… it's not about camp."

He collapsed onto the sand beside me, both of us staring at that damn moon that would never be covered by that tiny wisp of a cloud because rain was a thing of the past. Even the moon couldn't hide this summer.

Time passed. More than I needed, but maybe the right amount for him.

"I'm here for you," I said, though I knew how freaking lame it sounded. "What's going on?"

Lucas wasn't like me. He didn't need to process on his own. He needed someone to hear him.

"Well… my dad died a month ago."

"What?" Suddenly, the difference in how he acted since we got to camp made sense. The guys checking on him. Dana's concerned looks. The fact that he wasn't coming, then all of a sudden he was, and he'd been given preference over Eric.

Paige had even tried to tell me at the beginning of camp, hadn't she? I suppressed a groan. How unobservant could I be?

He sniffed; a sound so quiet I almost missed it. "I'm not crying because he's dead."

Focus. This isn't about how much you suck. It's about him. He needs someone. "Okay…"

He swiped at his eyes. "I'm crying because I feel guilty for not being sad."

My brain connected the dots from last summer. How his parents were divorced. How he only visited his dad in the summer, and when he did, he ended up at camp. "Lucas—"

"He wasn't abusive. He just didn't care. But I'm supposed to. And I do, but I can't… and Tyler…"

"How did he die?" I had to interrupt his spiral. He was beating himself up, and I couldn't let him.

"Car accident."

"Jesus."

"Yeah." A small breeze knocked a boat against one of the docks in a muted pattern. We listened to its *tap, tap, tap.* I couldn't say anything to make his problem better. Except… "You said something about Tyler?"

Lucas swallowed. "He's mad at me."

"What? Why?" From what I remembered last year, Tyler was the calmer brother of the two.

"I didn't go to the funeral." He made a frustrated sound in the back of his throat. "And I begged off team conditioning," he whispered.

"For your swimming scholarship?" So, pool maintenance was a lie.

He nodded once.

"Is that… are you still…" My stomach twisted. He didn't throw away his full ride, did he?

"My dad died. The coach gave me a pass," he said in a flat voice.

I nodded, relieved. "You should have one."

"Even if I ditched them to come here."

"Why *did* you come here?" I sure wouldn't if a tragedy like that happened in my life.

He stared at me for a long moment. "It's a constant," he muttered. "I always come here, and..." He sighed. "Maybe I didn't know what else to do. Maybe I wanted to see you."

"Lucas..." My throat closed. I didn't know what to say.

"I know. I'm sorry. I just wanted to pretend."

So, he just pretended to be attracted to me? Anger welled up in my chest, then receded. His dad died. "Pretend..."

"That it's a normal summer. That everything isn't falling apart." His voice broke.

I swallowed. "Do you..." I'd reached a mental space where a light touch might not hurt. "Do you need a hug?"

He stared at me. "Not if you can't right now. I don't know why I told you. I'm sorry. I'm having a..."

"Day." *Relatable.* "Me too."

"I know."

I itched my arm. Maybe I could distract him. I couldn't stand seeing him so defeated. "How did you know?"

"Know what?"

"That I don't want to be touched right now."

He sat up. "Do you remember what you told me last summer?"

I wasn't in the mood to guess. "We said a lot of things last summer." I sat up, too.

He pointed to the sand beneath us. "We met right here, and you said *I see you.*"

I was silent. He had compared himself to his brother at the time. I didn't realize it meant so much to him.

"Well, I see *you,* Andy. And you're not broken. I might've overheard the tail end of you talking to Eric, and it was crappy."

I glared at him.

"I didn't mean to."

I deflated. "I know." He had come out here to think. Like me.

"You're allowed to need what you need to be okay. We don't have to hug."

But he needed something. I leaned over. Slowly, so he would know my intention, I reached out to lay one hand on his cheek. It was smooth and rough at the same time. I focused on that instead of the damp tearstains under my fingers. Lucas crying made me feel so helpless I wanted to scream.

He closed his eyes and leaned into my touch like I was the only thing connecting him to reality. Maybe I was. And maybe he was that person for me.

We were tethered together so strongly under the light of the moon on this beach where we had kissed and fought and talked and just... were. I couldn't think about how messy, how inappropriate it was standing here holding his face in the dark. It was Lucas.

"Alright, Campers! It's time to head back to your bunks where your counselors will be waiting to tuck you in! Just kidding! But get there now, please. No detours!" Dana's voice, so full of laughter and happiness, carried to us on the lakeshore.

Lucas opened his eyes, and I dropped my hand. "We should go," he whispered. I nodded.

We walked together all the way back to the cottages, neither of us touching each other, but connected just the same. Once the door to his cottage closed, I snapped out of my funk and drifted back to my own. I pasted a smile on my face for the last thirty minutes until lights out. As I climbed into my sleeping bag in the dark, guilt over Eric didn't overwhelm me the way I thought it would. Lucas's tearstained face filled my mind instead, his eyes full of anger and sadness, leaning into my touch.

He might've been the first person to truly need me. And I'd been there for him. There was something in that.

17

Tug of War

"Five minutes to lights out," I reminded the girls the next night as I fluffed my pillow. Groans and boos sounded from every corner of the cottage. I smiled. No drama had occurred today. Eric texted me like normal. Lucas didn't seem any worse for wear. My Turtle Day had ended, and life had returned to normal. All that remained was lights out and... a subtle tapping? Someone was knocking on the door.

My heart jumped into my throat. *Lucas.* But when I opened the door, Josh from the Cheetah cottage stood before me holding a bunch of wildflowers that looked suspiciously identical to the landscaped ones next to the cafeteria. His hair stuck out every which way, and he smoothed it back as he tried to see past me. "Is uh... Destiny..." His voice cracked. "Is Destiny here?"

I smiled. Four minutes remained until lights out. I spied Lucas sitting on the railing of his own porch, watching his camper. Had he recovered from our talk? It was pretty heavy. Today had been so busy I hadn't had a chance to connect with him. Did he put Josh up to this, or was he being supportive?

I looked over my shoulder to where Destiny sat cross-legged on the floor playing cards with Summer and Sarah. "Destiny. There's someone here to see you."

She showed her cards and the other two girls groaned, throwing theirs down. "Neither of you have a poker face." She grabbed the mints from the center and popped one into her mouth, heading over to me in tiny terry cloth shorts and a tank top that didn't even reach halfway down to her belly button.

She brushed past me, and her face softened. "Hey, Josh."

I stared down at my own hoodie and ran my hand over the frizzy hair escaping my braids. She didn't even know he was coming over, and she looked gorgeous.

Josh pulled a long daisy from his bouquet before handing them to Destiny. "This one is for you," he said to me.

"You guys still might want to stay on the porch," I said with an arched brow. I knew this game. "Because lights out is lights out."

"Okay," he said, coloring.

Destiny rolled her eyes.

"But it's from my counselor," he said.

My eyes flew to Lucas, who now pointed to a cup of coffee steaming on the rail of my porch.

I stomped over and grabbed the cup. How did he always know what I needed when I needed it? He gave me a silent cheers with his own cup, his eyes burning with unspoken words that bridged the distance between us.

Destiny and Josh watched in open curiosity.

You're gorgeous, he mouthed.

My heart stopped.

You're ridiculous, I mouthed back, trying to play it off. Then, after a beat, *Are you okay?* I was here for him, for however long I could be. He chuckled and went back inside his cottage. I sighed.

"Wow. He wasn't kidding. You have a thing."

I jumped at Josh's voice. "What?"

"Uh, nothing. Never mind."

I pointed at him. "There's no thing."

Destiny gave me a wide-eyed look, then stared at the door.

"Enjoy your time." I flipped on the porch light and walked back into the cottage. My pocket buzzed.

Miss you.

My stomach knotted with guilt as I read Eric's text. Why did everything have to be so complicated?

The next day during the tug of war color war challenge, Lucas and I lined our campers up boy, girl, boy, girl. I shoved his stupid hat back into his hands, then ignored him as we took our stances at the end of the rope to be the anchors against the Dolphins and Tree Frogs.

As we placed our hands, I made sure not to touch him. I'd had all night to think about Josh's comment. What Lucas must've told his campers. How he didn't hide that he was trying to steal me from Eric.

"Are you mad at me?" he asked, his breath hot in my ear.

"What?" I lifted my shoulder to get him out of my space.

"You haven't looked at me all morning except to give my hat back."

The campers in front of us messing around jostled us back. Lucas held my arm to steady me, and I ripped it out of his grasp.

"Stop it," Summer complained, punching a kid named Brady in the shoulder. "I want to win!"

"I don't know what you're talking about," I mumbled to Lucas.

"If this is about what I said last night—"

"Did you..." I lowered my voice as Brady and Summer traded barbs. "Did you talk to your campers about us?" I hissed. "That's so inappropriate!"

"Ready... go!" Dana shouted.

We leaned back and dug our heels in.

"So, you admit there's an us," he said between gritted teeth as we strained.

"Not what I said," I grunted back. We gained a few feet of ground and my butt bumped against his hips, jolting me. I let go of the rope in shock. We lost a few inches.

"Andy!" he yelled.

"Don't yell at me!" I yelled back. I held on again and pulled.

"I didn't—"

"Come on, Beavers! You've got this!" I cheered to cut him off.

"I didn't mean to tell them anything. It all came out after capture the flag."

I snorted. I could imagine him telling his horny teenager campers about how I'd thrown myself at him on the beach last year. What a jerk. I pulled harder. So did he. We gained a few more feet.

Then suddenly, the rope went slack. Two of the Tree Frogs had gotten tired and let go, giving us the win.

I fell backwards, right into Lucas's lap on the ground. Like a bolt of lightning, every inch of my jean-clad body reacted to his. Tingles ran through me as his arms surrounded me to cushion the blow.

"Are you okay?" his voice rumbled in my ear.

I froze, unable to leave the heat of his embrace, the rock steady support of his arms. I needed to... do something... but I...

He didn't move a muscle. "Andy?" he breathed.

Our surroundings came back to me all at once, and I scrambled to my feet, chest heaving. No one saw that, right?

He got to his feet more slowly, dusting off his shorts with his gaze on the ground, but I could've sworn that his hands shook.

"Alright, Beavers?" I called to the girls as they stood.

"We won!" Destiny screamed. "We won! Take that, you froggy flippers!"

"Destiny. Sportsmanship," I reminded her. But the Tree Frogs and Dolphins didn't seem to give a crap as they melded into the crowd and four new teams arrived to take up the rope.

I backed off to the sidelines to watch as they fought over an arbitrary line, every cell of my body attuned to how ruffled Lucas's hair looked as he jammed his hat back onto it. It was a game. We fell. There was no reason for me to feel as guilty as I did right now.

18

Trade Me

We won the tug of war competition. Summer just about jumped out of her shoes as poor Paige led her unaffected team away, her brow furrowed with frustration. They were out in the first round, even though they'd been paired with the Iguana team, who were pretty strong. I wanted to call out to her to see if she was okay, but she waved me off the second she saw me frown. *I've got this,* she mouthed, her shoulders set. Okay, then.

As soon as I walked my back to the cottage, I swiped into my phone to text her anyway. She might need a friend right now. I was working out exactly what to type when the buzz of an incoming text from Eric stopped me short. I blew out a breath as I stared at the words on the screen.

> **Sorry about what happened on the beach. I'm just used to seeing you more.**

> **Are you okay?**

I clicked the button to text him back, but I didn't know what to say. We'd texted like nothing had happened since then, and I thought we'd made the silent decision to ignore the awkwardness between us. Now he wanted to talk about it? He wasn't responsible for my mental health stuff. Heck, he didn't even know about it. This was the type of moment I would talk to my counselor about, but Dr. Santos wasn't here. I had to figure it out by myself.

Sure, I was sweeping it under the rug, but I didn't have another solution. I should have texted him I was fine once I felt better, but I was too focused on being a counselor and on...

...Lucas.

I exited our conversation and texted Paige.

After a few seconds, she sent me a thumbs up. I bit my lip. That could mean anything. She could be busy with the girls or telling me she wasn't okay. I didn't know. Maybe I should take it at face value. I wanted to be a good friend to her, but I had a lot going on this summer, too.

The girls around me freshened their hair and re-did the makeup that had melted off their faces the second they stepped outside. I snapped back into counselor mode and managed to convince everyone to drink water and re-apply sunscreen, shaking the bottle in their faces.

Then I smoothed down my vest to exit the cottage for the next activity. "Come on, girls. Let's get to the archery field for the water balloon fight."

Bathing suits flashed by me as my last few stragglers sprinted out of the cottage, but my eyes snagged on a camper who hadn't changed yet—and who looked like she was nowhere near the right frame of mind to play games.

"Destiny? Are you okay?" I approached her bed. Only then did the tearstains on her cheeks register. She didn't answer me as she sat on the edge of her bunk staring into space with a frown on her face. Did someone piss her off? Was it—*oh*. "Did something happen with Josh?"

She glared at me.

I put my hands up helplessly. I didn't know what possessed me to think that at eighteen years old I would be able to deal with other people's emotions this way. I couldn't handle most social situations.

Destiny turned her tear-streaked face away from me as I sat beside her on her bunk. I didn't know what to do with her—like how last summer no one knew what to do with me.

I fumbled for something to say. "What do you need?"

"I don't know," she muttered. "Not you," she said in a flat voice, so unlike her normal tone.

"I—" My phone buzzed in my safari vest. I fished it out.

Wait. Josh was quiet, shy, more like me. Destiny was more like...

I placed a hand on Destiny's shoulder as her body shook with quiet sobs—ones she didn't want the other girls to hear.

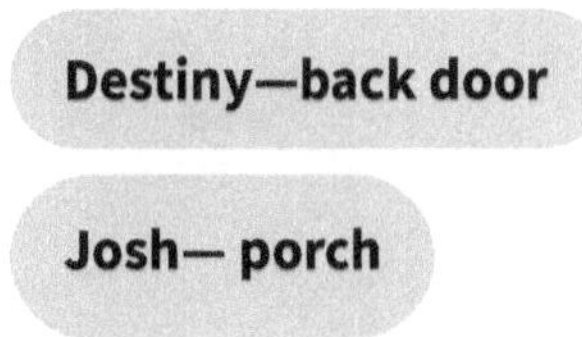

Oh, thank God. I leaned in close to Destiny. "I have a plan. Go to the back door."

"Now?" She pointed to where her makeup ran down her face.

"No one important will see you. Promise." No one important to her, anyway.

For a tense moment, I wasn't sure if she'd do what I said, but then she flipped her hood over her head and stalked to the back door. As soon as she passed through, I hurried to the front porch.

Josh sat on the lone porch swing, his grey hoodie also over his head. I sat beside him.

"I don't need a babysitter," he said, staring straight ahead.

"Maybe I need a break," I said.

"I'm not talking to you," he mumbled.

"Okay."

He turned his head to frown at me. "Fine."

I used the toe of my sneaker to rock us back and forth. He remained buried in his sweatshirt, the picture of teen angst.

Minutes passed. I texted Paige to cover my bases.

> Help my girls? Teen crisis over here.

> Destiny and Josh, right?

> I knew they wouldn't last through camp. Is it bad that my cottage bet packs of gum on it?

> Kind of, yeah.

> I'll help your Beavers, even if they don't need it.

> Thanks.

I shoved my phone back in my vest.

"I'm fine," Josh gritted out.

"Cool. Me too."

"I'm not going to the next activity."

"Okay."

We sat longer, me still pushing us back and forth on the swing. I closed my eyes. After a while, Josh's muscles started to relax beside me. When I cracked my eyes open, his were shut tight, but I knew by his breathing that he wasn't sleeping. I stopped rocking.

A long moment passed. "Thanks," he mumbled.

"No problem."

"I still don't want to talk to you."

"That's fine."

"I can handle it."

"I know."

He stood. Boy, was he tall. At least six foot two, if not more. I expected him to walk off, to retreat into his cottage, never to make eye contact with me or Destiny again. It's what I would do. But he remained standing, indecision written on his face.

Then, he whispered, "Can I hug you?"

Poor kid. I nodded.

He crushed me in his arms, and I hugged him back tight. We stood in front of the swing for a solid minute, longer than most hugs should be, but I understood.

When he let go, his ears glowed pink with embarrassment. "Sorry, I… is it weird to say you remind me of my mom?"

I bit back a laugh. "Not at all."

"Thanks." He headed back to his cottage, and I watched him go. Only then did I see Lucas standing on the porch, staring at me with a weird smile on his face.

I threw my hands out, exasperated. *What?* I mouthed as Josh closed the door of the cottage.

Nothing, he mouthed back, his blue eyes lined with mirth.

"Where's Destiny?" I called out.

He cupped his hands around his mouth to holler back. "At the activity."

"Don't make Josh go," I warned.

"Whatever you say, Counselor." He saluted me.

"Shut up."

He laughed and followed Josh inside.

19

Stop Pretending

By the time I jogged toward the archery field to meet up with my Beavers, the activity had ended. A flood of campers headed back down the path toward me. I nodded to Maria and Abby as they passed, feeling guilty that I didn't help them or cheer them on. I didn't regret my time with Josh. I just wished I could be two places at once.

Destiny shuffled down the trail, frowning at the ground.

"Did we win?" I asked to distract her.

She flinched. "Yeah... obviously," she said. At least she wasn't crying.

I sighed as she passed me, pivoting to follow her to the cottage.

"Andy!" Paige's voice rang out through the withered trees. She jogged to catch up to me.

"How did it go?" I asked.

She punched my arm. "Your girls smashed it, like always. But you missed Eric."

"Eric?" What was he doing on the archery field?

"Yeah, he came by to see you in action. Bad timing, huh? I told him where you were, though."

I kicked a rock down the trail in front of us. Eric had tried to come see me, support me as a counselor.

"He wrote you a note. I said I'd give it to you," Paige said. She fished a paper out of her vest.

I recoiled. Notes belonged to Lucas. "Why wouldn't he text me?" I wondered aloud.

"Something about you not answering your phone as much? I don't know. He's sweet, Andy. I'm sorry I haven't been more supportive."

I tuned her out as I pulled my phone from my pocket. I hadn't heard any texts come in—but there they were. Six missed texts from Eric, all timestamped from when Josh needed me. I didn't even feel my phone buzz. And if I had, I wouldn't have answered them. Not while trying to help. That would've been insensitive.

"I..."

"Open the note! Let's see what it says. Your life is so much more interesting than mine."

I frowned. Paige's reaction bordered on feverish obsession, which was a bit much for the situation. But her Clownfish were... well. I should humor her.

As I began to unfold the paper, my hands shook, and I stopped. What if he was annoyed that I wasn't there when he came to an activity? Okay, mad wasn't Eric's style, but camp hadn't been easy for him so far. The note might be too private to share.

I pocketed it. "I'll read it later."

"Suit yourself," she said, running to catch up to her girls on the path. One of them rolled her eyes as Paige talked to her, but the beginnings of a smile tugged at the camper's face. Paige might not see it yet, but it seemed like they were beginning to tolerate her cheeriness. It was a step. I didn't need to be worried about her, right? No one could hate Paige.

As soon as the path cleared out, I stepped into the woods and opened the letter.

His handwriting was neat, each letter closed and evenly spaced from the next like a typed font. It didn't come off as mad. He wanted to hang out with me. And this time, I'd have something real to say. I could tell him about how I'd helped someone who needed me. I wouldn't choke like I had before when I could've told him about... well, anything.

I floated through dinner, looking up every ten seconds, half-expecting Eric to appear and whisk me away. I didn't look over at Lucas once. It shouldn't feel like an accomplishment, but it did. Finally, the last camper exited the cafeteria for free time, leaving only a few counselors to loiter next to the juice bar.

Go away, I wanted to yell at them, but they had as much right to be here as me. I ducked into the staff lounge and poured myself a steaming cup of liquid courage. When I exited, Eric's serious face greeted me.

"You got my note?" he said.

Should I have texted him to confirm? He looked like he wasn't sure I would show up. Of course, I'd show up. We were dating.

"Yeah. Sorry I wasn't there. I was..." I waved my free hand.

"I heard about that," he said. "Want to sit for a bit?" He gestured back to the cafeteria where a woman wiped down the tables.

"Sure." I trailed behind him until he stopped at one of the long tables that had been recently sanitized. We sat facing each other.

I stirred my coffee with a shaky hand. "How are... things?" Why couldn't I get past that same question this summer? I asked him that every time we met up, and he never once gave me a straight answer.

He frowned and pulled my free hand across the table. "I could ask you the same thing."

So, he was going to dodge the question again. We'd continue to go around in circles if I also changed the subject. But I wouldn't this time.

"Things are... okay. Being a counselor is different—more than I thought it would be." More effort. More scary. More rewarding.

"And you're overwhelmed. I'm sorry," he said in a gentle voice. "I could tell the other night when you didn't want to hang. I wondered if this would happen."

"What?" My stomach dropped. The other night hadn't been my finest moment, but that didn't mean I was a failure, right?

"I'm here for you, Andrea. Whatever you need. Do you think you can make it to the end of camp?" He traced reassuring circles with his thumb on my hand.

"I... yes. I can make it." He was jumping to conclusions. He didn't think I could hack it. His words were supportive, but he didn't...

I blinked back the sudden moisture in my eyes. *He didn't believe in me.*

"Do you think I can do it?" I whispered. As soon as the words escaped my mouth, I wanted to call them back. What would I do if he said no?

Eric squeezed my hand. "I think you should only do what you want to do. You don't have to overextend yourself if it's hurting you."

I nodded, taking a large gulp of coffee to save myself from having to say anything. So much for bringing up my counseling win with Josh or talking about the Beaver girls. This wasn't that kind of conversation.

"I'll think about it," I said in a quiet voice.

He let go of my hand. "I've got you, no matter what you decide." He stood.

For once, I wasn't sad he had to leave so soon.

"I'll text you tonight, okay? Let me know if you need me before then."

I nodded again. And he was gone.

I don't know how long I sat there. Long enough that the counselors by the juice bar disbanded, leaving behind a thick silence. Long enough that I finished my coffee and stared, dry-eyed at the empty cup. Long enough that Lucas sat down beside me and pressed a fresh coffee into my hand.

I took a sip, then twisted to look at him. A frown pulled his eyebrows together. I slapped the table. "What? What, Lucas?"

"Nothing. I didn't say anything," he said in a gentle voice. Everyone talked to me like I was a minefield, like one mean comment would trip the wire. I was sick of it.

"You didn't have to. Your face says it all."

The idiot had the audacity to chuckle. "He doesn't know you at all."

I didn't ask who he meant. "Yes, he does."

"No. And he's not even trying."

"He does. He does all kinds of sweet things for me." Even while he tried to convince me to quit, Eric was the perfect boyfriend.

"Like picnics?"

I stared at my hands. "With my favorite food."

"He didn't even know which dish you liked. He had to get them all."

What a stalker. But I didn't have the energy to be upset right now. "It was sweet," I said in a tired voice.

"It was stupid."

"Like you know what my favorite Chinese food is." He didn't know anything about me outside of camp.

"That's the thing. You wouldn't have to tell me. I'd notice what you ordered. What you ate. It's not that hard."

I threw my hands in the air. "So, he's not taking notes on everything I ingest. That doesn't mean he's a bad guy. You don't get to tell me who to date."

"I know, because if I did, *Andrea*, you'd be dating me." His blue eyes blazed.

"I..." I couldn't speak when he looked at me like that, when he cared about me with such passion that it spoke to my very core. Why was he doing this right now? Like I didn't have enough to deal with.

"So, let's stop pretending, okay? Let's stop ignoring what happened between us last summer."

I swallowed and tried to push back the memories that surfaced of Lucas holding me at the rock-climbing wall during a panic attack, of our frenzied kisses on the beach, of the remorse in his eyes as he ended us before we even began.

"Fine," I said after a long silence. "We... we were attracted to each other during camp. I'm sure you're attracted to people all the time."

He shook his head, but not out of anger. Like he was disappointed. "It was more than that and you know it. It *is* more than that."

"Lucas..." I wanted to support him, to be his friend if he needed me. God knew his summer was off to a terrible start with his dad dying. But this... *this*, I couldn't handle. I'd barred off talking about us in my mind. It was too painful, too real. All my emotions were busy dealing with other responsibilities at camp.

"I want to *know* you, Andy. I want to figure out why you like Lo Mein better than any of the chicken dishes. Why you fold your socks over instead of wearing ankle socks. Where you go in your head when you get overwhelmed. What career you're going to smash with all that romance book knowledge. I want to touch you every second, not just kiss you, but touch you. Hug you. Hold your hand. And you're so far away."

I blinked rapidly, pushing back the tears that made no sense right now. "I'm right here," I whispered. How could Lucas see me so clearly? Not even my parents knew that much about me.

"You're not. But you're not with Eric, either. You don't let him in at all."

Guilt gnawed at me. This whole conversation was wrong to have when Eric was my boyfriend. "I..."

Lucas's hands pulled the coffee from mine, forcing me to face him. "What do *you* want?"

It wasn't that easy. He made it sound so black and white, but life was gray. And I was a mess. "I..."

"You need to think about it." He stood and set the coffee before me again. "And it's your relationship, but if you're not going to be real with a guy, you probably shouldn't be with him."

Anger welled within me. How dare he? "You don't get to tell me what to do, Lucas Thompson!"

He stared at me, unaffected by my outburst. "I never would. I'll be here when you decide. But Andy?"

I tilted my head up to stare at him. Let him talk. Let him say whatever. It wasn't like I could feel any worse.

Lucas leaned in close until my whole world was filled with his face. "I wouldn't let you pretend if you were with me."

My mouth fell open as he strode away. The actual audacity of that guy. He showed up unannounced at camp and blew up my whole life. My relationship. Everything. He was totally out of line, but...

...But was he wrong?

"What do you want?" I repeated in a nasty voice after the door to the cafeteria banged shut behind him. "If I knew that, I wouldn't be so screwed up right now." I stood and threw my coffee cup in the trash. "Stupid."

I didn't know if I was referring to Lucas or myself.

20

I'm Not Doing This for You

I rarely saw sunrises at home. I was either in a class or sleeping, especially in the dark winter months. Today, the blazing summer sun followed me into the land of the awake. I watched the slow glow of fire begin below the horizon and streak into the sky from the cottage porch swing. Splashes of pink and orange and even red heralded its arrival. *Here I am to scorch your day.* Well, I already felt burnt up from yesterday. Eric didn't believe in me, but he supported me. Lucas believed in me but was frustrated with me.

What matters the most is how you *feel about you*, I could hear Dr. Santos saying. *How does Andy feel about Andy?*

Well, Andy felt like a fraud.

Sometimes, I thought I had the hang of being a camp counselor. My ability to lead came in bursts of energy, but I could never be sure I was doing the right thing, saying the right thing. And after what Eric said yesterday…

I hugged my knees to my chest. I should have gone for a run this morning instead of sitting on the porch. It might've helped me purge some of this nervous energy. The kind of energy that made me feel like maybe I shouldn't be here. Maybe I was ruining both of our summers, not to mention the summers of the girls I led. Would they be better off with someone like Paige?

My phone buzzed. *Speak of the devil.* I swallowed the lump in the back of my throat before opening Paige's text.

You ready for today?

As opposed to yesterday?

Totally.

I sent a thumbs up emoji. *Fake it 'til you make it, right?*

You sure? I can take the girls to the rock wall if it brings back bad memories.

I rubbed my hand over my face. I should've looked at the itinerary. As a counselor, I couldn't avoid the stupid, scary rock wall. They had us scheduled down to the minute the whole camp. Even if I could get out of it, my girls would have a ball climbing the darn thing. I couldn't deprive them of that.

I'm fine. Promise.

As long as no one makes me climb it.

When the girls awoke minutes later to get ready for breakfast, I broke the news.

"Yes!" Summer said, pumping her fist. "I've been waiting."

"I'm going to beat you to the top," Destiny challenged. It looked like she'd somewhat recovered.

"So competitive!" Maria teased. "My money's on Abby, though. She has the longest legs."

Abby grimaced as she threw on a hoodie that would likely be discarded halfway to the cafeteria.

What was that about? Normally she was right in there with the girls, teasing and jeering. *Oh, no.* Did she have a camp romance I didn't know about that ended, too? No, that couldn't be it. She and Maria were attached at the hip.

I walked behind them and frowned as she hugged herself all the way to the cafeteria. She picked at her food during breakfast, only responding to conversation when addressed by name. Something was up.

When we made it to the wall, Lucas and the Cheetahs were waiting for us. Paige and her Clownfish and James and his Jaguars waited on the other side of the tower.

Paige leaned around the corner when I rolled up with the girls. I held my coffee cup like a life preserver in front of me. No one could make me climb. I had a beverage.

Of course, Paige noticed. "You've got this, Camper Andrea!" she teased in a falsetto, making fun of Counselor Suzie from last year.

"Your name is Andrea?" Sarah said.

"What did you think Andy was short for?" Destiny asked, rolling her eyes.

"Nothing. I thought that was it."

The girls laughed.

I stared up at the rock-climbing wall as Destiny and Summer trash talked their way through placing their hands and feet. They made it look so easy. They made most everything look easy.

With a huge smile, I cheered on camper after camper as they each scaled the wall. "You got this, Maria! Go Taylor!" I called in my loudest voice, proud of them for facing the fear I couldn't. It didn't stop the manic energy that threaded through my voice. My heart hammered in my chest every time they left the ground. *Don't fall.* I even drained my coffee extra fast so I could set myself up as an unnecessary anchor at the end of the rope, just in case. No one would get hurt on my watch.

I side-eyed Josh when he stared at Destiny's butt in the most obvious way possible when it was her turn. He caught me looking at him and suddenly found the woodpecker in a nearby tree fascinating. Maybe their summer fling wasn't over, after all. Or maybe it was complicated. I understood complicated.

Soon everyone had climbed the death trap but Abby.

"I'm good," she said, her face a mottled shade of red when Sarah started pulling on the straps of the first harness. She'd volunteered to go again so Abby wouldn't have to climb alone.

"Really?" Now, her silence at breakfast made a ton of sense. Like me, she was scared.

"Yeah, heights aren't my thing."

"Give us a minute," I called to Sarah and gestured for Abby to walk with me into the woods to talk.

"You're scared of heights?" I asked as soon as we were out of earshot.

Abby rolled her eyes. "No. I'm scared of falling from a huge height and dying."

"Death is scary," I agreed, cramming my hands into the pockets of my jean shorts.

"I heard you didn't climb it last year," she said defiantly, staring at the forty-foot square peg of a tower.

I picked at the shriveled leaves of the nearest tree. "It doesn't matter what I did last year." Or it shouldn't. Not to her.

"I'm allowed to be scared."

"Totally. You don't have to climb it if you don't want to. But…" I shook my head.

"What?"

Should I say it? I was going to say it. "I see you look at it like it's beating you, and that kills me. No wall can beat you, Abby. Not if you don't let it."

She made a frustrated sound in the back of her throat. "It's so high."

"It is."

"This isn't making me want to climb it!" she yelled.

"See, that's the thing. You want me to pep talk you into climbing it. That means you do want to climb it. You need a push, and you're going to do it. You know how I know?"

She was silent for so long I thought I had lost her. Then: "How?"

"Because you haven't looked away from the wall the whole time we've been talking. Someone who's given up wouldn't still be looking at the wall."

She took a deep breath and dragged her gaze away from the tower to look at me. "You're right."

I spread my arms. "And if you make it halfway up, that's still brave."

She balled her hands into determined fists at her side. "No. I'm doing it. The whole thing."

"Yeah, you are." I smiled. I wanted her to conquer it. For both of us.

When we re-entered the clearing, the Beavers were waiting for us. Abby gave a weak thumbs up and they exploded into cheers.

"That's my girl!" Destiny screamed.

I stepped back and let them take over while she got strapped in. By the time she put her foot on the first rock, she grinned from all their comments. I already knew she'd make it.

"Ready?" Sarah asked.

"Hell, yeah," Abby said.

She climbed slow, but even I couldn't hold myself back when she stumbled during a hard crossover in the middle.

"You've got this, Abby! Show that wall who's boss!" I yelled.

The girls around me cheered harder even as we all held the rope.

"I won't let you fall. You can do this!" I called again.

She nodded to herself and tried the crossover again, this time getting a handle on the next rock. Seconds later, she'd made it to the top where counselors pulled her onto the roof of the square tower, and she got to do a mini victory dance with Sarah behind a rope before rappelling back down the wall.

I couldn't keep myself from jumping up and down, uncaring that I had held the rope so tight that the fibers had indented themselves into both my hands. She did it. All my Beaver girls did it.

"Hey," Lucas said, walking over from his side. "You okay?"

Darn. I thought I might get through this without him noticing me. Without him bringing back memories of what happened... last time.

I turned a bright smile on him. "Why wouldn't I be?" *My Beavers slayed this rock wall, and I'm happy. Don't bring up my panic attack last summer or I will kill you.*

He pulled his hair back and fastened it at the nape of his neck with a hairband. "Uh, because you turned into a version of my sister-in-law during this activity which is very not-you."

"Your sister-in-law?" I smacked his chest. "I am *not* Suzie."

"Uh huh," he said.

"No one's making me climb anything this year. It's all about the kids, and my team is competitive." I smirked.

"I noticed." He didn't say anything else as we stood shoulder to shoulder, staring at where Sarah and Abby now unbuckled their harnesses. The warmth of his arm leaked through my T-shirt and into my side. He had that smile on his face like he wanted to say something.

I caved. "What?"

"If no one *makes* you do it…"

"Yeah?"

"I might climb it. Kind of missed out on it last year." He nudged me.

"Shut up." My face was probably as red as his shirt right now. He wouldn't rehash that in front of everyone… would he?

He sighed, long and loud. "But it's a two-person thing. I can get Paige to do it with me, I guess." He kicked a rock.

I narrowed my eyes. It didn't have to be a two-person thing. "Peer pressure doesn't work on me."

"My dad's dead?" he tried.

I covered my mouth in horror.

He scratched the back of his head. "Yeah, that was bad. Sorry."

No. I was sorry.

He shrugged. "I totally killed the mood, huh?"

I frowned. He needed distraction. I pointed to the top of the tower. "It's forty feet high."

"Ridiculous, you're right," he agreed and latched back onto our earlier conversation.

I folded my arms. "I'm not doing it."

"Okay." His eyes squinted as his smile grew.

"I'm not."

Lucas held his hands up. "I didn't ask you to."

"And if I did decide to face this fear, I wouldn't do it in front of half the camp."

"Yeah, who needs that?" He continued grinning.

"No one thinks I'm a wimp after beating your team in capture the flag."

"Correct." We both folded our arms and stared at the wall again.

Parker from the Cheetah team jogged over. "Hey, Lucas. Can I get some help with…" He gestured to his tangled harness.

"Sure." Lucas bent over and helped him out of the labyrinth of straps, pulling them apart to step into correctly. Parker returned to the Cheetah side of the wall and clicked in.

I refused to look up at the forty-foot tower of climbing doom. Instead, I shielded my eyes from the sunlight that broke through the treetops and looked back at my Beavers. They were all sporty and had on sturdy tennis shoes. I had a heck of a lot more faith in their ability to hold the rope than I did in the campers last year.

"Are you going to go?" Summer called to me.

I waved to her, grinning, and pretended not to hear her. Blood rushed to my head. I'd be crazy to put myself in a position to fail in front of my campers the way I failed last time.

And Lucas...

Lucas was still here, chatting with his campers like he hadn't just egged me on. Why was it such a big deal to him, anyway?

Maybe it wasn't. Maybe it was a big deal to me.

I'd feared a lot of things this year, but I survived. I took swimming lessons, and that was embarrassing to do as a senior, but I sucked it up. I joined a new friend group, had a boyfriend for the first time. Social activities never came easy to me, but I managed. What was one more hard thing now?

I stared at a caterpillar brave enough to try to inch up the side of the tower with no harness at all. Reaching out, I let it crawl onto my finger and set him in a tree nearby. Last time I stood here, the girls on my team were less fit, and they still managed to lower me to the ground safely. There was no reason I shouldn't try now. No reason but the stomach-sinking anticipation of not being safe on the ground. Of not being in control.

If I could conquer this, maybe I could take some of that control back. I could show my campers that I cared about what they did. Show Abby that I could face my fear like I'd helped her do. And maybe Eric was wrong. Maybe I could do this.

Before I could talk myself out of it, I strode over to where Lucas stood harnessed into the straps.

"Here to cheer me on?" he asked.

"I'm not a cheerleader," I snapped, grabbing a harness for myself. A sturdy, black, reinforced looking one. Now, if I only knew how to put it on.

Lucas stared at me. His voice lowered. "Are you..."

"Don't make it a thing," I said under my breath.

"I wouldn't dare." His mouth twitched.

"I'm not doing this for you."

"I hope not," he said. "I hope you're doing it for you."

He sorted me out, his hands sure and strong as he tightened and adjusted the harness. I barely noticed the brush of his hands against me. I was too busy staring at the death trap in front of us. Then Lucas clicked us both into the correct carabiners and nodded at our campers.

"Yeah, Andy! Show him who's faster!" Sarah yelled.

Lucas stared at me, his gaze steady. "We can go slow."

But slow was the worst thing I could do for myself. If I did it faster, wouldn't that mean I'd be done faster?

"Sure." I gave him an innocent smile.

"You're already so brave for trying," he encouraged.

Now he sounded like a kindergarten teacher. I may not know what I wanted between us, but it wasn't that. Not pity. In my head, I tracked the route I needed to take on the rocks above me, my brain feeling sloshy as I stared up, up, up. I could do this. I didn't need Lucas. I didn't need anyone but me. In fact, Lucas could eat my dust.

"Go!" the campers screamed.

Lucas braced his foot against the first rock on the wall, turning toward me to show me how to place my hands, but I was already off, scrambling up the thing as fast as my awkwardness would allow.

"Hey! What happened to going slow?" he called from below me.

"This is my slow!"

"You little…" He laughed.

But I wouldn't turn back to him to gloat. I made that mistake last time. Hand, foot, hand, foot. I had to keep my rhythm because if I stopped, I'd embarrass myself and ruin my six month no panic attack streak. I refused to go back down that road. I would conquer this damn wall. Halfway up, my legs strained as I sprang up to a difficult hold, but I didn't care. If I fell, they'd catch me. I had to trust them to catch me.

And I did. The Beavers and Cheetahs cheered from the ground.

"Go, Andy!" Summer yelled.

"You're kicking his butt!" Destiny called.

"Come on, dude. She's wasting you!" Tanner's voice echoed from the Cheetah side.

Lucas drew nearer. I could hear his labored breathing, but only three more foot placements separated me from the top. *Almost there.* I looked over to where his arm now gripped a rock level with my thigh and glimpsed the ground below.

"Is that Andy?" I heard Paige ask, but I couldn't concentrate on that. My heart had jumped into my throat. Oh my God, it was so far down. What the hell was I doing? What was he doing? What were any of us doing? We were going to die! A familiar tingle of panic started in my fingers. My foot slid the wrong way on a rock, and I lost my footing.

But I hit something solid. Lucas's palm. He braced my sneaker with his free hand.

"Back to the wall," he gritted out, straining to keep his own precarious hold. Why would he...

I stepped back onto my rock.

"You're going to let me win?" he asked as he pulled himself up another level.

I snapped back into beat-Lucas mode.

"No!" I yelled and pushed myself up the last three feet and touched the top of the wall. A chorus of screams and groans echoed from the ground.

"Why'd you help her, man?"

Lucas ignored his campers and helped me over the lip of the square tower where a couple other counselors milled around behind the rope.

"You... I..." I couldn't string together a thought as I faced him, chest heaving. "You didn't have to do that."

"Andy..." His hand brushed mine on the side away from the campers, not wanting to make more problems for me.

Tears escaped my eyes and tracked down my face.

"Are you okay? I'm so sorry. I should've never..."

I didn't let him finish. I flung myself into his arms and hugged him so hard I was sure he'd never breathe again.

He stumbled back a step and crushed me in his arms as I wrapped my legs around his waist. "You did it. You were so brave. Andy, you did it," he kept repeating. The cheers below us roared in my ears, and I couldn't separate the ones that were for team Landy from the ones that were for my crowning achievement of not being scared of heights.

"You helped me," I cried into his shoulder.

"I didn't. You put your foot right back on the same place on that wall."

"I did it," I said as adrenaline spiked through my veins. I did it for me. Not Eric, not Lucas—me.

He hugged me tighter. "You did it."

21

Time to Let Go

Lucas and I rappelled down the rock wall. Refusing to look down made it less frightening. I rejoined my cheering campers as if in a trance. The comments of the Beaver girls and the fist bump from Paige blurred together as we walked to the cottage. All I could see was Abby's wide, accomplished smile ahead of me, the way Maria and Destiny high-fived her. She won. She defeated the wall.

So did I. And just like that, the cottage emptied out for free time.

The logical side of my brain took over. *I should find Paige and see if she needs help with her campers. I should see if Eric is free. I should read.* But I didn't want to do any of those things. My dramatic mother would gasp and clutch her chest if she was here. Me, not wanting to read? But my body thrummed with energy, and even with the escape reading always delivered, I didn't think I'd be able to sit still long enough to enjoy it. I didn't want to escape right now. I wanted to think.

I shucked my jean shorts and replaced them with running shorts. Time to tighten my ponytail and go for a run. It might be a million humid degrees out, but I needed it. I'd have to hope the trees on the forest trail would provide enough shade.

I pulled up my running playlist on my phone and stretched in the blistering heat of the afternoon. Then I popped in an earbud and jogged down the path to the forest. I passed a couple of campers straight away, which was a little awkward when one of the guys mouthed *crazy* as I ran by. I blocked him out. Sure, my sweat already drenched my shirt, but I wasn't as out of breath as I would've been last summer. A little practice and a lot of music helped me build my confidence back up this year.

I'd never be the fastest runner, but I'd liked sharing my interest with a team this last season. They'd welcomed me back with open arms even though I'd been MIA. Like it was no big deal I'd taken a two-year break.

I veered left, sweat dripping down my face and neck. I could almost drink the air it was so humid, but the burn of my muscles felt so good, I didn't care. My tennis shoes hit the well-worn dirt path to the beat of the song pulsing into my ears. When it became hard to breathe, the emotions came.

I'd climbed that stupid wall. I'd faced my fear and won on my own terms. And I did it with... Lucas. I could still feel his strong body holding me up as I jumped on him, his muscular arms surrounding me, protecting me, building me up. *"You did it."* He wouldn't even take credit for helping me. He was proud of me. I was proud of me, too.

Sweat stung my eyes, and I wiped my forehead with the back of my hand. Lucas was right. I needed to be honest with myself.

A stitch in my side stole my breath and I paused, bracing one hand on the rough bark of the nearest tree. It would never work. After summer he would attend college in West Virginia, where he was from. He wasn't even in the right mental place to like me right now, between the drama with his brother and his loss. We'd never see each other again. It made no logical sense, but...

I paused my music.

"I still like Lucas," I gasped, holding my side. No wind carried my words away. No chattering birds talked over my soft declaration. It made it all that much more real.

My stomach clenched. That wasn't it. I had to say it all.

"I *only* like Lucas," I confessed, every cell of my body rebelling at how horrible and mean that was to Eric.

But it was true. I believed I liked Eric. Genuinely, I did. I liked the way he pushed his glasses up the bridge of his nose, the way he always smelled so fresh. How courteous and kind he was in every situation, always thinking of others. He fueled every fantasy of mine for the past four years, but it wasn't enough. And if I was being honest with myself, I never felt like me around him. I thought he made me a better person when we started dating, but now that I was here, I wasn't sure.

I started to jog again, slower this time.

I didn't need a guy. All of middle school and three years of high school proved that. But this past year had been equal parts wonderful and terrible. I'd learned to swim, gotten my driver's license, and rejoined the track team. I didn't need anyone to make those decisions for me. Though it had caused me a lot of stress, I'd persevered.

Lucas didn't mind when I was short with him or overwhelmed. He adapted. He accepted. I was myself with him. Always had been. It was unfair to compare the guys, but maybe I wasn't comparing them. I was comparing myself when I was with them.

I couldn't fault Eric because I never gave him a chance to prove he could be that for me. But I couldn't be me with just anyone. Only... Lucas.

Was it sweat or tears on my cheeks as I looped back toward the cottage? Did it matter? The result was the same: it was time to grow up. Time to let go.

For all our sakes.

22

Stalling

I wanted all of camp to stop. When I got back to the cottage, soaked with sweat, my new, horrible knowledge about myself knocked around in my chest like a bird struggling to get free.

But that's not how life worked. No sooner had I rinsed off in the shower than the girls trickled in, and I had to be their leader again. The pages of Dana's counselor manual blended together as I flipped through them. We'd done so many cottage activities.

"Can we, like, play something? I want to be outside," Maria said.

"Like basketball?" I asked. My brain flashed to Lucas's game of HORSE from last year. The way he teased me, how we chased each other around a bench. My heart clenched.

"Or soccer." Megan shrugged.

"I'm sure we could make that happen," I said, pulling my phone out to text Paige.

> **Feel like a Beaver/Clownfish soccer match?**

> **Yes! See you at the front field in five.**

"The Clownfish will play us," I told the girls and showed them my phone screen.

"Really?" Taylor asked. "I didn't think sports were their thing."

I shrugged.

We walked to the front field, my phone burning a hole in my pocket. I should text Eric. Or Lucas. Or... No. They both deserved to hear from me face to face.

My girls met up with the reluctant Clownfish, and I collapsed on the sideline with Paige as my girls taught some of hers how to play. I tried to distract myself with their game, but the teams were lopsided. A million UV rays beat down on us, and the Clownfish, though good sports, didn't have their hearts in it.

I picked at the grass as Paige hollered to her girls. "Get on the ball! You can't *all* wait to be passed to. Who's on offense?" She turned to me. "What's with you? Oh." She lowered her voice. "Did Luke finally tell you?"

Oh, great. What now? "Tell me what?"

"About his dad," she whispered.

"Yeah." It was the most real thing any guy had ever shared with me, and... "It sucks."

Paige tilted her head. "That's not what's bothering you though, is it?"

"It's become this huge mess." I adjusted my sunglasses. "Eric and Lucas."

Destiny scored another goal. I gave her a thumbs up, but she rolled her eyes. What? Thumbs up was good, right?

"Just because something's a mess doesn't mean you throw it all away. Are you even seeing your girls right now? Defense, Clownfish! Come on!" Paige yelled.

I leaned back on my elbows. "They are pretty great." I winced as Destiny body checked one of the Clownfish girls to the ground and ran full speed with the ball to the goal.

"How did you end up with the sportiest team? Come *on*, girls!"

"I feel so bad." My voice broke. How could I tell Eric that I'd rather have a few days with Lucas than a whole, perfectly planned relationship with him?

"Why do you feel bad? Because you feel nothing for Eric or because you feel something for Lucas?"

I lowered my sunglasses to glare at her. "Both."

"Yeah, that sucks, but... the solution seems obvious, Andy."

"What?"

"You like Lucas. You've always liked him. Let it run its course."

"But its course is the end of camp just like last time." He would go to college back home, and I would stay in Vermont.

"Long distance relationships can work. Look at my parents. They lived two states apart for like, five years, and ended up getting married. What better reward for them than my perfect presence?" She gestured to herself.

I laughed. "True."

"Talk to Luke. See what he says."

I fell silent, staring at the bald patch of dirt in front of me where an ant colony had moved in. They were busy creating a mound, so motivated and organized. They didn't wonder whether they were doing their job correctly or working with the right partner ant.

Paige let me simmer for a minute as she leaned back on her arms in the itchy grass.

"Why does everyone always call him Luke?" I whispered after a while.

She stared at me. "Maybe you should ask yourself why you're the only one he wants to call him Lucas."

I hugged my knees because I couldn't think about that right now. "And Eric?"

"You already know it's not fair to him to act like this." She lowered her voice. "Andy, you can't string him along as your back up plan. That's not okay."

"It's so hard, because..." I rocked back and forth.

She placed a hand on my knee, stopping me. "Because you like him too."

I blinked back tears, glad that my sunglasses hid them from my Beavers. "Just not..."

"Like you like Luke. That sucks."

I nodded. The Beavers won the soccer game.

23

We Need to Talk

My heart stopped. I'd taken the girls back to the cottage after my chat with Paige. We were gearing up for free time activities now, but those four simple words stopped me cold. I had to text him back, but the urge to throw my phone across the room and smash it overwhelmed me. Everyone knew what that meant. *We need to talk* was break up language. He wanted to break up with me?

I mean, I had thought about doing it myself, but this felt different, like I was in trouble. I couldn't breathe.

Only for another ten minutes, but if I could stall, I would, because I didn't want to know what I'd done wrong. How I'd failed as a girlfriend. Maybe I'd been failing all year. I still wanted him to like me. Not like that, but in general. The blunt delivery of his texts came off cold and angry. I racked my brain for what to say, but he beat me to it.

> **You have a break in 9 minutes. I checked the schedule.**

> Okay.

> **Meet at the car.**

> Okay.

The car? He needed it to be that private? What did... *oh, no.* The rock wall. Someone told him about me and Lucas.

"Andy, are you okay?" Destiny asked behind me.

It took a second, but I managed to turn on my fake counselor smile. "Fine. Listen, do you all want to go to free time a few minutes early?"

"Uh, sure. Hang on." She gathered the girls one by one, and by then we had two minutes until free time anyway.

"You need a minute?" she asked carefully. God, how must I look right now? I couldn't feel my face. I needed to get to the car or dive in the lake. I needed a hug.

"Yep. I'll be waiting for you when you get back from your break. We have a color war to win!" I injected fake excitement into my voice.

"Uh, okay. We'll see ya." She frowned.

The girls left, talking in low tones. Maybe about me. I didn't have it in me to care. I pulled my safari vest off and walked with measured steps to the parking lot. Eric sat in his car, the engine idling. I opened the passenger side door and slipped in.

"So," he said, his facial expression neutral.

I pressed my hands together in my lap. "So."

A long silence stretched between us as my heart rate doubled.

"You ready to tell me what's going on between you and this Luke guy?"

"Lucas," I corrected before I could stop myself.

He sighed. Not in a confrontational way. More like he was tired.

I licked my lips. "What did you hear?"

"Really, Andy? You want to know what I heard so you can do damage control?"

"No, I—"

"Hang on." He closed his eyes and gripped the steering wheel, color draining from his knuckles. I sat beside him, trying to make myself smaller in the space.

"That's not what I meant," I said after a second. Though maybe it was.

He released the steering wheel. "I need you to talk to me."

"I... think we should break up." The words poured out of my mouth before I could phrase them right, before I could put other words around them that would somehow make it less hurtful.

"Me too," he said softly.

"This isn't working." My nails dug into my hands as I clasped them.

"Because you like him."

I took a deep breath, but it got caught in my chest. "We were... we had a thing last summer."

"Why didn't you tell me?" he asked in a tortured voice.

"Because it didn't matter. I'm with you now." Or I was.

"It mattered."

I didn't dare look over at him. "I know that now," I whispered. "I'm sorry."

He blinked a few times. "I feel blindsided."

"You heard about the rock wall." It was the only thing that made sense.

"I heard a lot of things, Andy. It's a small camp. I just didn't..."

"You didn't believe them."

"I didn't want to. I trusted you." His voice broke.

I pressed the heels of my hands into my thighs. Pressure pulsed in my chest. I hurt him. I was a monster. "I'm sorry."

"I think..." He stared out the windshield. "I think I've always liked you more than you liked me."

"That's not true!" I said, my voice loud in the cramped space of the car. "I liked you since freshman year."

"What?" He turned to me, his eyes wide.

"I was too scared to say anything, but I liked you even then." I didn't know why I felt the need to say this now. It wouldn't change anything, but it felt wrong that he didn't know. He deserved the truth, even if it was too late.

"You..." He stopped. "You had a crush on me but didn't tell me for *three years?*"

I swallowed. "Yeah."

"I had to ask *you* out."

"It was a great ask," I said in a meek voice.

"We could have been dating for four years, Andy. We could have been miles ahead of where we are now. Or we could have figured it out way sooner."

"Figured what out?"

"That we're not right together."

I sucked in a breath.

"You're not comfortable around me. I've been trying to figure you out, but I can't. I kept thinking maybe she'll open up if she knows me better. She's shy. She'll get there. But..." He ran a hand through his short hair. "You act different with him. Uncensored."

"You like me better censored." I didn't mean to say it, but then the words were out, and they hung there in the car. All along, I'd been pushing myself into a box of what I thought a perfect girlfriend should be without giving us the chance to figure out our relationship together. I was so scared of losing him, so scared of any friction that I'd done everything in my power not to make any. In the end, I'd never let Eric see the real me. He had no idea that I was working on my mental health, that I struggled with friendships. All he ever got was a carefully curated, polite version of me that didn't exist.

"The fact that you think that really puts a nail in the coffin of this relationship. I need to... I need to leave."

"You're quitting?" Now the meeting in the car made perfect sense.

He met my eyes. "I was only here for you."

I nodded, the pressure in my chest increasing. This was my fault. I wanted to believe that leaving the kitchen shorthanded made him selfish, but how could I feel that way when he'd sacrificed so much to stay here with me?

"I helped prep the next few meals. Camp is almost over. I can't stay. Not now."

"Okay," I whispered.

He tapped the wheel with his fingers, waiting for me to get out of the car, but I couldn't do it. Not yet.

"You're a good person, Eric. I never deserved you."

"You didn't let yourself deserve us."

I had nothing to say to that. I nodded, unlatched the car door, and got out. He drove in his usual careful manner around the dirt circle drive, turned onto the main road, and disappeared behind the trees.

I walked with numb legs to the nearest picnic table, one off the beaten path away from the happenings at camp, my vision blurring as moisture gathered in my eyes. I climbed on top of the table, sat, and looked after the boy who did everything right, who treated me like I was perfect and precious. And I let myself cry.

I cried because I hurt him. I cried because I was hurting Lucas. And I cried because most of all, I hurt myself by not knowing what I wanted—I never intended to lead on someone I cared for. At least last summer, I never ruined other people's lives.

Time passed, and the lazy summer breeze shifted. My tears slowed, but the soul-crushing guilt remained. The wooden table groaned as another person sat beside me. I was too scared to turn and see who it might be. But then the person pulled me into their arms. *Paige.*

"It's okay. It's going to be okay," she repeated over and over as she rocked me.

No, it wasn't. I sobbed into her T-shirt. I didn't care how hot it was, that we were sweating all over each other. Paige didn't push me to talk. She let me cry for I don't even know how long before I sniffled my last.

I pulled away from her. "Thank you."

We sat in silence for a long moment. "It's been a tough summer, huh?" she murmured.

I wiped my face with shaky hands. "For both of us."

"Mmm." She bumped me with her arm in solidarity, and I laid my head on her shoulder.

"We're only eighteen, you know? We don't have to have it all figured out. You're allowed to change your mind, Andy."

I sighed, but it came out in a rattle. "It didn't feel like that. It felt like I handled everything wrong from the start."

"There's still time for you and Lucas," she said, gripping my hand. "You know what to do."

I did.

24

You're Not My Rebound

The day passed in a blur.

Though I'd reassured Paige that I knew what I had to do next, I didn't. In a summer this intense, I had no way to figure out my next move.

I clapped for my Beavers as they acted out a silly skit for the talent show Dana used as another color war activity. Through bleary eyes, I watched Leah slip into the crowd, late as always. I said nothing to her. I moved them from activity to activity, passive and silent between instructions. After, I drank coffee and sat with Paige and the other counselors instead of the campers during dinner, but the Beaver girls didn't say anything to me, content to let the conversation flow around what they wanted to do with their free time and who was cute and whose tan lines stood out more. Maybe they sensed what happened. Maybe they knew. Like Eric said, it was a small camp. I didn't think about it.

I didn't think much at all. Regardless, I found myself walking to Lucas's cottage during evening free time as if magnetized to the comfort he could provide.

For the longest time, I stood in front of his door, overwhelmed by guilt. I shouldn't talk to him. I needed to let my time with Eric breathe, process that I threw away an entire year. But it was Lucas, and I needed him. Thoughts jumbled together in my head as a mosquito buzzed in my ear and I absent-mindedly slapped my neck.

As if in a trance, I watched my hand knock on his door with zero plan, the thud muffled by the long sleeve hanging over my knuckles. He wouldn't be here. Why would he stay in his cottage when he could be spending free time with campers?

Energy thrummed through me, my heart in my throat. I should go. What would I even say?

The door opened.

"Andy," he breathed, leaning on the doorjamb. "Are you okay?"

He'd heard. He had to know about me and Eric.

When I looked up at him, all the heartbreak faded into the way his jaw squared, a hint of stubble on it I hadn't noticed last year. I reached my hand up to touch it.

His eyes searched mine for a hint of what was happening. I stared back, every emotion this summer had pulled out of me now transparent. After a long minute, he closed his eyes and leaned into my touch the way he'd done on the beach.

"I can't..." he gritted out. "I can't keep doing this when I want more with you."

"I know," I whispered.

He blinked, a tortured expression on his face as I dropped my hand.

This was it, then. He wanted more. I wanted more. But should we have it? I stood on my tiptoes and pulled him in by his shirt until his lips met mine in an explosion that I had waited so long for, I felt it in my toes.

His fingers threaded through mine between us, and he pulled me in tighter; the kiss became more demanding, more volatile than I'd thought possible. Lucas was oxygen, and I'd been locked in an airtight car the whole summer. I needed him more than I needed anyone else ever.

He ripped his lips from mine, and I fell into his chest.

"Wait," he said breathlessly, his arms catching and wrapping me in his embrace. "You don't want to do this, Andy. You have a boyfriend."

My heart beat so loud in my ears that I almost couldn't hear him. *Boyfriend?* I had a—

"Not anymore," I whispered. He needed to kiss me again. I'd do anything to feel that way again. I couldn't think when he touched me like that, and I desperately didn't want to think about anything right now.

His eyes closed for one painful second. "I can't be your rebound."

I stiffened. "You can't... What? This whole time, you've been trying to steal me from Eric, and *now* you grow a conscience?"

He stepped back and let go of me. "Yeah. I mean no. I don't know." A frustrated sound escaped his lips.

"I do." It might have been the most assertive comment I'd made all summer. I finally knew what I wanted. Enough of this back and forth between us. Time to get on the same page.

Lucas froze, his hand halfway through his hair.

I sucked in a deep breath. "You're not my rebound. Eric was."

Lucas recoiled in shock. "Excuse me?"

I nodded in admission. My crush on Eric existed way before Lucas ever appeared in my life, but when the void of Lucas's smile crushed me last fall, it was so easy to turn to Eric. And that wasn't fair. Not to any of us.

"No, wait. Hold on. You didn't return my texts," he said. "I texted you."

"It wouldn't have worked," I whispered. "That didn't keep me from missing you." Everyone said that camp relationships were doomed to fail, and we lived states apart. I had no way of knowing I'd ever see him again, but fate had dropped us right on top of each other, and now... I couldn't ignore it, and neither could he. There was something here. Something big.

Lucas groaned. "I shouldn't. We shouldn't." Then he muttered, "But I can't help myself."

He pulled me into his cottage and locked the door. His kisses were blistering, starting at my mouth and trailing to my jaw, my neck. I gasped, my back bumping against the door. It was so wrong. A camper could knock at any moment. They could look through the windows. There were a thousand ways we could be caught and then we'd both be fired.

He made a low sound in the back of his throat, somewhere between a moan and a grunt, and all my anxiety fled. I'd never heard anything so sexy before in my life. His big, warm hands cupped my shoulders, then slid down my body, and I got lost. I got lost in the sensation, the realization that finally it felt right. My body was an electrified socket that Lucas plugged into, every touch jolting me out of my insecurities and back into a place where I was confident, wanted, needed.

And if this was all I got, I would make it count.

His hands trailed over the bare skin of my back where my cropped shirt ended and my shorts began.

"Andy..." he said in a rough voice.

"Touch me," I begged.

"You don't know…"

I smacked him on the chest. "I know more than you do. Smutty romance novels, remember?"

"It's not the same in person. It's way more…"

"Real? It's always real with us."

Big blue eyes searched my own. "You need to tell me if it's too much. I couldn't stand it if… I'm worried."

"You're killing the vibe right now, Lucas."

He frowned. "I don't care. I'll bring it back."

I laughed. *Always confident.* "I'll tell you if I want to stop. I trust you."

He pulled me in by my belt loops, his expression serious. "I love you, Andy Stevens."

All the air in the room disappeared. *He loves me.*

And then his lips found mine again. Kissing me so calm and sure that I melted into his arms, a puddle of happiness. His hands inched under my shirt, every millimeter a thrill sending chills up my spine and over my arms. I might die before we ever made it to second base.

I took matters into my own hands and pressed my body against his, creating a blissful friction that sang in all corners of my brain. His breath caught.

Every moment we'd had together flashed through my mind as his hands traced heated paths on my bare stomach. Lucas throwing his arm around me last summer as we walked to another activity, his crushing hug as I cried at the base of the climbing wall, his hands on my body under the stars on the beach, the pain in his eyes when he told me he lived nowhere near me, his voice this summer when he yelled at me that we weren't over, the brush of his hand as he placed my millionth cup of coffee in my hands, his look of pride when I helped Josh.

Lucas saw me. He understood me. This moment wasn't two hormonal teenagers hooking up. It was never like that with Lucas. We were connected.

My shirt disappeared along with my shorts until I stood before him in a black sports bra and unmatching purple-striped underwear. His eyes swept over my body, all the soft places I kept hidden. Heat flooded my face. Did he like what he saw?

Lucas cleared his throat. "I..." His eyes burned into mine. "I need to get the blinds." He scrambled over to the windows and pulled the blinds until the natural light disappeared from between the slats. When he turned back, all I could hear was the sound of my own breathing. And all I could see was his shadowed face, dark with an intent that made my heart pound. His brows drew together as he crossed the space between us.

As soon as he stepped close enough, I pulled his head down and pressed my lips to his. I didn't want him to talk us both out of this.

My hands locked at the base of his spine, and he rested his chin on my hair. "Andy."

"Lucas."

"Are you sure?"

I nodded, dislodging his chin from where it rested on my head. There weren't many things I really, truly wanted for myself. That I felt sure about. This might be the first time I'd ever wanted anything with every cell of my being. My heart jumped into my throat as we moved to lay together on his bed. Every second felt individual and important and full of emotion now.

He brushed a stray piece of hair from my face, tucking it behind my ear. "I'm sure, too," he whispered in the semi-dark.

Later, when I returned to my cottage, that was the moment I'd remember. Not the fumbling, the too-narrow bed that squeaked, the laughter as we figured out what made each other groan. I'd remember the moment of safety and overwhelming connection right before my body lit like a struck match, and we chased the pleasure we'd been denied all summer.

Even though I had to re-dress in a hurry and sprint out of his cottage to lead my campers afterwards, I didn't regret it. Not one awkward, tender moment.

It was the single-most amazing experience of my life so far.

And it couldn't have felt more right.

25

The Bonfire

It seemed like only yesterday Paige and Emma sat me down at the camp-wide bonfire and told me Lucas was a player. The night ended with me punching him and then, somehow, cuddling in his lap.

I'd had it so bad then. But it didn't compare to how I felt now.

Nerves gathered in my stomach as I dusted on a peach blush and selected my best ripped jeans and fitted flannel. My Beaver girls and I laughed as we primped in the bathroom mirror—in no time, we all smelled like hairspray and happiness.

We stepped out the door a few minutes later than we planned, but it didn't matter as we made our way to the archery field. A riot of red and orange painted the evening sky, and a massive fire crackled into the early night air. The girls flocked to the s'more station to talk to the boys who'd already stuffed their cheeks with marshmallows.

I sat on one of the logs surrounding the fire and watched the flames glow brighter as the sun disappeared behind the trees.

Paige sat beside me. "All good?"

I smiled as Dana fed another log to the fire. Like we needed more heat. "So good." My knee shook, and I couldn't help but overthink everything now that I had some distance. I had no idea what to say to Lucas. Could I even look at him after what we'd done? What if he regretted it? Maybe it didn't mean as much to him as it did to me.

Paige hugged my side. "Finally! You two are so stubborn."

I snorted.

"Okay, mostly you."

If I was anyone else, I'd spill all the details of what Lucas and I had done and said in his cottage earlier. But I didn't want to dissect it. I wanted to keep that moment forever, private and preserved in my memory. Even if he did end up regretting it, I never would.

"How are your campers?" I asked Paige.

She sighed. "I think I'm starting to get them."

"And by that you mean…"

"They're not competitive. They only want to have a good time. That's okay, too." She turned and showed me her intricate braid with ribbons of different colors threaded through her hair. "I wanted warrior women and got princesses instead. But princesses have skills, too."

"Truth." I nudged her.

She grinned. "And my hair has never looked better."

"You look very nice," I said, wiggling my eyebrows.

She squinted at someone over my shoulder. "I'll let you have your moment, Counselor Andy," she said, bounding away.

I didn't have to look up to know that Lucas was heading my way. Tension rippled through me as I turned to where he stood in well-fitted dark wash jeans and a long-sleeve baseball tee, looking all kinds of leading man hot. He smiled at Paige, who knocked knuckles with him before disappearing into the crowd.

When his eyes found mine, I didn't look away. Instead, I watched the way his shirt stretched across his chest. He was so hot with his hair swept back into a low bun, the firelight dancing over the shadow of his jaw.

"Checking me out?" he teased, sitting down.

"Yes," I admitted in a soft voice. I didn't need the campers to hear how we'd made up, how all their Landy efforts had panned out. I didn't want to field their satisfied smirks right now. All I wanted was him.

Lucas tucked a piece of hair that had escaped my ponytail behind my ear. I shivered.

"Cold?" he asked.

"No," I said, staring up at him. "It's hot as hell."

He threw back his head and laughed.

I giggled, too. Maybe we were okay. Maybe more than okay.

"I'm glad you're not making this weird," he said after a minute.

My heart thumped painfully inside my chest. "Me, weird?" What was that supposed to mean? He said he *loved* me. That meant everything to me. Was it not supposed to? I scrunched my hands together in my lap.

He covered my knot of fingers with one hand. "Never," he said. "And if you are, so am I."

I smiled, my throat tight. No, he wasn't weird, unless his taste in girls counted.

"I'd ask if you wanna get out of here, but it seems we might be needed."

I followed Lucas's gaze to where Dana struggled with the s'more station. Too many campers grabbed what they needed without making a line. She did her best to organize everyone, but she was fighting a losing battle.

"You get the line; I'll help with the food?" I suggested.

"Ready, break," he said.

I put myself in charge of opening the graham crackers and Hershey bars while Dana doled out sticks and marshmallows. Lucas pushed everyone back into a line, and it went smoothly for the next hour while the fire crackled behind the campers.

Every so often, he'd stare at me, and I'd glance at him, then blush. That look encompassed everything, the memory of what we'd done earlier, our heartfelt conversations, and maybe not being at each other's throats now, unless it was for fun.

I adored him.

"Looks like you finally saw the light," Maria said as she accepted a graham cracker and chocolate from me.

"Hmm?"

Lucas mouthed something at me, but I couldn't quite figure it out. He put his hands on his hips in fake exasperation. I rolled my eyes, smiling.

"You two are so obvious. We knew it was only a matter of time."

I smiled at Maria. "Maybe you were right." No point denying it when everyone could see how something had shifted between us. I didn't want it to be a big deal, but I wouldn't hide anything, either.

"Landy forever," she sighed and took a marshmallow from Dana. "Right?" she said to my boss.

My blood ran cold. Would Dana think involving campers in my romance with Lucas was unprofessional? I didn't need another problem this summer.

"Right," Dana said, distracted by opening another bag.

I exhaled. *Thank God.*

When the line trickled down and the campers began to disperse, a pair of arms circled my body from behind. "I love it when you're not mad at me," Lucas murmured, nuzzling my neck.

I squirmed in his embrace. This amount of PDA made me uncomfortable. Not because I was against it, per se, but because of how my body responded the way it did to Lucas. We had jobs. And how did he know the right pressure to hug? Not too loose, like a cage, but not so hard I couldn't breathe? My muscles relaxed against my better judgment as I leaned into him in the dark. This guy was so much more than my boyfriend. It felt right.

After what seemed like no time at all, he pulled away. "Walk you back to your cottage?"

"Okay," I said in a small voice. I was thrown off by all the touching.

He frowned, searching my face. "Don't mind if I do," he said, stooping over.

Oh, no. I knew that stance. I backed up a few feet. "You wouldn't—"

"Dare? That sounds familiar." He flipped me over his shoulder.

"Lucas!" I cried, beating on his back as blood rushed to my head. I dissolved into laughter. If he wanted to act like a cave man for a second, I'd let him. It wasn't like he'd throw me into a lake this time. Right?

After a minute of stomping down the path back to the cottages, he set me down.

"What, you don't want to carry me a quarter of a mile?" I teased.

"Nah," he said and grabbed my hand, threading his fingers through mine. "I'd rather hold your hand."

My heart melted.

All the way back, we didn't talk—we didn't need to. We communicated with small squeezes of our interlocked fingers and heated looks under the light of the moon. I wanted it to last forever, but eventually, we stopped at the tree line before our cottages.

"I had fun tonight," he said in a low voice.

"Me too." I didn't have to wonder if that was the right thing to say because Lucas was always real with me. He never hid behind politeness. He had zero problem calling me out. This night hadn't been perfect, but I never needed perfection. Just him.

I tilted my head, and his lips met mine. Warm, reassuring, a hello, and a goodbye. An I-love-you kiss, but with an underlying heat that promised more.

When he pulled away, I was breathless.

"Goodnight, Andy."

"Goodnight," I whispered.

I floated all the way back to my bunk before remembering I was in charge of lights out. I counted all my little Beavers; one was missing. *Leah.* It figured.

I waited, toe tapping, until she sauntered in five minutes late.

"What? I'm on time!" she said.

I didn't have the heart to reprimand her. Not on a night full of stars and fire and Lucas. I laughed and closed the door. That night I slept better than I had all camp.

26

It's Not Okay

The breakfast line the next morning moved fast—too fast. What was going on up there? I tried to peek around the girls in front of me, but their height prevented me from seeing beyond them. It didn't matter. I didn't have long to wait to find out why.

Destiny groaned in front of me. "Cereal? Seriously?"

Little cafeteria-style cartons of milk and five different choices of cereal greeted us as we slid our trays down the counter. A pitiful bowl of bananas and apples sat at the end of the line. We'd gotten used to a variety of amazing breakfast food this past week. To say this was a letdown would be a massive understatement.

"Too bad you broke up with our only source of decent food," Abby said.

The lady scooping cereal into my bowl paused, and our eyes met. Disappointment clouded her eyes.

I nudged Abby. "That was rude."

"Sorry," she mumbled.

A tidal wave of guilt threatened to capsize me as I thanked the woman for my Cinnamon Toast Crunch and fled to the nearest table. While campers talked around me, I watched the sugary squares in my bowl drown themselves one by one. I wasn't hungry anymore.

The cafeteria lady hated me. Eric was a great guy.

I'd gotten so caught up in Lucas that I hadn't considered Eric's feelings for more than the briefest of moments after we broke up. I kind of hated me too.

I obsessed over it through camp activities. It didn't keep me from doing my job, from helping the girls, but the fact that he might be suffering distracted me.

"You okay?" Lucas asked when we teamed up for a walk-the-plank activity, which ended up being glorified trust falls. Hadn't we already done trust falls? I guess these were the "planned" ones.

Destiny flopped into our arms. "Fine," I grunted to him. But when he tried to make conversation, my thoughts were too loud. I smiled to reassure him I was, in fact, fine.

When free time rolled around, I'd made a decision. I needed to call Eric. Maybe he was okay, and I was stressing for no reason. I had to find out. But when all the campers emptied out of the cottage and I was left standing alone, my finger hovered over the call button in apprehension. Maybe this wouldn't solve anything. But maybe it would.

I tapped the screen. The phone rang once, twice, three times. He never let it ring more than twice when we dated. But now we weren't. Would he ignore my call? On the fifth ring, I leaned against the log wall inside the cottage and sighed. Yep. He was sending me to voicemail.

But then the sound of his voice echoed through the phone. "Hi, Andrea."

Andrea. It didn't thrill me at all now that he called me that. It never should have. I was Andy. "Hi."

"What's going on?" His voice couldn't be more monotone.

"I..." My mouth dried up. *I want to make this right. I don't want you to be mad at me. I want to feel like we're well and truly over.* "I wanted to say sorry."

He didn't say anything for a moment. Then: "I'm guessing you're not calling to get back together."

"No," I said in a small voice.

Lucas tapped on the open door to the cottage and walked in with a big grin. "Andy, are you sure you're o—" When he saw that I was on the phone, he paused. "Who are you talking to?"

"Then why are you calling?" Eric asked.

"Eric," I said to both Lucas and Eric. Lucas would understand. I shouldered the phone for a second. "I'll tell you later," I said.

He nodded once and exited the cottage. *Crap.*

I should have closed the door. I should have done this somewhere else. But I didn't have anything to hide.

"I wanted to... I don't know. Clear the air," I said to Eric.

"The air is clear," he said, returning to that calm, monotone voice.

"It doesn't feel like it is," I whispered.

He sighed, long and loud. I'd never heard him sigh like that before. "What are you looking for from me? Haven't I given you enough?"

"I want you to understand. I want..." *I want you to forgive me.* This was so much more painful than I thought it would be.

"Well, you don't get to control that, Andrea. I do understand. That doesn't mean I don't feel hurt. That doesn't mean we can be friends if that's what you're looking for. I have to trust my friends."

I picked at a crack in the wood of my bunk post. "Eric..."

"You shouldn't have called. I'm sorry. I can't do this." He hung up.

I sat down on my bed. That was not how I hoped it would go. Something ugly twisted inside me. *God, I suck.*

I stayed frozen that way, stuck in my feelings until the girls trickled into the cottage. Then, I snapped out of it and stowed my phone under my pillow, since it only seemed to bring me trouble. *Focus on them*, I told myself, but it was impossible.

I smiled in all the right places, laid out the directions for the activities we'd do as a cottage, everything that was necessary of me, but I was going through the motions. I didn't tease Leah for being late or Taylor for tripping over her untied shoelaces. I didn't check in with Destiny about her romance with Josh. I didn't do much of anything beyond the bare minimum. I couldn't help it.

And boy, did they notice.

"Are you okay?" Maria asked me after we finished a knot-tying activity in the courtyard. Maria, of all people.

"Fine," I said, my fake smile stretching even larger as Lucas passed by. I should talk to him. Explain why I was on the phone with Eric, but I didn't... I needed time. I couldn't do another difficult conversation right now. I needed to focus on being an excellent counselor. Maybe then, I could do one thing right this summer.

"What's the next activity on the list?" I asked. I grabbed the schedule from my pocket and sighed.

"Looks like we're teaming up with the Cheetahs again," Destiny said, reading it over my shoulder.

"Yes!" Taylor cheered. We all looked at her, and she shrugged. "What? They're kind of fun."

Lucas's face when I told him who I was on the phone with flashed before me, and I shivered under the blistering heat of the sun.

Yeah, fun.

27

Figure It Out

When we got to the archery field that night, we weren't teamed up with the Cheetahs after all. The schedule had been changed so the camp could participate in a Glow-in-the-Dark Duckie Find. Where did Dana come up with these activities?

She said that due to the uneven team pairings, the competition would now be individual cottages. When she narrowed her eyes at us, Lucas stuck his hands in his pockets and whistled like a doofus. I shrugged helplessly. She created the cottage assignments.

I kept trying to catch Lucas's eye after that, but he was in Counselor Mode, always talking to a camper. I guessed my Beavers were more self-sufficient than his boys. But when the black light flashlights came out and the girls streaked their cheeks with phosphorescent paint, I had to admit that it was odd Lucas and I hadn't made eye contact even once.

Soon I found myself sitting in the dark with my own flashlight, mothering a bunch of little ducks that my girls found while they went to grab more before Dana called time.

I wanted to laugh with Lucas about how the Beavers were gunning for his team. The majority of their gathered ducks glowed a very neon yellow. But he talked to James and Derrick in a hushed voice halfway across the field. With his arms crossed, he rocked back on his heels, his face the picture of seriousness. I needed to talk to him about the fact that I'd called Eric, but every time I summoned the courage to do it, embarrassment coated my throat. I didn't want him to think me pathetic for wanting closure that wouldn't happen. Poor, naïve Andy, who couldn't let someone dislike her. Calling him had been a mistake.

Lucas glanced at me before responding to something Derrick said.

I swallowed. He wouldn't talk to them about *me*, right?

Ears burning, I focused on organizing my ducks—four rows of four made sixteen. Abby and Leah arrived with more. Orange this time. It looked like Paige's team would take a hit in this game, too.

I strained my eyes looking over my shoulder at Lucas. If he turned, I could beckon him over. But he didn't turn. The activity ended without us talking even once. His team won.

The next day broke cooler than the previous morning, and I pushed my arms through the sleeves of a sweatshirt. I didn't try to tame my hair, preferring to put it up in a bun so I could get to breakfast early. Find Lucas. Make sure we weren't weird or whatever that strange feeling was that I felt last night.

When I got to the cafeteria, I found him eating at the Cheetah table. I slid my tray next to his, and his campers went quiet. Like, actual tomb quiet. Not a sound.

"Gotta go," he said, though he still had half a plate of greasy bacon left. "Catch you later, yeah?" He smiled, but it wasn't at me. Not exactly.

I sat with the Cheetah boys in complete embarrassment as he left me there. Then I stood. I couldn't do this. Not after how hard he fought for us to be together. I followed him out the door. I had to half-jog to catch up with him as he speed-walked toward his cottage.

I fell into step with him. *Just say it.* "You're avoiding me." The words came out softer than I wanted. Weaker.

"Am I?" He still didn't look at me.

I stopped. "Yeah. I think you are," I said in a stronger voice.

He stopped, too. Ran a hand through his hair. "Okay. Maybe. I don't know."

I waited for him to explain.

He didn't.

I hugged myself. "Okay." I didn't mean for my voice to crack, didn't mean for tears to spill down my cheeks, but he was avoiding me. On purpose. I didn't know what that meant. And I couldn't dismiss the pain that ripped through me knowing that I might be the reason for that. Not when I cared about him the way

I did. Not when I wanted him to feel the same way about me. His words at the bonfire still knocked around in my head. *I'm glad you're not making this weird.* He regretted sleeping with me, didn't he?

Now, when I looked like total shit, he met my eyes. His face fell.

Anger ignited inside me. He saw me crying. He made me cry. If someone walked by, they'd see me crying over him.

"Are you happy?" I whispered through my tears.

"Happy?" he replied, incredulous. "That you're upset? How could I ever be happy about that?"

"Well, I dumped Eric for you. He was perfect and good, and—"

"Boring," he interrupted.

I gritted my teeth in frustration. This wasn't coming out right. "And I broke his heart for *you*. Because this *thing* between us won't go away. You still have this... this horrifying hold on me! And for what? For one more week? You won't even give me that! I'm stupid. So stupid, and I can't..."

"Is *that* what you're crying about? You think I made that decision for you?"

A frustrated sound erupted from the back of my throat. We were in public. Campers could be done with their breakfasts at any minute, and then they'd see us making a scene out here.

Lucas stepped closer to me. "That's bullshit, Andy, and you know it. You never liked him the way we like each other. He was never right for you."

"He was amazing," I said, "but I chose you."

"Great guy. Wrong guy. You can't blame me for that. But do it if it helps you feel like it's not your fault."

How dare he? "You're an asshole."

He shrugged. "So are you."

I smacked his chest. It was like smacking a rock. My wrist bent back at an unnatural angle.

"Ow!"

He rolled his eyes. "I suppose that's my fault, too."

I hiccupped, trying not to cry harder.

Lucas sighed. "Let me see it."

"No." I didn't need him poking it, hurting me even more. I held my hand against my chest.

"Andy—"

"You're not a doctor," I said.

His eyebrows rose. "Do you need a doctor?"

"No." He knew I didn't.

"Want some ice?"

I sniffed. Not if he was going to say it in that tone.

He chuckled. "Wait 'til I tell Dana we need ice because you hurt yourself slapping me."

Oh my god. I totally did. I slapped him. In the chest, but still. Shame made my heart pick up speed. "I'm sorry."

"For what? Hitting me?"

Well, when he put it that way, I felt even more terrible. "Yeah."

"I could care less. I didn't even feel it." He pointed to his chest. "You know what I do feel?"

I shrugged, unable to speak, guilt clogging my throat.

"Mad. At you. Don't make what we have seem like less because you feel guilty. You said it yourself when you came to my cottage. He was never right for you."

"I didn't say that, exactly." Even though it was true.

"Are you taking it back?"

I glared at him.

"That's what I thought. You're so... argh!" He threw his hands in the air. "You're so frustrating. Stay here." He jogged to the Snack Shack. I could see him from here, flashing that fake megawatt smile at Dana.

He was mad at me. I didn't know how to process that. Lucas was always the seducer when it came to me. This was unfamiliar territory. Did it mean... were we over? My mouth dried up.

He jogged back, a sandwich bag of ice in his hand. Gently, he placed it over my injured wrist. I wiped my tears with my arm and took the bag from him.

He stepped back, his eyes blazing. "Let me know when you figure it out." He turned to go.

"Wait!" I called out.

He stopped but didn't turn back.

"So, this isn't... you're not done?" I hated that my voice sounded weaker than I wanted it to.

He didn't look back, but I heard his next words as clear as if he stood right next to me. "I don't give up on people that easily."

Was that a dig on me for bringing Eric to camp? For moving on? I thought we'd been over that!

"Figure it out," he said. "I'll be here when you do." Then he walked off and left me in so much pain, I wasn't sure how I was going to find the strength be the Beaver den mother in ten minutes.

28

The Talking Stick

I muttered to myself as I walked down the gravel path. "*Figure it out.*" What a Lucas thing to say. I stomped back to my cottage like an angry T-Rex, my chest tight with emotion.

Summer chose that moment to sprint up to me. "Hey, Andy! How much time do we have before the next activity? Because I saw the Clownfish circling up and..." She drew closer to me. "Are you okay?"

"Uh, yeah. Hang on." I fished my phone out of a pocket in my safari vest. *Crap.* We were supposed to start a cottage activity ten minutes ago. Would we have enough time to do anything on the list? What if the Beavers weren't all at the cottage? The pain in my chest grew sharper.

"How do you feel about a little extra free time today?" I asked with what I hoped was a winning smile.

"Um, sure," Summer said. "We can... do that." She backed away.

I gave her a tired thumbs up as she headed back to the cottage.

They'd be fine. Free time was a gift, right? *Right.* After a few minutes of standing there, holding my chest like a frozen, angsty Andy statue, I unglued myself from the path and took a shortcut to the back of Paige's cottage. She knew about relationships and campers and everything I struggled to navigate. She might be able to help me.

But when I approached her cottage, I spied her sitting cross-legged in the grass with her campers, laughing at something one of them said.

Of course. It was cottage-activity time still. What was I thinking?

I wasn't.

Lucas and I were falling apart, and I wanted my friend, but we had a job to do. Lucas was probably doing his job right now, too.

I sighed and headed back to my cottage. I longed to be able to smile in the face of all this the way my counselor last year had. She was so bubbly, happy, so down for anything. But I wasn't Suzie. I'd have to grit my teeth behind my smile until it turned into a real one. I could do that.

But if I thought my cottage would be a safe haven from drama, I needed to think again. No sooner did I close the door than Destiny approached me, her expression wary.

"You're just in time! We're calling a cottage meeting," she said as the girls circled up on the cottage floor.

"Okay, sounds good." Did they want to add more activities to our schedule or make up for lost time? That would be on brand for them. If Destiny wanted to redo an activity we'd done or come up with something on her own, I wouldn't say no. I appreciated her taking initiative since my mind was… preoccupied.

Unease prickled in my stomach as I sat down cross-legged in the circle—the vibe was off. They were too quiet, and most of them had avoidant, sour expressions on their faces. I opened my mouth to ask Sarah if she was okay when Destiny took over.

"We called this meeting because we want to talk about something touchy. We're invoking a talking stick," she said, producing a branch that looked like it had been snapped off one of the trees outside.

"A talking stick… is a great idea." Why didn't I think of that before? It was perfect for a bunch of girls who always interrupted each other. This way all their ideas could be heard. I smiled, proud of Destiny for thinking of it.

"So, when someone has the talking stick, they get to talk. No one else can. You can raise your hand if you want the stick, but you have to wait for it to be passed to you to speak. Everyone got it?"

Nods all around the circle. I'd never seen these girls this quiet. I relaxed a little. This was great.

"Who wants to go first?"

"I will," Summer said and took the stick. "I'm having a great summer, but I wish…" She bit her lip. "I wish here at camp, there was a bit more structure. Like sometimes I'm not sure where I'm supposed to be or what to wear until we're already on our way to something. Like maybe I don't feel super prepared?" Her eyes skated sideways.

I frowned. I hadn't been telling them what to wear, but I didn't think it mattered much. It was hot. Wear shorts. They all did. This wasn't about me, anyway. Was it?

Destiny raised her hand. The stick made its way to her.

"I loved how competitive we were during capture the flag, but it kind of turned into a romantic vibe here at camp. It's been distracting... some people from what they're supposed to be doing." She stared at me.

I nodded slowly. Her romance with Josh had been painful, but it surprised me she wanted to throw it out to everyone. Was this conversation a review of their camp experience? What was touchy about that?

Caralyn raised her hand for the stick. "I feel like Taylor and I have gotten super close lately." She nudged Taylor. "Like when we hid the glow in the dark ducks. I guess I wish my leader cheered me on more when I did something cool."

I sat back. Okay, *that* was about me. One by one, each of the girls listed an aspect they liked about camp, but at the end, they tacked on something I could've done better. Been more present. Noticed when they got hurt. Been more consistent. Asked what upset them. Hung out with them during free time so they could have a real conversation. The list went on. Even Leah, who never showed up to anything on time, grabbed the stick and had something to say.

"I love the way the girls in our cottage have become friends this year, but it feels separate from our leader. Like maybe she's going through the motions and doesn't care."

A bomb went off in my chest. *I didn't care?* It took everything I had not to react. I blinked back the moisture in my eyes as the stick made its way to me. I hadn't raised my hand, but they'd all said their piece. Now it was my turn.

"Um... I don't know what to say," I whispered. "I think I need to process."

"See?" Maria said. "That's the problem, she's always—"

Destiny held up her hand. "You don't have the stick."

Maria folded her arms and stuck her tongue out.

"I feel a little blindsided by this conversation." I swallowed. "I'm glad for the happy things that have happened to you all during camp, but I need to think about the other things that were said. I can't absorb it all at once, and I want my reaction to be constructive." My throat closed on the word constructive. *Don't cry.*

A long silence stretched in the Beaver cottage. "That was very... diplomatic," Destiny said.

I nodded, willing the tears in my eyes to recede. They hated my leadership style. They thought I was a bad counselor. I had failed them. Everything I had done made them think it was about me and Lucas or me and Eric, and not about them. I needed to step back and think. But not in front of them.

I got to my feet, and they all followed suit. "Thank you for... being honest with me."

Destiny nodded, but none of them looked at me. Then Dana's voice over the speakers announced free time for real. I did my best impression of a smile and retreated to the bathroom to take a shower where I could cry in privacy.

Thankfully, none of the girls followed me.

29

Somehow

S calding water from the showerhead cascaded over my body. I bit my fist and willed myself to make zero noise as my shoulders shook with sobs.

The Beaver girls had an intervention for me. They *hated* me. I could get *fired.*

I rubbed my eyes until spots clouded my vision. Would that be the worst thing in the world? *Yes.* Getting fired meant I was a failure. That I didn't belong here. Maybe I *didn't* belong here.

I rested my forehead against the cool tile of the shower. I had fooled myself all summer. How did I ever think I could be a counselor in a place like this? The girls were right. I was aloof, uncaring, too much inside my head. They needed someone like Paige. Someone the opposite of me. Last year should have taught me that.

My tears mixed with the water streaming down my face. The only place I'd ever felt confident was this camp, and now I'd ruined the one memory I had of it being special. I'd also ruined it for an entire cottage of girls. I wrapped my arms around myself, shaking. I couldn't think about anything else except that I failed, failed, failed.

I sucked in one rattling breath after another as the water ran cooler. *Stop. Think.* I needed to get out of the bathroom. Get dressed. Go to the next activity. I couldn't miss another one. The girls would revolt.

With wooden movements, I dressed and followed them to the color war challenge, a version of freeze tag that took up the whole archery field. It didn't require me to do anything but stand on the sidelines, so I did. I didn't seek out Paige. I didn't look for Lucas.

I clapped when Destiny tagged out three Clownfish girls and wordlessly handed Taylor a Band-Aid when she scraped her knee. Again. On the outside, I was serene.

On the inside, I wanted to scream.

I skipped dinner. What did they hope to get out of their circle-attack? I couldn't turn into a great counselor overnight, and honestly, I wanted my mom.

On my bunk bed in the cottage, I stared at the mattress above me. I'd never been good at confrontation. Guilt overwhelmed me every time. I never felt like I said the right thing at the right time. I found it easier to shut down. I squeezed my eyes closed. I couldn't keep doing that. I'd come so far past that this year. I needed to deal with my problems. Yes, they were overwhelming. Yes, they were my fault. I swallowed. That didn't mean I couldn't handle them. I might not know how right now, but no one was in physical pain. No one was dying. This could be solved.

I took in a shuddering breath. My mom would be able to help me figure it out. I grabbed my phone and scrolled through my contacts. Involuntarily, my finger paused on Lucas's number, which came before my mom's. I sat there and stared at his name. He always got me. He was even trying to give me space to figure everything out right now. But for the first time in maybe ever, I didn't want space. I wanted Lucas's arms around me in a hug so tight I could block everything else out. He'd done that for me once last summer.

I put my own arms around myself. A pitiful substitute. I needed to grow up. I needed to...

I sat straight up. I knew what I needed to do. What would make him understand I was still with him, even if I had screwed up.

Grabbing the counselor binder, I tore off a corner of a page the girls and I had already done. In my best handwriting, I wrote:

Canoes. 8pm.

Now I had to get it to Lucas. I sprinted out of the cottage and bumped into one of the Cheetah boys on his way back from the lake.

"Hey, can you give this to Lucas?" I asked.

He smirked, taking the folded scrap of paper from my hand. "Sure."

"Thanks."

Only three more hours until eight. I could make it that long. Then Lucas and I would... I didn't know what we would do or say, but the note and the canoes at eight was our thing. Somehow, I had to believe it would all work out.

I stopped pitying myself long enough to plan out the next Beaver activity, but when I got the girls situated, Destiny jumped in.

"We haven't played Never Have I Ever yet, and I've been waiting all camp," she said to the others like I wasn't even there.

"Bring it!" Taylor said.

"I will own you in this," Abby cheered.

I pushed the baggie of bouncy balls I'd brought behind my back and opened my mouth to give them directions on the game they'd rather play.

"Everyone knows how this works, right?" Destiny asked instead.

Nods from around the circle.

"Okay, five fingers up. I'll start," she said. They laughed as they went around the circle, each of the "Never have I evers" getting more ridiculous by the minute.

I was ousted. I bit my lip and shrugged when my turn came around. "I'll watch," I whispered, but either they didn't hear me, or they didn't care. It took all my effort to keep a composed face until they left for free time. I didn't even clock who won the game.

I sat alone in the middle of the room until seven-fifty rolled around, and I could walk to the canoes. I waited in Lucas's and my spot, staring at the cloudless sky for I don't know how long. Until a rising moon took the place of sunset. My legs grew stiff, and I blinked as the stars blurred together. He was late.

I checked my phone. 8:23.

He wasn't just late. He wasn't coming.

I stood, smoothing out the indent my butt had made in the sand. If he did show up later, I didn't want him to think I'd waited for him. That I was pathetic like that. I made it back to the cottage, counted the girls, waited an extra five minutes for Leah, and flicked off the lights.

Somehow, I didn't cry myself to sleep.

Somehow, I didn't feel anything at all.

30

Kind of Intense

Walking to breakfast behind the girls the next morning was torture. Every step required effort, like walking through sand. I didn't want to go. I didn't want to see Lucas shooting the breeze with James and Derrick while I sat in the middle of the Beaver girls, surrounded and discluded. From him. From them. From camp.

But I didn't have a choice. I couldn't let Lucas see how his rejection last night affected me. Also, I was hungry. I hadn't eaten since lunch yesterday. Hadn't had any coffee since then, either.

I split off from the girls and went to the staff lounge to make myself a cup. I had just snapped on the lid when the door opened. *Lucas.*

He walked in, the room shrinking around us as I averted my eyes to step around him.

"You don't even talk to me now?" he asked.

I froze. "What?"

"I told you what I needed, and you…" He trailed off, eyeing the way my fingers clenched my cup. "What's wrong?"

"I waited for you last night," I whispered and held my coffee even tighter, like the heat from it might cancel out the pain of this conversation.

"Last night," he echoed.

"You could have texted," I said. I should stand my ground. Sure, it was an invitation. He didn't have to go. But he could have let me know so I didn't wait for him.

"Texted? About last night? What was supposed to happen last night?"

I stared at him. He was pretending he didn't get my note? I thought he was so much better than that.

"*Eight pm. Canoes.* I thought it..." I swallowed the lump in my throat. "I thought it would be romantic. I can see now that I was wrong." I swept past him.

"Andy—"

The door swung shut in his face.

I grabbed a bagel and fled the cafeteria. What was I doing? I pulled my sunglasses out of my hair and set them on my sweaty nose. When had every moment with Lucas become difficult again? It wasn't supposed to be this hard, not when you really liked someone. Was it?

I ripped off chunks of the bagel and shoved them into my mouth, concentrating on chewing methodically until I pushed through the Beaver cottage door to change into my bathing suit. The girls couldn't stop talking about the blob this morning. If I couldn't be a good counselor, maybe I could be a piece of furniture in their summer. I didn't know what else to do.

But when I got to the cottage, they left as soon as they saw me, slamming the door on the way out. I watched through the window as they threw their arms around each other and walked down the path to the lake. Here I stood in a bathing suit that I loved with a new fluffy towel instead of the lame Little Mermaid one I brought last year, and I was... useless.

I should text Paige. If there was ever a time for an S.O.S., this was it. I shut my eyes. But I didn't want to. It was embarrassing. She bonded with her campers even when they were her literal opposites. My campers didn't want me around and now, I didn't know how to fix it. My chest constricted. This was the end, wasn't it? I needed to quit. I needed to let someone else be a better counselor, a better person for these girls. I was screwing it all up.

They deserved better.

I turned and headed toward the main building. The one with Dana's office. My head swam as I trudged up the porch stairs. Even last year, I never came here. Never thought to give up in this way.

My heart constricted in pain when I thought of Eric climbing these steps to do the same thing. I had cost her two workers. She was going to be so stressed.

And Lucas? I couldn't even think about him right now.

But this was the right thing to do. I knocked, and after a scuffle, the door swung open.

"Andy Stevens, hi. Come on in," Dana said, smelling like soap and woods. She flashed me a polite smile. I was such a jerk.

I followed her inside, but she didn't sit behind her desk. She crossed to the window and pulled the blinds open so that the sunlight splashed in and over the sofa on the opposite wall. She sat on it, beckoning me over.

"How are you doing?"

I perched next to her, at a loss for what to say.

"It's been so hot out, huh?" she continued, scrutinizing my face. "Kind of intense."

I stared at Dana, and she arched an eyebrow. She wasn't talking about the weather.

"Very," I said.

"The weather's like that sometimes. It's all about adapting. Making sure we're prepared."

"What if... what if we're not prepared? For the intensity, I mean."

She sat back. "Sometimes we think we know what we're about, but the sun takes us a bit by surprise. It's true."

I nodded and laced my fingers together. I couldn't look at her.

"But surprises aren't always terrible. Maybe they hurt our pride bit, but the great thing about amazing leaders like all my counselors here at camp is that if they aren't prepared, they think on their feet. They figure it out."

I swallowed. Maybe this conversation had gotten too abstract for me. I didn't figure it out. The girls had lost complete faith in me. So had Lucas. I couldn't hang onto Eric—I didn't end up wanting to. I didn't know what I wanted, but it wasn't to ruin anyone's summer.

"I've failed you," I whispered.

She shook her head. "If I was worried about the safety of those girls, you would already be gone," she said in a sharp voice. "If I thought you were leading them to do destructive things, same thing."

"They don't need me."

She leaned back on the couch and laughed.

I flinched. She was laughing at me? *Great.*

"No, no, sweet girl. I'm sorry. It's funny because I hand-picked your cottage this year. I thought these girls specifically could learn from you."

I twisted my hands together in my lap. "But they haven't."

"Haven't they?" She placed one of her small hands over mine.

I shook my head, looking at a bare spot of carpet she'd tried to hide in the corner. I wondered what happened there.

"They're learning how to work with someone who isn't like them. They're learning how not to talk over each other. They're learning to root for someone. I think you're not seeing it because it isn't what you thought you'd be teaching them this summer."

"I thought I'd get someone more like me," I admitted. "That I'd have to help them fit in."

"And you didn't, so you think they don't need you?" She snorted. "They need you, Andy. Trust me."

I shook my head. I guess I didn't see it the way she did. Maybe my feelings about... people were getting in the way.

"I think you knocked on my door to quit," she said, "but it would be a mistake. In fact, I was going to come get you for something else."

I looked her in the eye for the first time.

"I wanted to do something different than the dance this year. It seems a little antiquated, and the campers this year are so much more competitive than they have been in years past. I thought you'd be the perfect person to come up with a final activity for the color war. Something fun that pulls their summer together."

"Me?" I squeaked. "Why me?"

"Because you see people, Andy. You know what they like. And since you're into books, I bet whatever you come up with would be creative."

While that might not be true, a flicker of hope ignited within me. If I planned the best activity of the summer, the girls might forgive me. On the other hand, if it flopped, they'd hate me forever. "Um..."

"But if you want to throw in the towel and call it quits because it got a little difficult... If you don't want to prove to the girls that you've got this..." she said in a casual voice.

I frowned.

She smiled.

Oh, she knew exactly what she was doing. "You're kind of evil. You know that, right?" I stood.

"Evil? Or a good leader?"

I laughed as she closed the door in my face. "Pitch it to me tomorrow, yeah?" she called through the screen door as I trotted back down the path. My stomach clenched. I couldn't believe I was going right back into the lion's den. She'd played me. But maybe I needed to hear that I hadn't botched things as much as I thought. And I needed to hear it from my boss.

I sighed. What would a good last activity be for these kids? I had always liked puzzles. But first, I needed to talk to my Beaver girls.

If I'd attached lead weights to my feet, it wouldn't have made me any slower walking back to my cottage. I tried to pep talk myself on the way there.

They're just teenagers. Own your mistakes and take back the reins. Destiny will be mad, but she'll get over it. You can do this. You can.

As the cottage came into view, Destiny's voice became clearer and clearer. "The binder says we have three things left to choose from, and all of them are physical."

"But I pulled my leg at the last activity you made us do. I want to be fresh for the color war." Taylor held up a bag of ice.

"I don't know what to tell you. Those are the rules. Now are you going to suck it up and play nice with us, or do you want to sit out?"

Taylor ducked her head, grimacing.

"Wait a minute," I said when she started to get up. She shouldn't be doing anything physical if she didn't think her body was ready.

The girls in the cottage did a double take. I would think it hilarious if it weren't for the fact that they appeared shocked I was about to do my job.

That hurt.

"The activities on the clipboard are suggestions. They're not a checklist. We can pick something we've already done or come up with a new activity that will include all of us in a way that won't hurt. It's about bonding and leadership," I said.

"Says who?" Destiny said and propped her hand on her hip. "You? You haven't been around or helping with anything. We've had to figure it out on our own."

A couple of the girls nodded, but nobody else chimed in.

"Maybe we should talk first. Circle up?"

The girls looked at each other, then shuffled into a crappy oval on the floor. I sat with them, but Summer and Sarah, who sat on either side of me, avoided bumping knees with mine. It would take a hot second to get them to forgive me.

I swallowed. *If* they forgave me.

"Okay, here's what's going on. I... haven't been completely honest with you girls. Maybe it's time we do that."

"That would be a switch." Maria snorted.

Destiny rolled her eyes.

"I've never been a counselor before."

"That's pretty obvious," Abby said.

"Would you let her speak?" Blair said. "Go ahead, Andy."

"And well, I think it might come more naturally to people who are more outgoing than me, but Dana convinced me last year that I might be able to... to show a different side of leadership. More of a lead by example thing. Except... I didn't know how to do that."

Destiny nodded.

"Bringing Eric with me was a mistake. Seeing Lucas again when I thought he wouldn't be here... The whole Landy thing..."

A couple of the girls shifted uncomfortably.

"It seemed like I was screwing up everywhere. Like I couldn't do anything right, and the harder I tried, the worse it got."

"Not with us. You were awesome at the beginning of the week," Destiny said. The other girls nodded.

"Was I?"

"Yeah, you helped us stick it to the Cheetahs in a big way. You were so competitive." Abby smiled.

"I didn't know if that was okay or not," I said quietly. "It's so out of character for me."

"And the wall? You smoked him. You were so strong. What happened? Was it all guy drama?" Taylor asked.

"I don't know... it seemed like you girls didn't need me, that you'd rather go for it yourselves. It threw me."

"We didn't want to. We wanted you," Summer said.

"Okay." I picked at the carpet. "I'm sorry."

"We like how you see us. How you notice what we need," Taylor continued. "I don't want to do a physical activity, but it doesn't mean I don't want to be a Beaver. I'm hurt and I'm trying to rest for the big end-of-camp thing, whatever that is, now."

"You heard we're not doing a dance?" I raised my eyebrows. "Are you upset about it?"

"Upset that we get to compete instead of dress up and be awkward? I'm real broken up about it," Taylor deadpanned.

I laughed. "Okay. So... what now?" I shouldn't let them control the conversation; I should step back into leadership, but it was their summer, too. Their leadership camp. Whatever they needed from me, I would give them.

Destiny, who'd been sitting in sullen silence, spoke up. "Be our counselor. Don't flake again. Promise us that, and we'll forgive you."

"I promise," I said, holding my hand over my heart.

"And help us beat the Cheetahs," Maria added. "They're ahead."

I winced. The leaderboard stood outside Dana's office. I saw how they'd jumped up. It would take a pretty good win to grab the title back from those boys, now. "I'll do my best."

"Okay, then, oh wise counselor. Which activity should we do over?" Destiny asked.

"It doesn't have to be a do-over. Hmm. Do any of you know cups?"

Half the girls raised their hands. "That's perfect. Buddy up and teach someone else. By the time we're done, we'll be able to do it in a circle. Should be chill, but also help you work on one-on-one communication."

Taylor beamed at me. Instead of being the lame one out, she'd be teaching Destiny the rhythm of cups.

I settled in across from Sarah. Maybe I had a little leadership left in me, after all. By the time we left for the next color war activity, the girls laughed and joked with me again.

"I'm glad you're back," Blair whispered as we walked down the trail to the archery field. "Destiny was getting intense."

I nodded, but I didn't want to throw Destiny under the bus. She did what she felt like she had to do. They were lost without a leader. I'd done that to them.

"Destiny," I said as the girls broke through the trees to the field. "Can I talk to you?"

She hung back. "Are you going to yell at me?"

Where did she get *that*? "No, I wanted to apologize to you. And say thank you. You stepped up when no one else did, and that couldn't have been easy."

Silence sat heavy between us for a long moment. Then she sighed. "It's fine."

"It's not. You took on a lot."

She smiled and looked up at me. "They're not easy, are they?"

"Are *you*?" I laughed.

"I don't envy you. Thanks for taking them back."

"I got you. Go be a kid."

"Thank you." She crushed me in a big hug, then ran across the field to catch up with the girls. "I'm back, bitches!"

"Language!" I called. Then I jogged to join them, laughing.

Volleyball nets stretched in an X shape across the field. Paige and I had played this activity last year. Dana finished her instructions as I walked up. She made eye contact with me, lifting her eyebrows a touch.

I nodded, smiling. She smiled back at me.

When my girls set up to push the gigantic clear "volleyball" over the net, they were so hyped, I wondered if they'd chugged energy drinks.

"Stay on the balls of your feet. It will make you move faster," Summer said.

"We're going to need at least two or three of us under it every time," Destiny called.

Even Leah showed up on time today. "We've got this, Beavers!"

The boys from the Cheetah cottage squared off against them. After a couple of false starts, the guys figured out how to serve, and trash talk got flung over the net more than the ball. Most of it made me laugh, so I didn't step in.

My pocket buzzed.

I never got the note. Ryan forgot.

I'm sorry, Andy. Meet tonight?

I swallowed, relief and regret coating my throat. Maybe he was telling the truth, but I'd just gotten the girls back on my side. I wanted to see him, but I couldn't let that distract me from cheering on my Beavers.

I scanned the sidelines so I could give him some sort of signal, but I didn't see him. And where was Paige? I shifted around other counselors and managed to spy her. She waved at her girls like a woman trying to land a plane. Two sat on the field. One picked flowers for a dandelion crown.

I snorted.

Like a laugh-seeking missile, she met my eyes. She looked to where my girls stretched between games like they were preparing for the Olympics. They'd already eliminated the Porcupine team, and it was barely five minutes into the activity. *Not fair,* she mouthed at me.

I shrugged, grinning.

"You suck!" she yelled at me. Then she jogged over to where I stood. "You doing okay? We haven't talked since..."

"The bonfire. Yeah."

"Where is Lucas, anyway?"

"I have no idea." I shifted my feet.

"Really?"

"Yeah, he's been..." Yelling at me. Standing me up. Texting me to meet him. I hugged myself.

"Looks like your Beaver girls are in it to win it."

I dropped my hands. She was right. The next game would begin any second. This activity wasn't about me or Lucas—it was about them. "They're great."

"I think they've learned a lot from you this summer."

"Come on. I've been a terrible counselor."

"Part of the time, but yesterday I saw Destiny check on a girl sitting by herself. Two weeks ago, she wouldn't have done that. Maybe you've taught them to listen a bit more. To notice."

I stood dumbfounded. Had I? Finally, I said, "They're great girls." In the end, they got to decide what kind of leader they'd be.

Paige nodded. "I'm glad you're back."

"I didn't go anywhere."

"You know what I mean." She grinned.

"Yeah."

"And go!" Dana pushed the huge volleyball off a ladder with the help of Lucas and another counselor named Tony. Had she done that last year? I was so unobservant when it came to those types of things. But Paige was right. When it mattered, maybe I was perceptive.

And maybe Lucas couldn't hang out with me because Dana asked him to help her. I was sure he'd be along any moment to stand next to me on the sidelines.

Paige yelled encouragement to her girls, but it didn't last. They were the second ones out. My Beavers knew a weak team when they saw one, and they took zero prisoners.

Paige shoved me when they ran back up the hill to continue working on the flower crowns they'd started earlier. "You suck!" She laughed.

I resisted the urge to look for Lucas again. Maybe he didn't see me. But I knew, even as I thought that, that it wasn't true. He always saw me, always pursued me. If he wasn't standing with me now, it was to make a point. Probably that I should text him back. I pushed back a wave of guilt. I *would* text him back. After the game.

"Go Beavers!" I called. I didn't scream as loud as the other counselors on the sidelines, but my girls still heard me. Summer grinned, flashing me a thumbs up. "For Andy!" she cried, heaving the ball up with the help of Sarah.

"Aw, they love you," Paige said.

"I'm not sure why."

"I am." She threw her arm around my shoulders. Ten seconds later, she snaked her arm back. "Yeah, it's way too hot out here for that crap."

I couldn't agree more. Sweat dripped from my body as it had so often this past week. The Beavers defeated team after team, but never the Cheetahs. Those boys knew something about strategy. They rotated their players so there were no weak zones on their court. Smart. So very smart.

But my girls mirrored their intensity. They huddled between every round, talking to each other like they were in a life-or-death grudge match instead of at a Leadership Camp. Man, I loved that about them. All in, always.

"Mine!" Caralyn yelled as she dove for the ball time after time. Destiny jumped in to support her. And Sarah. And Maria. They had each other's backs.

Lucas didn't call out to his team at all. Of course, the moment I found him in the crowd, I couldn't help watching him. He stood on the opposite sideline, his muscular arms crossed, his sunglasses an impenetrable wall between us. I couldn't tell if he was looking at me or watching the game.

From across the court, he reminded me a lot of his brother. I'd never tell him that, though.

I turned my focus back to the game; I had some Beavers to support. The next time they huddled up, I ran to join them, and they included me in their circle.

"They're good," Maria puffed.

"Not good enough to beat the Beavers," I said. "If you can control the ball at all, hit it to the left. Every time those two boys are supposed to defend, the others have to jump in to help. Tire them out. They can't keep going forever."

"That's so devious. You really have been watching," Abby said.

I scoffed. "I always watch you."

The girls grinned at each other.

"Beavers on three?" I said.

We all stuck our hands in. "One, two, three, Beavers!"

They scattered back into their positions.

I tried not to laugh as the boys threw tiny cups of water over their hot faces. My girls were single-minded. They were going to crush this.

I stuck my tongue out at Lucas. And even though he had his counselor face on, I thought I saw the corner of his mouth twitch.

Five minutes later, the Beavers edged out Lucas's campers and won the game. They cheered, then raced across the field to slap hands with the Cheetahs. It was a far cry from the "in your face" attitude of a week ago.

"Who taught you all to be such good sports?" I joked when they joined me on the path back to the cottage.

"You did. Duh," Destiny said and skipped ahead. It was almost like I could see the weight lifted from her shoulders now that she no longer had to try to lead the Beavers by herself.

Wait a minute. *I* did? That wasn't right.

Or was it?

A slow smile spread over my face.

31

We Should Talk

The Beaver girls and I rehashed the game on our way back to the cottage. They'd owned everyone and reclaimed their spot at the top of the leaderboard. When Destiny and Abby looped me into their conversations, it felt like this summer could be salvaged, after all.

As my campers departed for scheduled free time, I pulled my phone out of my vest and texted Lucas back. We *should* meet tonight. I needed to stop avoiding talking to him because it was hard. That wasn't fair to either of us. I should be braver than that.

The energy that thrummed within me slowed as I sat on the beach and watched the watery glow of the sun's last rays fade into the tree line. I leaned back on my arms and breathed in the smell of tree and water, the warmth of the sand warming my legs. A few minutes later, Lucas sat beside me. He used one finger to draw shapes in the sand but remained silent.

I would have to speak first. That was fine. I breathed in and out slowly. I could do this.

"Are you okay?" I asked.

"Andy…"

I didn't want to assume the weirdness between us was about Eric since he had so much more going on. And maybe I didn't want to talk about that at all. "Are you still upset about Tyler? Do you want to talk about your dad? I'm sorry I haven't been a better listener this summer. I want to be here for you. You need to let me." I dug my fingers into the sand. Most of our relationship had been Lucas supporting me, but he needed someone to lean on, too. I wanted to help. Not so it would be fair, but so he could be okay. I wanted him to be that teasing, smiling Lucas again.

He sighed. "It's not my family. It's you."

"Me?" I squeaked.

"I feel like I've been fighting for you all summer. And last summer. I'm always fighting for you." He looked over at me, but as much as I wanted to say something, I knew he wasn't done. He *had* fought for me. It was the major difference between him and Eric.

"I want you to fight for me, too," he whispered.

I swallowed. What had Eric said? That he liked me more than I liked him? It might have been true for our relationship, but it didn't apply to Lucas.

"I might not fight the way you do, but I'm still fighting. I'm here. You're not more..." All the things I wanted to say and couldn't jammed together in the back of my throat. "You're not more invested than me. Honestly? You could shatter me."

He stopped drawing in the sand. "What?"

I shifted until my arm pressed against his; I needed the contact. What I was about to say wasn't polite. It might even make him more upset. "Last summer, you hurt me. I know you didn't mean to and there was no way around it, but... I've been working on myself a lot this year."

He swallowed. "I know that."

I took in a shuddering breath. "And now that we see eye to eye, I'm scared... it's always there, this overwhelming need to be near you. And..." I reached over and threaded my fingers through his. "No one can hurt me as much as you."

"Wow." He looked up at the sky.

I leaned my head against his shoulder. "No pressure."

I felt, rather than heard him swallow. Once, twice. "I think we should talk," he said.

My skin went cold. Those weren't the words I thought he'd say. I'd opened myself up, been so vulnerable and now we needed to talk? "Isn't that what we're doing right now?" I asked. My heart hammered in my ears. If this ended up being a repeat of last year, I would never recover.

"Sure, but not really. Why do you keep running away? Why do you keep avoiding me? I'm not Eric, Andy. I can't accept that from you. I won't. Not when I'm this..."

I took a deep breath when it became clear he wouldn't finish the end of that sentence. He wanted the truth? Okay, I was ready to tell him. Something I wouldn't even admit to myself until right now. "I feel like we're not together. Everything this summer has been screwed up, and you stopped talking to me, but maybe that was my fault. Is... is what happened that day in your cottage all you wanted from me?" I blinked back the burn of tears.

"What?" He surged to his feet. "No. How could you think—"

"You said you were glad I didn't make it weird," I whispered.

Lucas pushed a hand through his hair. "I said... okay, we both might need to chill out for a second. We're having communication issues."

"Okay," I said, hating the vulnerability in my voice. I hugged my knees.

"You came to my cottage having broken up with your boyfriend and we... I maybe took advantage of you when you weren't ready."

I opened my mouth to interrupt him.

He held up his hand. "My turn, remember?"

I closed my mouth.

"And then I said this thing that was huge, and I meant it." He stared at me until I nodded. "I still mean it. I love you. But it seemed like you might not have been ready to hear that."

I sighed. I was ready. I just forgot to say it back. I thought he knew I felt the same way, and that was on me.

"Then you call your ex-boyfriend and tell me you'll talk to me about it later."

Crap. Yes, that had happened.

"And you don't. So, I don't know what to think. That's where I'm at. I'm waiting for you to clarify, Andy. I'm waiting for you to make some decisions. Because I'm all in if you are, but I can't... I can't commit if you won't. It would hurt too much."

I stared up at him. He looked like he'd just run a mile, his hair messed up, exhaustion furrowing his brow. This was the deepest, most difficult conversation we'd had. We weren't shying away from it, either. Relief that we could be transparent like this spread through me. I swallowed. *Don't screw this up.* "I…" I didn't know where to start. All I knew was that…

I rushed to my feet and pulled his head down for a kiss.

His lips were unsteady on mine, like he had to hold himself back. I stood on my tiptoes and pushed my hand through his hair, slanting my mouth against his.

He relaxed into the kiss, and I pressed against him. We made out for a long minute before he pulled back and touched his forehead to mine. "That didn't solve it, you know," he rasped.

"I know, but it started to."

He chuckled.

"Okay," I said, detaching from him. "Let me help with this. I'm sorry, I'm so bad at…" I waved my hand between us, "but I'm trying."

"Okay," he said and sat back down.

"First, you should know you didn't take advantage of me. I knew what I was doing, and I don't regret it at all. Second, with Eric? I was trying to clear the air with him, to see if he was okay." I sucked in a shaky breath. "I'm sorry if it hurts you, but I care about him as a person and what I did… it was so shitty. I wanted to try to make it less…" I waved my hand in the air again. "Just less. Never, for one second, did I consider making up or getting back together with him. I'm sorry I didn't talk to you about it after. I got embarrassed. I'm sorry."

He stared at me, silent for a second. Then his mouth twitched. "That was a lot of words."

I blew out a shaky breath, sinking to my knees in front of him. "How did I do?"

He pulled me into a crushing hug. "You *are* trying."

"For you. Anything for you." *Even if it only lasts until the end of camp.* The words hung around us, the impermanence of this moment crystallized in the night sounds of the cicadas and crickets chirping from the forest.

"I love you, Andy Stevens," he whispered against my hair as we lay in the sand.

I sucked in a breath, my heart hammering. "I love you, too."

Lucas drew away enough to stare into my eyes. "Yeah?"

"Yeah," I whispered.

He squeezed me tighter. "I would never ditch you after all we've been through. I'm sorry if it seemed like that was what was going on."

"I'm sorry that we've been wasting the time we've gotten together," I murmured against his chest.

"Would you rather be making out with me?" he teased.

"Twenty-four seven," I deadpanned.

He pulled back to look at me. "You little deviant."

"Just when it comes to you."

"That's so hot." And then he pressed his lips to mine.

32

Working Together

I tapped my pen against my notebook for the millionth time and tried to ignore the burning behind my eyes and the tightening of my chest. Dana would want to talk about the end-of-camp activity at breakfast, and I'd been up since five planning. A few of the girls got up at six to go for a jog, but otherwise, even breathing filled the cottage as the sunrise poked through the blinds. I was running out of time. And it had to be perfect.

I stared down at my sloppy handwriting. What I had planned used everyone's strengths. It would transform the camp into a race of epic proportions. But due to the number of stations, it required all the counselors. What a mess.

I wanted it to be impressive. Something cool enough to make up for the mistakes I'd made this summer. Something that showed the girls I was worthy to be their counselor. But could anything do that?

Breathe. Start back at the beginning. What does the first station need?

But I didn't know. I didn't know how many staff were lifeguard certified, how many of them could jog alongside kids, or who might be best at paintball versus egg toss. I knew my campers inside and out, but the other counselors? If I had known I'd be planning something like this, I would have paid more attention to their strengths.

I flipped through the papers on my clipboard again, one by one. Maybe twelve stations were too many. Well, no. If there were less, we'd have too many campers waiting their turn. Everyone needed to do something at the same time.

It was a lot to pull off. And I didn't know if I could do it. Maybe I should rewrite it. More legible handwriting might make things clearer. I wished I'd brought my laptop to camp with me. Organizing this would be easier in a doc.

"Hey, Andy?" Sarah stumbled into the cottage. "I don't feel so good." She lurched toward the bathroom.

Whoa!

I shoved a wastepaper basket under her less than a second before she vomited. I held her hair back and tried not to gag as she bent over and let go of all her dinner last night and probably more. When she stopped, I asked, "Are you sick?"

She shook her head. "Running with the girls."

I frowned. "What happened to a light jog?"

"Have to stay... competitive."

"What? No." I sat with her on my bunk, pushing the trash can out of smelling range. "What do you mean stay competitive?"

"Destiny says..." She shook her head.

"Destiny isn't in charge of you. You're in charge of you. You have talents she doesn't have and vice versa."

She sighed and pushed back her short hair. "I know."

I patted her back in circles the way my mom did when I felt sick or sad. "I'm sorry you felt pressured."

She flopped backwards onto my sleeping bag. "It's not bad pressure."

I huffed. "If you're not having fun at summer camp, yeah, it kind of is."

She rolled her head toward me. "Fair point."

"This is your summer, too. What would you rather be doing today?" Because it sure wasn't running and then puking her guts out.

"I wanted to make bracelets," she murmured.

I slapped my knee. "Then let's go make bracelets after breakfast. Running be damned."

She laughed, then groaned, holding onto her side. "I don't think you're supposed to swear as a counselor."

"Well, we all know what kind of counselor I am, anyway." I offered her a hand up.

Sarah took it. "You're a good counselor," she murmured as I pulled her up and we started for the door. Maybe she hadn't intended for me to hear it, but it mattered—a lot.

Now, if I could get this last activity to work, they'd know how much I cared about them.

As we entered the cafeteria, noise welled around us. Sarah gave me a weak smile, then skipped the line to sit with the other Beaver girls. Her stomach must still be upset. I made a mental note to grab some crackers for one of my many vest pockets before we left. She shouldn't try doing anything physical again with no food in her stomach.

My feet carried me to the staff lounge first, though. Coffee before anything else. I had just added creamer to my cup when Dana stepped into the lounge.

"Thought I'd find you here," she said with a smile. "Do you have an activity for me?"

I inhaled, then let out a shaky breath. This was it. She could tell me I'd taken on too much, that the idea sucked. That would be the end of it, and my chance to prove to her and everyone else that my position here as a counselor wasn't a mistake.

She gestured for me to sit, and I did, grabbing my clipboard from the counter where I'd put it during coffee-making time.

"Okay, so I'm thinking a relay race. A massive one. Involve every cottage. Every team. They'll be rotating through stations and checkpoints. And there will be time limits at each station to keep them moving, but the best time will win. Like the other activities, we can award points according to what place they get. But more, since this will take a lot of effort."

"What about our three campers who can't run because of physical impairments?" she asked.

I blew out a breath. "They can be waiting at the stations that aren't physical and then rejoin their team at the end—though it isn't necessary since the time of each team will start when they reach a station and end when they leave it. They can also choose to travel with their teams at their own pace if they're comfortable with it. We can put those teams first or last to keep the flow appropriate for them."

"You seem to have thought this through. Do you know who will be in charge of each station?" She flipped through my chicken scratch pages, and I wished again that I'd had enough time to rewrite them before she saw them. Stick figures decorated the activity descriptions and rules in cramped handwriting curved around the margins. Could she even read it?

"I'm sure I can figure out who would be best for every activity," I lied. She smiled when she saw that the swimming race already had a counselor name above it: Lucas.

"It's a lot to plan in such a short amount of time. If you think you can handle it…" She broke off and looked at me, her smile gone. "Can you handle it?"

"Of course." I gave her a winning smile, my hands shaking around my coffee cup. I'd find a way. I had to. I'd spent too long leaning on everyone around me. It was time to step up.

"Okay," she said. "This is great. If it works out well this summer, we can bring it back next year. We can even call it the Andy Relay."

Blood rushed to my head. "Oh, no. Please don't do that."

She laughed. "I'm kidding. I know how you love the limelight."

I swallowed a scalding sip of coffee so I didn't have to answer her.

She stood and waved to me, the light tinkle of her laugh following her out of the lounge as the door swung shut behind her.

I slumped over in my seat. What had I gotten myself into?

I stayed in the lounge going over my plan, penciling in names and scratching them back out. I made a list of all the materials we would need and hated that I should have asked Dana where all the sports stuff was located so I could use the equipment we already owned at the camp. After another cup of coffee, my body buzzed and the sound in the cafeteria had lessened. Breakfast was ending. I needed to get to Sarah so we could make bracelets together.

I rushed out of the lounge and to my relief, Sarah still sat between Maria and Abby, fiddling with the straw to a juice cup. *Good.* Juice would give her a little sugar.

I sidled up to the breakfast bar.

"We're closing," one of the cafeteria ladies said, her face solemn. I bet she hated me because it was my fault they were now short-staffed. And who didn't love Eric?

I muscled through the heat that sprang to my cheeks. "I know. I'm sorry. I have a camper who isn't feeling so well. You wouldn't happen to have a few packets of crackers anywhere?"

The lady's face softened. "I'll see what I can find." She disappeared behind a door in the kitchen and came back with a few of those two-pack saltine packages. "Tell your camper to feel better."

"Thank you so much," I said gratefully.

She nodded at me. Not an I-forgive-you-for-making-Eric-leave nod, but I would take it.

I shoved the crackers in my vest and jogged over to the Beaver table. "Ready to make some bracelets?" I asked Sarah.

Her face brightened as the other girls looked at me in mild shock. I should've done more activities with them this summer.

In the end, Abby, Caralyn, and Summer followed Sarah and me to the bracelet-making hut. I tried to mask my smile when Sarah's shoulders straightened now that her friends were doing an activity she wanted to do for a change.

The bracelet counselor gushed over how many girls were suddenly interested in the "art of knotting," so it felt like an overall win when we sat down and selected our colors. I picked blue and a soft yellow, humming as I threaded them between each other. Bracelet-making soothed my nerves. Now in her element, Sarah talked a mile a minute with Summer about the color war and their friends back home who would love this and that about camp.

"Why did you choose those colors?" a familiar voice asked from behind me.

I turned as Paige sailed through the door.

"Thought red was more your thing?" she said with a smile as she slid into the seat next to mine.

I smiled too, the stark red of our bracelets from last summer crisp in my mind. "I don't know. I felt more like these colors today."

Paige didn't pick any string to make her own bracelet. I smothered a smirk. She'd been terrible at bracelet-making last year.

"So, the fact that you've chosen the color of Lucas's eyes and hair has nothing to do with it?"

I froze, then looked more closely at my bracelet. She was right.

"Pathetic, right?" I whispered.

"You? Never."

"Make a bracelet, Paige," I taunted.

She laughed. "No, thanks. So did you hear that we're not doing a dance this year at the end of camp?"

I pressed my lips together as I knotted off my bracelet, acutely aware that my Beaver girls had fallen silent to listen to our conversation. "Yep. There's going to be a relay race instead to decide the color war once and for all."

"Oh, really? Where did you hear that?" Paige said.

"I'm planning it," I said in a casual voice.

"You're planning a campwide activity where every single person is being used and you're not catatonic with panic right now?"

"Have a little faith," I said, laughing. But my laugh sounded hollow in the small bracelet hut.

"You need help." A statement, not a question.

"Did I say I needed help?" I still couldn't look at her.

"You don't have to. Let me help you."

I sighed. "No." If I let her, I might lean on her too much, and how was that any better than how I acted at the beginning of camp? I needed to show the girls that I had changed.

"No?"

"Is there an echo in here? No. You can't help me." I had to do this on my own.

"Why the hell not?"

"Paige!" I hissed. "There are kids here."

Sarah rolled her eyes. "I'm literally one year younger than you."

"I already have all the activities planned," I said.

Paige brushed some imaginary dirt off the bracelet table. "Then why do you look like the slightest noise or problem will have you running for the hills?"

"I do not look like that."

Paige stared at me.

"Want a bracelet?" I asked and offered my finished product to her.

She batted her eyelashes. "You mean, does Lucas want your bracelet?"

I punched her in the shoulder.

"Seriously. You need to let us help, or it's not going to be good." She wouldn't let this go.

"Who is *us*? And are you saying that I can't handle it?"

"Andy. Of course, you can but come on. Do you know where all the stuff is? Do you know how long each activity will take? What order it should go in? Who should be in charge of each thing?"

I swallowed. Those were my exact problems right now.

"You know who does know all that stuff?"

"You?" I asked. She'd been coming here for a few years.

"Me? No way. Who has been here every year of camp since forever? Come on, you know this."

"Lucas," I whispered.

She nodded. "And who is good at spatial relations?"

"You are," I said. She'd organized all of us campers for multiple activities last year.

Paige tied my bracelet around my wrist. "Part of being a leader is delegating, knowing who is good at what so things can happen in the most efficient manner. You didn't think Dana wanted you to do this all on your own, did you?"

I blinked back the moisture welling in my eyes. "Maybe she does."

"Yeah, because that's why I'm in this hut of tangled strings right now."

My eyes flashed to hers. She hadn't sought me out as a friend today. "Dana sent you?"

"And before you get down on yourself, it isn't because she doesn't think you can do it. Use your resources, Andy. Be smart. Let's do this together."

I sighed. "Fine."

She nudged me. "Because it's the most horrible thing ever to talk to your new boyfriend."

I would see him tonight, anyway. I smiled at her.

"That's what I thought. Now can we get out of here? Your girls are on bracelet number three and not slowing down anytime soon."

I looked over to Sarah and she nodded, still chatting with Summer. Before leaving the bracelet hut, I placed the crackers next to her.

She looked up at me with shining eyes and mouthed *Thank you*.

Anytime, I mouthed back.

"You're a good counselor. You know that?" Paige asked once we were back on the trail.

I was trying to be.

She left me at Lucas's cottage with my clipboard and waning confidence. I wanted Lucas to see me as more competent than last year—as a fully adjusted counselor. Admitting I needed help felt vulnerable. But Paige was right. He was a resource. He knew everything about this camp and working together made sense.

I knocked, knowing he'd be in there. We had five minutes left until the next activity, and I needed to get back to my own campers in a second.

He popped his head out. When he saw it was me, he opened the door and hugged me. "Hey, Andy. What's up?"

I took a deep breath. Lucas wouldn't think I was wimping out by asking for his help, right?

"You okay?" His brows drew together in a sexy, concerned way. It made me want to... *No! Focus.*

"Can you help me?" I blurted out before I lost my nerve.

He blinked. "Help you..."

"With an activity. I have an idea for how to tie together the color war, like a grand finale." I shook my clipboard at him.

"Does Dana know..."

"She assigned me to it."

He blew out a breath. "Yikes."

"Yeah, but I think if we..." I pointed to the first page of my clipboard.

He took it from my hands and flipped through the activities, his eyes scanning each page. "Whoa, this is intense."

"You think it won't work?" I chewed my bottom lip and resumed tapping my pencil, this time against my leg. I'd never planned a camp wide activity before. If I was honest, I never planned anything outside of this summer. I wasn't a go-getter, but I'd thought this one through.

Lucas covered my hand with his, and I stopped tapping.. "I think it's perfect. What do you need me to do?"

I couldn't contain my broad smile. "I thought we could have a counselor at each checkpoint." I ran my finger along my map. "Like here, and here, and here, and obviously this one would be yours."

"Obviously." He nudged me.

"What?"

"I want to kiss you right now. You're so happy. It suits you."

"Don't kiss me or I'll be a big failure because we'll never get it done in time."

"Oh, I'll kiss you. After." He grabbed the notebook and scratched names under each section.

As soon as I recovered from the promise of Lucas's lips against mine, I watched him match the counselors to the checkpoints they'd be more passionate about. *Smart. So smart.* I could've kicked myself for panicking over this, for thinking of it like a school project where I was the only motivated one. It was leadership camp. We were all motivated. We should be working together.

"Oh hey," I said, untying my perfectly knotted Lucas-colored craft from my wrist. "Want a bracelet?"

"Heck yeah," he said and fastened it to his own. "Anything from you."

33

Ready, Relay!

I spent the rest of the day obsessing over the big relay. It blurred together with team challenges with the Beavers and high fives from Paige. My phone buzzed and I had to check it and reply about a thousand times to iron out all the details, but it was coming together.

And when Lucas's hand brushed mine as we pored over the ever-growing stack of papers on my clipboard during free time, the whole world froze. Soon, half an hour remained, and the day was almost over. Even after everything that had happened this summer, I didn't want it to end. Camp was funny that way.

"Come swimming with us!" Destiny called to me as she slammed out of the cottage with Abby and Maria, towels thrown over their shoulders. "It's the last day!"

"You totally should," Summer said from inside the cottage as she slipped her feet into flip flops. "It would be a blast."

"Sure. Why not?" I wasn't ready to let go of them yet. I wanted to soak up every minute we had left.

Leah came running into the cottage, late again.

"Can I ask you a question?" I said as she rummaged around in her suitcase for her bathing suit.

"Sure," she said.

"Where do you go all the time? Why are you always late?"

She dropped her clothes. "Can I ask *you* a question?"

"Um, sure."

"Why do you feel the need to always be on time?"

I laughed. "Okay, keep your secrets."

"No secret to keep," she said, finding her bathing suit. "I like to go at my own pace. Sometimes wonderful things distract me."

"Wonderful things?"

"People. Nature. Thoughts." She threw her hands out. "Camp is great, and I don't want to miss it."

"But doesn't that mean that you're always rushing at the end to get to things? That maybe you're missing them?"

She cocked her head to the side, thinking. "Meh. That just makes life interesting. Are you swimming with us?" she asked as she disappeared into the bathroom, not waiting for my reply.

Did she even have enough time to swim? Did she care? I smiled.

As I walked the familiar two-minute path to the beach, I tried to take a page out of Leah's book. Why bother being the first one down there? Why bother rushing? The water would still be there. So would the girls. Instead, the warmth of the baked earth beneath my thin sandals soaked into the soles of my feet and the whisper of a breeze tickled my exposed shoulders. I'd always thought of this path as a means to an end. It got me somewhere I needed to be. But now I saw it for its beauty. The leaves rustled against each other, streaks of light cutting through the humid summer air. This path could be the destination if it wanted to.

Maybe Leah had a point.

When I broke through the trees, the sight of most of the camp crammed together on the small strip of beach greeted me. In the past, that would make me feel claustrophobic. People were a big nope to me. Crowds, even more so.

But not today. Today, I'd enjoy every too-close, too-hot moment with my Beavers, who were waving me down.

"Andy came!" one of them called.

"Of course, I came," I said and sat in the sand next to them. There wasn't enough room to spread out my towel.

"It's so hot," Summer said. "Let's go swimming."

"Beat you there!" Destiny said.

"Not if I get there first!" Taylor yelled.

And they were off, even Blair and Sarah, who weren't the most competitive of the bunch. Only Leah drifted between groups, laughing and chatting. The rest of them splashed into the water like it was their job, and I guessed it was. Their job was to squeeze every bit of joy they could out of the last day of camp.

I brushed the sand they'd kicked up off my legs and leaned back, tilting my face to the sun. Summer was almost over. In a few weeks, I'd be packing for college.

A shadow blocked the light, and I opened my eyes. A dark cloud drifted overhead. After a camp of nothing but heat and blazing challenges where sweat soaked through all my clothes, I now worried it might storm on the race I'd spent so much time on.

"Ah, finally. A little shade," Lucas said as he sat beside me.

"You're everywhere. You know that?" Of course, he'd see the bright side of a raincloud.

"She notices me! Finally!" he joked.

"You're impossible to ignore," I teased.

He nudged me. "Admit it. We've got this today."

"If it doesn't rain." I squinted at the sky again.

"If it rains, it will be even more fun."

"You *would* say that."

Over at the floating dock, Josh's arms surrounded Destiny from behind. She squealed as they fell into the water together. I smiled.

"Looks like they made up," Lucas said.

"The magic of the last day of camp."

His hand covered mine, rough with sand. "Yeah."

I looked over at him. His sharp jaw, his shaggy hair, the dusting of a sunburn starting on his cheeks. He was so... Lucas. "Yeah."

The time at the beach ended too soon. We packed everything up in the cottage, and as they waited for the final activity, the girls vibrated with nervous energy. The relay was worth a hundred points. We were currently still ten behind. Their time today would determine the winners.

"You've got this," I said to them as they strode beside me, a united front against the Cheetah cottage.

"I know," Destiny said, her jaw set. Her love for Josh only went so far. This was war.

At the archery field, Dana laid down the law. "It's time for the ultimate competition that will once and for all determine the winners of this color war!" she yelled through a bullhorn.

I winced at the sheer volume of her voice.

Paige laughed as she sidled up beside me. "How are you not used to her by now?"

I shrugged.

"This activity comes to you courtesy of Counselor Andy who has spent a lot of time putting together the most unique competition we've ever seen here at camp. Are you ready to accept that challenge?"

I could feel my girls' eyes on me.

"Are we having a reading contest?" Abby snarked. Sarah punched her in the arm. "Ow! I was kidding."

"Be nice," Sarah hissed.

"The competition includes every camper, every counselor, every activity director, and every available location here at camp. The team with the best overall time will win a hundred points. Everything you've been doing together has led you to this point. How competitive are you?"

"Yeah!" Paige yelled. Her campers looked at her, nonplussed.

"Seriously?" she muttered under her breath. "I can't catch a break this summer." Despite the complaint, a huge smile stretched over her face.

I giggled.

"You suck." She shoved me.

"And we have a special surprise for you all today, too!"

I turned my attention back to Dana in time to see two very familiar figures sidle up to her.

"Two of our former counselors will make a guest appearance as your final judges. They'll be circulating to make sure there are no shenanigans at the stations!" She wagged her finger at all of us, but I was too busy picking my jaw up off the ground. None other than Suzie and Tyler stood before us. Suzie was my counselor in the Beaver cottage last year who butted heads with me at every turn.

My eyes flew to Lucas. Tyler was Lucas's brother. Was he still mad about Lucas skipping their father's funeral? Lucas looked as flummoxed as me. He hadn't been expecting this either. From what I remembered, they were supposed to be on their honeymoon this week. Maybe they'd come back early?

"Counselors, to your stations!"

I wanted to protest, to call a time out until I could see how this would all go down, but I had a job to do. We'd all worked too hard to put this together. The counselors jogged away from their campers, and I headed toward the beach, running next to Lucas, who looked down at me with an eyebrow arched.

"Are you—"

"It's fine," he said, giving me a light shove.

I recovered my balance. "Jerk." I broke into a sprint, laughing. His long legs caught up to me easily, and he pushed our pace until the lakeshore appeared, both of us stopping at the same moment.

"Good luck, Counselor Andy. See you after."

"You too, Counselor Lucas."

He pulled off his shirt, and I didn't bother averting my eyes from the lean muscles that flexed under his tanned skin.

When he caught me staring, he laughed. "Focus on your station!"

"What?" I asked innocently, but I retreated to the horseshoe pits. Did I make my station close to Lucas's on purpose so I could watch him? Maybe. And maybe that wouldn't end up being the worst thing, since I'd put money on the fact that Tyler would visit him.

Before I could think any harder about that, the first group jogged down the hill to the pits, and I gave instructions as fast as possible.

"Three ringers and your team can move on, but no one steps over the line here," I pointed, "and you have to rotate who goes." Easy enough, but not everyone excelled at horseshoes. It was an equalizer. I loved that.

"Let's do this!" one of the Tree Frogs cried. It took them a few minutes, but they finished before their cut-off time, and then I had to explain the activity to a new set of campers.

At the lake, Lucas oversaw the swimming relay. We'd told all the campers to wear suits, but only their two fastest swimmers with deep water swim bands would compete under his sharp lifeguard eye.

Paige would be working the obstacle course with a mini rock-climbing wall and complicated ropes that the campers would have to shimmy under and over to get to a flag. James was in charge of the three-legged race. And Garrett would be the relay's midpoint with a water balloon fight.

Other counselors supervised life-size puzzles, riddles, and even a trivia contest. There was something for everyone, and not everything was physical. The team that won would have to excel in both mind and body challenges.

I had no way of knowing how the Beavers were doing. They blew by my station, so I assumed it had gone well, but their final time would tell. Before long, I got wrapped up in my duties, calling the ringers and scooting kids back over the line when their feet strayed too far. Their groans and cheers gave me life. I loved horseshoes.

During one slow point, I shielded my eyes and looked toward the lake. Lucas stood with his arms crossed, watching as campers swam. A guy with darker hair and a similar build stood next to him in the same exact stance. Tyler. Their mouths moved, but I couldn't figure out what they were saying from here. Were they mad? Happy? Figuring it out? As the campers exited the lake, the brothers gave out high fives, and the team ran to the next station.

Then they turned to each other and exchanged a brief, manly hug.

My body relaxed. They'd be okay.

Paige's Clownfish stomped up to the pits next. Their ever-present flower crowns sagged in their hair, and they looked a little worse for wear.

"Okay?" I asked them.

One of the girls waved for me to go ahead with the directions. Another girl braced her hands on her knees to breathe.

I recited the same run-down I had for the previous teams. "And... go!"

The two girls looked at each other and the rest of the Clownfish. "For Paige!" they yelled in hoarse voices.

Aw. If only she were here to see this. Her Clownfish were rallying for her. They were trying to be competitive! I pulled out my phone and took a picture of them to send to her later. They took longer than the Beavers, but they still were able to complete the challenge. I grinned as they rushed to the next station. After that, team after team passed through and I fell into a rhythm until the last group of campers appeared at the horseshoe pits, sweaty and laughing. That was also when Suzie hiked my way. Sweat coated her brow. It seemed she'd been assigned to the rear of the competition, but they were still running. Good for them.

She placed her hands on her hips when they crested the hill. "Hey, Counselor Andrea."

I mirrored her. "It's Andy," I deadpanned.

She laughed. "Some things never change."

I gave the same swift instructions to the last team. Suzie smiled during my entire spiel. "And... go!" I yelled, clicking the timer.

Victory yells rang out from pit number three after a few seconds. Suzie came to stand with me and took the watch from my hand so I could concentrate on counting the number of ringers they were able to achieve.

"That's one!" I called, squinting against the sun with a wide grin on my face. "Two to go!"

"Some things do change," she said in a gentle voice. "Good for you, Counselor Andy."

I turned and saw nothing but genuine support on her freckled face. I nudged her.

"You've got this, girls!" I cheered. In my heart, I knew I was exactly where I needed to be.

34

Team Landy

Faster than I wanted, the last team passed through the horseshoe pits and got their three ringers. I jogged with Suzie through the rest of the stations until we made our way to the archery field—the place where everything always began and ended at camp. I cheered as the last team crossed the finish line and collapsed in the grass.

Paige sat nearby with her Clownfish, who were sweating buckets and grinning ear to ear as they placed a flower crown on her head. She laughed and leaned back on her arms in the field.

I waved at them. Then I went in search of my Beavers. They weren't hard to find since they were the loudest group.

"That was awesome!" Caralyn cried.

"Did you see me at the obstacle course?" Taylor flexed her biceps.

"You flew under those ropes!" Abby said.

"I thought you were gonna botch that horseshoes thing, but you owned it!" Maria high fived Sarah.

I grinned with pride. They worked hard this year.

"I can't believe you organized this whole thing!" Summer said, running over when she saw me. "It's not like you at all!"

I took it as the compliment it was intended to be, but she was wrong. Figuring things out, figuring people out—it *was* my thing. It's what made me a leader. It wasn't loud or in-your-face, but that never had been my style. Dana was right.

As if magically summoned by me thinking of her, Dana chose that moment to yell through the bullhorn: "We've tallied all the times, and we have our winners of our first ever color war!"

The girls and I cheered at the top of our lungs.

Lucas looked over from his group of Cheetahs and smiled.

You're going down, I mouthed at him.

Probably, he mouthed back. Then he winked.

I was stunned. No trash talk for me? The brotherly love must be strong today.

"In third place, with one thousand, two hundred and twelve points, the Tree Frogs!" Suzie cried through the mic. I clapped along as the campers cheered for them. She handed the microphone to Tyler.

"The race was tight between our top two contenders," he said, glancing between Lucas and me.

We both waved innocently at him. Tyler rolled his eyes. Destiny sat forward, anxiety lining her face. I wanted it for her. I wanted it so much for my badass Beavers. Those Cheetahs better not win.

"In second place, with one thousand, six hundred and two points, the Cheetahs!" he said.

Groans from the Cheetah crew. Lucas caught my eye and shrugged, but my girls were already screaming and jumping up and down.

"Which means that our winners are the Beavers!" Dana said, her voice drowned out by the sheer volume of the girls' celebrations.

"We won, we won, we won!" Abby kept repeating.

Taylor high-fived Blair as the girls went up to accept their trophy. And me? I screamed my guts out for my Beavers. This moment would be imprinted on my brain forever, a core memory of how happy we all were. No one deserved this more.

Then, with only half an hour until parent pick-up, they all had no choice but to calm down and leave for the cottage along with all the other campers. I hummed as I helped the other counselors clean up, then jogged back to the cottage. When the Beaver girls had all their bedding and bags packed twenty minutes early, I wasn't surprised. In fact, I'd been counting on their efficiency. I pulled a pile of papers out from inside my pillowcase and grabbed a small bag I'd been hiding underneath my bunk.

"Who wants to circle up one last time?" I called in the loudest voice I'd used all camp.

"Me!"

"Yes!"

"Me too!"

Within seconds, all the Beavers sat in a perfect circle surrounding me, cross-legged on the dingy floor that had seen better days. I looked into the faces of these eager girls who would no doubt someday be counselors themselves, or senators or doctors or motivational speakers. They'd learned a lot. They taught me a lot.

I pulled the first paper from the stack I'd created yesterday. Was this stupid? Too late, now.

"My first award is the Stick with It Award, and this goes to Abby."

The girls clapped as Abby bounced to her feet. "For your undying perseverance at the climbing wall, I present you with five whole sticks of chewing gum." I pulled a pack of gum out of the bag of last-minute snack shack stuff I'd procured this morning.

The girls *ooh-ed* while Abby grabbed the gum from my hand. She gave a big bow and flounced back to her seat.

"The next award is the Better Late Than Never Award, and this goes to Leah."

The girls laughed as she stood. I stepped back in shock when she reached for her paper. "You're on time? Someone call a doctor!"

She grinned and grabbed the page from me. I passed her a candy bracelet with a fake watch face on it.

"This will help for sure!" she joked as she sat back down.

The awards continued with the Accident-Prone Award for Taylor, the Extra-Miler Award for Sarah, and even a Positively Positive Award for Caralyn. Each time I called a name, the catcalls probably echoed all the way across the lake. I didn't even try to shush them. They loved it, and I loved celebrating all their crazy antics throughout camp. Let people hear how much I cared about these girls.

Finally, I pulled out my last award. It felt more important than the flimsy paper and plastic toy in my hands. I didn't know how she'd take it. I hoped well.

"Last but never least, the I'll Do It Myself Award goes to Destiny, for her excellent team management skills."

Destiny burst out laughing so loud, I thought she might be crying instead. She rushed forward, bypassing the tiny plastic hammer and paper to throw herself into my arms.

"Thank you," she whispered in the softest voice I'd heard from her all camp. "For everything."

Despite the obvious tear streaks down her cheeks, we all pretended we didn't see her cry.

"We got you something, too," she said.

Summer stood. "My mom works at a T-shirt shop in Richmond. I was scared she wouldn't send it in time, but it came yesterday." She pulled a baseball cap out of her back pocket. In big, gaudy pink letters it read, TEAM LANDY.

I groaned, and they all laughed. I put it on my head and pulled my ponytail through the hole in the back.

"We knew you'd see it in the end!" Sarah said.

"Landy, Landy, Landy!" they chanted.

"Alright, Alright," I said, cutting them off. "You were right. One last huddle?"

They all stood, and we packed in together with our hands in the center of our close-knit circle and shouted, "One, Two, Three, Beavers!"

After that, the hugs were plentiful and the goodbyes so equally tearful that Destiny's emotional reaction earlier fit right in. And then suddenly I stood alone in a way-too-empty cottage, staring at my own blank bed with watery eyes. It was hard to feel like I'd never be here again, that this summer could never be repeated—that I'd never be in charge of a group so perfectly wrong and perfectly right for me ever again. Soon, it would only be a memory of a pivotal summer in my life. I'd move on.

I touched the worn wood frame of my bunk bed, content to stay in the bittersweet of goodbye for just one more moment.

I spent the next two hours checking things off the counselor To-do list. Sweep, look for lost items, make sure the bathrooms were clean. Not the most glamorous part of my job, but I was happy to pitch in. I found two abandoned, mismatched socks under the bunks and a half-full travel tube of toothpaste in one of the bathroom drawers.

I sprayed everything down with Lysol and wiped it clean. By the time I packed up my own duffel, everything looked the way we had found it this summer. No scent of hairspray or make up lingered, no laughing voices, no one chanting "Landy." I smiled a watery smile.

"Knock, knock!" Paige sang out as she tromped through the door. "Aw, you're getting emotional."

I opened my arms, and she sank into them, smelling of sunscreen and body spray and everything summer and Paige. "I'm sorry we didn't hang out more this summer. That it turned into all kinds of drama."

"Girl, that is your M.O., but I love you anyway." She squeezed me tighter. "Have you said goodbye to Lucas yet?"

I shook my head. "I don't want to say goodbye to either of you."

"You could always take a road trip to see me in Maine."

"I know."

"I looked it up and our breaks match up for most of the holidays."

"Sounds like a plan." I'd have to get a job to afford a road trip like that, but Paige was worth it.

"Text me."

"I will."

She left, and I turned to grab my duffel and sleeping bag. It was time. I ran my hand along the rough log-cabin walls before turning off the light and shutting the door.

The trudge to the parking lot felt long. Because Eric had driven us to camp, I had to call Dad to come get me. It was super embarrassing since I had a driver's license now, and none of the other counselors would be picked up by their parents. But as I rounded the corner to the parking lot, my parents' minivan was nowhere to be found. I sighed, my sweat evaporating in the relentless sun.

When I dialed Dad's cell, he picked up on the second ring. "Andy. Did you have a fun time at camp?"

"Yeah, it was memorable," I matched my dad's chill tone. "Were you going to pick me up?" I guessed I could wait a bit. We didn't live that far away.

Dad cleared his throat. "I got a call from a boy at camp who said he'd drop you off on his way home. I thought you knew."

"I... didn't." I wasn't on anyone's way, was I? I opened my mouth to protest when a very tall, familiar head appeared over the hill.

Eric.

What was Eric doing here?

"Never mind, Dad. I see him. I'll be home in a while."

"Okay, honey. I love you."

"Love you, too." I pocketed my phone.

Eric approached me, but I didn't look at him until he stood beside me.

"Hey," he said.

"Hey." Why was he here? He said he didn't forgive me. My heart beat a double rhythm in my chest.

"I didn't know if you had a ride, since..." He toed the ground, an oddly vulnerable image for a guy his height.

"Since we planned to ride together." Of course.

"Yeah." He scuffed his shoe at the ground again, and I wanted to tell him to spit it out, but that wasn't fair. He'd never been like that. Neither had I.

In the next crowd of people, Lucas's head rose above the rest. When he spotted us, he pushed down his sunglasses and stared at me. *You okay?* he mouthed.

I shrugged. I didn't know what would happen when Eric found his voice. What he'd say to me or how.

Lucas's mouth tightened and he nodded, pushing his sunglasses back onto the bridge of his nose. He sat on a nearby picnic table out of earshot and waited.

"I know it's a bad time, but I wanted to see you before I left," Eric said in a quiet voice. "I didn't want to end it like—"

"Before you left?" Didn't he already leave camp? I knew I didn't hallucinate that whole painful conversation in his car.

"Yeah, I..." He swallowed. "I got the chance to move into the dorms early, and I decided to take it."

He was forfeiting the rest of his summer to go to college early. Because of me? I stared at him. He stood straight the way he always did, but a sadness that hadn't been there before pulled at the corner of his mouth.

My stomach hollowed out. "You treated me so awesome, and I couldn't... I wasn't right for you. I'm sorry," I said. "I could have handled all of that better."

He shrugged, but it looked wrong on him. His posture was too perfect. "I was your first boyfriend."

"I couldn't have asked for anyone better."

He squinted against the sun, maybe to look away from me. "So, there's nothing there anymore."

"Eric..." I didn't want to hurt him again. I shook my head. "I've got a ride home." It might not be true, but I didn't know what else to say.

Eric glanced at Lucas, who saluted from the picnic table. Then he smiled, trying to rally. "You seem more you now."

"More me?"

"More comfortable."

Funny, since this whole conversation was the definition of *un*comfortable.

"I guess I needed to see you for myself. To make sure it was over."

He was right. I was way more myself here. Way more myself alone, or with Lucas—Lucas pushed me to be better. I didn't get a sour feeling in my stomach when I talked to him about serious stuff.

"It's over," I whispered.

Instead of acting the way he had last time, Eric opened his arms, and I hugged him. For a second, he petted my hair the way he used to. The gesture hurt in the worst way, but I couldn't take back what I said. I didn't want to.

"Goodbye, Andrea." Still Andrea. Never Andy.

"Bye."

He walked away, and I watched him go. He was the best person, so handsome and intelligent and polite. He'd be the perfect boyfriend for someone. I didn't regret my crush on him, dating him, any of it. He wasn't the right guy for me, and that was okay.

As soon as he was out of sight, Lucas approached. "You okay?" he asked.

I smiled. "Yeah."

He raised his eyebrows. "Really?"

I shook my head. I didn't want to talk about Eric when I'd been waiting to hear about his important moment. "Where's your brother?"

He covered his heart with his hand, pretending to be wounded. "You want my brother?"

"It wasn't funny last year, and it isn't funny now," I said in a stern voice.

He put his hands up in surrender. "Sorry, sorry. Suzie and Tyler took off a minute ago. He was…" He scratched the back of his head, staring up at the dark clouds that now darkened the sky.

"Checking on you. Making sure you guys are okay." I stepped forward and touched his arm.

He looked down at me. "Yeah."

"Are you? Okay?" I braced myself for his answer.

"Yeah. We are."

I searched his face, relieved to find some of the tension had faded. "I'm glad."

He smiled. "So, you ready?"

I shook my head. "I'm not on your way home at all, you know."

"I don't care." He shook back his hair.

"Me neither," I whispered, our faces inches from each other. If this was his way of prolonging the inevitable, I was one hundred percent in.

Lucas took my duffel and headed to a black car on the other side of the parking lot. I followed in his wake and shoved my stuff in the trunk beside his. It was a tight fit with the pillows and sleeping bags taking up so much space. We laughed as we smashed it all in.

"You ready?" he asked.

"Almost." I shielded my eyes to look for Dana as the first raindrops touched my hair. I spied her by the camp entrance.

As I dashed over to her, the rain picked up speed. This summer had been the definition of hot and bright, and now, as we all piled into our cars to leave, it chose to rain. The poetic side of me wondered if the camp mourned our absence the way I would mourn leaving.

"Andy, hey," Dana said, the rain plastering her blonde hair against her head.

"Hey," I said.

She shielded her blonde curls with her clipboard. "You did it, Andy Stevens," she said, bopping my head with her free hand. "I knew you could."

I swallowed the lump in my throat as I stared at her. She was more than a boss to me this summer. She was a mentor. I wasn't great with words when nervous, but I could do one thing. I leaned forward and hugged her.

She laughed, patting me on the back. "Will you come back next year?"

"I don't know," I yelled over the rain and released her. "It's a long time from now. I don't know what will happen."

She nodded. "Adulthood does that to you." Her wide smile told me she was okay with that.

"I'm so happy to have spent the last two summers here. Thank you..." My throat closed again. This should have been a conversation inside, where I could take longer to tell her what it all meant to me. "Thank you for everything."

"You're a leader, Andy." She pointed at me with one of her perfectly manicured fingers. "I know whatever you do next, you've got this. Don't forget us."

"Never," I whispered.

"Andy!" Lucas shouted over the rain. "Come on!" He laughed.

The sight of his wet shirt clinging to the planes of his chest was worth forcing him to wait for me, but he didn't need to know that. I sprinted back to the car and jumped in the passenger's side as he sat in the driver's seat.

Lucas looked behind him as he put his hand on the back of my headrest to back out, the muscles in his biceps bulging. It was so sexy, I thought I might combust in the small space we shared in the front seat of that car. "There's a backup camera, you know."

"I know," he said, flashing me that trademark Lucas smile as we drove out of the camp.

I giggled, and as we pulled away, I couldn't resist looking behind us for one last glimpse of the Welcome to Camp Follow the Leader sign. I watched the rain stream down its sturdy wooden face and smiled. The heat might've broken, but summer wasn't over yet.

Over the pounding of the rain, Lucas and I blew through topics and dried our clothes in front of the heaters. If we didn't say the words, would goodbye even exist? But when he pulled into my driveway after forty minutes, it was time. He shifted the car into park and looked over at me.

"It's not goodbye," I said, watching the swish of the windshield wipers, "so don't say it."

"Of course not," he said seriously. He reached for my hand, and I squeezed his fingers between mine.

"I'm not going to cry," I said through blurry eyes.

"Because you're going to video chat me tonight."

I stared at the dark behind the rain. "It's already night."

He laughed. "I know."

"And we'll figure it out. I know you're…" I swallowed. "We can make it work." I wanted to believe that. I needed him to tell me that.

"We can and we will," he said, full of that Lucas confidence that made me want to hit him and hug him at the same time.

We both opened our doors, and he walked me right up to the front of my house. I wouldn't put it past Mom to spy on us right now, but I couldn't care as he pulled me close and kissed me sweetly. Not a goodbye kiss. It was more like a promise.

"Video chat. Nine o'clock. Don't stand me up."

"Okay," I whispered against his shoulder.

And I didn't.

Epilogue

The rest of the summer flashed by like scrolling through pictures. Swipe to me on the beach with Brynn, sipping a coke. Then me checking in library books for the last time until next summer—Joan said she'd hold my job for me as long as I wanted it. Scroll to the silly moment I cried as I touched the big tree in my backyard. I'd miss the sanctuary of reading in its shade. Then my father tearing up when Mom and I came home with the bedding and towels I'd need for college.

And throughout all of it, video chats with Lucas. Texting Lucas. Trying not to lose Lucas. We'd be long-distance since he would attend college states away. He couldn't just throw away a full scholarship for Division One swimming. He'd worked so hard for it. We could meet up during Christmas break, and even Thanksgiving. We'd make it work, somehow. Nothing could separate such stubborn people.

The last day of summer dawned, bright and hot. After a short car trip and a tearful goodbye on the part of my mother, I watched my parents drive away. Until my roommate arrived, I'd be alone in the brick building of my new dorm at Middlebury College. I placed my hand on the glass window that separated me from the life I'd always known. They'd abandoned me. They'd set me free.

I sighed, picking up my phone and perching on my unmade bed. My new room stretched before me, blank and sterile. It smelled like books and paint, and I wished Lucas could be here. When I saw I had an unread text from him, I opened our message chain.

Settling in okay?

I smiled. He was always one step ahead of me.

> **Sure. I walked through the door. That's all you have to do, right? Furniture is optional?**

> **Completely optional. I have this great futon that Tyler gave me. I might get tetanus from a spring.**

He attached an image of a blue futon that sagged in the middle. God, what I'd give to see him again. It seemed every college dorm had the same fake wood floor. Maybe we could bond over that.

> **I wish you were here.**

A knock on my door jolted me out of my longing-filled text exchange. "One second!" I called in a cheery voice. It had to be my roommate. She hadn't shown up yet, but I was early.

I bounded over to the door, opening it wide to find…

"Lucas?" He'd cut his hair! It was so short—did he do that today? But his eyes crinkled the way they always did, like he was on the verge of laughter. Lucas was here. He was here!

He picked me up and twirled me in the hall. "Surprise!"

"Surprise you're visiting?" I asked when he set me down. Confusion swept through me. "But you need to be at freshman orientation."

"Of course, I'm visiting you. You're only one building over."

"You…" I took in his navy-blue hoodie. Middlebury College. That meant…

"Yep."

"You switched colleges?" I whispered.

"Looks like it."

I searched his face. He wouldn't joke about something this important, would he? "They don't even have a D1 swim program." I'd secretly checked when I thought maybe he'd be able to transfer here. Middlebury was Division Three, so I'd never mentioned it.

Lucas stared down at me, his blue eyes blazing. "Looks like you matter more."

Tears pricked my eyes. He did this for me? *Wait.* "You're not swimming?" I wouldn't let him do this. He couldn't throw it all away.

He scratched the back of his head. "I called up the coach here. Turns out, they're happy to have me."

"And give you a scholarship?" Excitement bubbled within me, but I knew how important that had been to him from our chats.

He nodded.

"But it's not Division One." I bit my lip.

"Andy." He spread his arms wide. "I'm still swimming, and now we get to be together. I can't think of anywhere else I'd rather be."

Lucas was here. This was really happening right now. I smacked his chest. "Why didn't you tell me?"

He laughed. "I wanted to surprise you."

I groaned. "I hate surprises."

"I'll convert you one of these days." He pulled me in by my belt loops. "You can't get rid of me that easy, Andy Stevens," he murmured against my lips.

"I would never want to," I whispered. When we kissed, it struck me that this was the first time we weren't on a time clock. The end of camp didn't loom over us. No misunderstandings stood in our way. The future stretched out in front of us, full of the promise of a thousand more conversations and kisses. It was just the beginning.

Acknowledgments

Thank you to Valerie Brodbeck, Nicole Atherton, and Tara Brodbeck for doing a lightning-quick beta read on this book for me. Your input was invaluable, and I'd never be able to smooth out the rough edges of my writing without you.

A big thanks to Michael at Winding Road Stories for taking a chance on another Andy book, and to Vanessa, for sticking with me through the millionth time I used ellipses and my fixation on adverbly adverbing everything. I love our supportive Winding Road Stories family, and I'm grateful to be a small part of it.

I also want to thank my school family and my students for the outpouring of support for *Andy and the Extroverts*. I've cried more times than I can count at this point. I never thought we'd make it this far, and I'm absolutely floored by all your wonderful comments and how you show up to my events over and over again.

To the bookstores that supported my first novel: The Book Cellar in Grand Haven, Schuler's Bookstore in Grand Rapids, Reader's World in Holland, 2 Dandelions Bookshop in Brighton, Hooked in Lansing, The Bluestocking Bookshop in Holland, the Barnes and Noble locations of Holland, Grandville, Grand Rapids, Battle Creek, and Portage, and Books Revisited in Sanford, Maine: you were the first to carry my book and promote it to people who happened to be looking for a YA summer read. I will never forget that you took a chance on my first novel, and I am so, so grateful that you did.

As this duology comes to a close, I'd be remiss if I didn't give a shout out to Lake Ann Baptist Camp and Central Michigan University's Leadership Safari for giving me a lot of material to draw from. They were both formative experiences for me, and being a Safari Guide for a summer in college was so incredibly fun, even if I lost my voice for most of it. Go Hippos!

When I think about the books that "made" me a writer, my brain always reverts to the Nancy Drew series, Sweet Valley High, and historical romance novels. So, thank you to Carolyn Keene, Francine Pascal, and Jude Deveraux for shaping me as a reader and a writer. Your books got me through middle school, high school, and college. They're still on my shelf for when I need a comfort read.

I'm lucky enough to be a part of a really supportive and fantastic family. Thank you to Andrew, the love of my life. You and me against the world. And to Sterling and Samson, my hilarious, kind boys: you make every day bright and wonderful. It's such an honor to be your mom.

To Kimber, Baer, and Lolly McGee, our current crew of rescue animals: you didn't help with this book at all. You kind of got in the way, to be honest. But I love you just the same, you high-maintenance fur-balls.

Finally, my heartfelt thanks to everyone who has read my work. Your support makes me want to keep writing. Words can't express how happy I am that you've chosen my books to read.

About the Author

Jessica K. Foster is the author of Young Adult Contemporary Romance books *Andy and the Extroverts* and *Andy and the Summer of Something.* She is a middle school Language Arts teacher with a penchant for hot tea and romantic beach reads. Jessica lives in West Michigan with her husband, two boys, and their ragtag crew of rescue animals. Check out jessicakfoster.com for more information.